The watchtower was the strongest line of defense around earth.

Superman's gaze froze on one of the dozens of screens. There was a blip. Too small to be an asteroid. Space vessel? No, too small even for that. Superman's telescopic vision zoomed in on the object, his heart sinking as he realized what it was.

A man on a bike.

And not just any man. It was Lobo—the self-styled Main Man—the Last Czarnian. The black sheep of the whole galaxy. Lobo was an amoral, aggressive, sometimes downright evil bounty hunter who killed others in return for cash. Lobo had fought the Man of Steel to a standstill in a long, exhausted battle in the past, when the Main Man threatened to cut an inebriated swath of death and destruction through the world's cities.

And now he was headed for Earth. Again.

DC UNIVERSE
LAST SONS

Alan Grant

WARNER BOOKS

NEW YORK   BOSTON

Copyright © 2006 by DC Comics
All rights reserved. No part of this book may be reproduced in any form or by any electronic or mechanical means, including information storage and retrieval systems, without permission in writing from the publisher, except by a reviewer who may quote brief passages in a review.

Superman created by Jerry Siegel and Joe Shuster

Cover illustration by James Jean
Book design by Stratford Publishing Services

Warner Books

Time Warner Book Group
1271 Avenue of the Americas
New York, NY 10020
Visit our Web site at www.twbookmark.com

Printed in the United States of America

First Paperback Printing: February 2006

10 9 8 7 6 5 4 3 2 1

For my granddaughter, Millie Marinello

DC UNIVERSE
LAST SONS

CHAPTER 1

They killed us.
The thought rippled out of nowhere.
The dead do not know they have been killed.

"What d'ya call a Sirian with a frag grenade wedged up his butt?"

Kiram Claaw almost choked on his whisky. He took a step back from the bar, his heavy-lidded saurian eyes opening wide with shock as he recognized the tall, muscular figure who'd suddenly appeared at his side.

"L-Lobo," he whispered.

Just his luck. Lobo. The self-styled Main Man. The most feared bounty hunter in the whole stinkin' galaxy.

"At yer service, pinhead," the bounty hunter drawled, in a voice that sounded like bloodstained gravel. He stood six-foot-six, but his heavily muscled torso made him seem even taller. He wore a battered, black leather biker jacket over a tee shirt and skintight pants. Claaw didn't like to think about what weapons he kept in the pouches slung from his skull-buckle belt.

Lobo's shoulder-length black hair, tied back from his forehead by a greasy sweatband, looked as if it had been styled by a psychopath posing as a barber. His face and skin were chalk white, with black markings around the eyes and mouth.

Incongruously, Claaw found himself wondering if the markings were natural, or if the bounty hunter was vain enough to wear facial makeup. Not that it was the kind of thing you could ask Lobo unless you were actively looking to spend some time on a casualty ward.

Besides, Lobo was the one asking questions.

"Ya never answered me, dude," Lobo said, almost affably. His red eyes glittered in his pale face as he pulled a battered cigar from the pocket of his leather jacket, then extracted a single match. Slowly, deliberately, he leaned closer to Claaw. "Are ya deaf, or just pig-ignorant?"

"I-I heard you," the Sirian muttered, recoiling from the foul odor of the bounty hunter's breath.

"And . . . ?"

Lobo held the match up to Claaw's scaly face. Then, with a quick flick of his wrist, he scraped it down Claaw's cheek. Claaw winced involuntarily as the match head flared into life. Lobo fired up his stogie in a cloud of evil-smelling smoke, then dropped the match into the remains of Claaw's whisky. There was a loud hiss, like a terrified Sirian pissing his pants.

Claaw's mind was racing. It didn't matter what answer he gave, the end result was going to be the same. Lobo had a terrifying reputation, and word in criminal haunts was that he was even *worse* than everybody said.

All around them, other drinkers were moving away, giving them space. Everybody in the bar could see that trouble was brewing, and none of them wanted any part of it. The bartender reached for the panic button, but Lobo's malevolent glance caused his finger to freeze in midair. He smiled weakly and stuck the offending digit up his nose.

Ahhh, shoot! Claaw cursed quietly under his breath. He should never have told Xemtex he'd take his chances alone. The gang had been together nearly five years, and every job they'd ever done went off smooth as silk. Walk in—point guns—shoot protestors—walk out with the cash. Best work Claaw had ever had.

But now, only hours after he told Xemtex he wasn't running, it was all starting to fall to pieces. He was supposed to be drunk as a lord, fighting off the attentions of the bar's shapely hookers; funny how, the more he drank, the more shapely they seemed. Then he was off someplace where nobody knew him, to settle down in a new, anonymous life, with no more paranoia about being hunted by cops . . . or psychopaths like Lobo.

It sure hadn't worked out as per schedule.

Surreptitiously, verging on desperately, Claaw cast his eyes around the bar. Lobo's hulking frame blocked any chance he had of making for the exit. There was a window only a dozen or so feet away. Maybe if he turned suddenly and dived full length, he could get out and away before Lobo realized what was happening.

Light glinted dully on the cruelly curved butcher's hook that dangled loosely in Lobo's right hand. It was attached by a length of chain to the bounty hunter's wrist. Claaw's twin stomachs performed twin somersaults. He'd heard a lot about that hook . . . and none of it was pleasant. Despite Lobo's love of hi-tech weaponry, it was said he always preferred to use the hook when possible. He liked to work on his targets up close and personal.

For one crazy moment, Claaw wondered if he'd be able to draw his own gun and shoot his tormentor before that hook came looking for him.

He decided that he couldn't.

The only escape was over the bar and out the back entrance. Claaw steeled himself, ready to burst into sudden action.

"Don't even think it," Lobo said casually, blowing a cloud of cheap tobacco smoke in Claaw's face. "In fact, ya *still* haven't answered my question. So lemme refresh yer memory, chuzzlewit. What d'ya call a Sirian with a frag grenade wedged up his butt?"

"Uh . . . unlucky?" Claaw ventured.

Lobo drew the number "1" in the air with a forefinger. "Strike one."

"An arms smuggler?"

"Strike two." Lobo's voice dropped an octave, and the temperature in the bar seemed to plummet by ten degrees. "Think carefully now."

"I g-got it," the Sirian stuttered. "The answer is—a squealer. Right?" He laughed shakily, feeling like he'd just swallowed half a canister of helium. He struggled to keep his voice level as he went on, "No need to go bringing grenades into this. I'll tell you everything I know."

"Yeah, ya can take *that* to the bank, dude."

Claaw risked another glance around the bar. Half the clientele seemed to have disappeared—probably afraid there were arrest warrants out on them, too. The remainder had put as much distance between Lobo and themselves as they possibly could without actually leaving the bar. A lot of folk liked to watch a cold-blooded killing.

"I'm waitin'." Lobo's voice was quiet, but it carried a dark undercurrent of violent menace.

Claaw shrugged. Okay, so he'd been a member of Xemtex's gang. Okay, so they'd killed dozens of people, most of them innocent victims, and stolen a lot of money. But it wasn't like he and Xemtex were *friends*, or anything. Claaw didn't owe the gang leader a thing. Especially not loyalty.

"Xemtex said they'd be heading for the Radlands. Couple of hundred klicks from here," Claaw blurted out. He saw Lobo nod approvingly and rushed on. "Wanted me to go with them, too. But I said no. I've had my fill of killing and looting. Figured I'd stay here, maybe settle down with a nice girl . . ."

"Yeah? An' establish a refuge for orphans, right? Save it for somebody who gives a crap." Lobo took a last, deep draw on his cigar, the tip flaring fiery red. He dropped the butt into Claaw's whisky. "See, it's like this, Kiram: the warrant on you says '5,000 Creds . . . Dead or Alive.' Now—"

"Alive is good," Claaw interjected hurriedly, nodding like he'd just contracted palsy. "Very, very good!"

Lobo ignored him. "—that'll take care o' my booze 'n' babes bill fer a couple of weeks. But ya gotta appreciate my position here, dude. How can I go after that fragger Xemtex an' his freaks with you taggin' along to cramp my style?"

"I got an idea!" Claaw exclaimed. "You could leave me

here—then pick me up on your way out again. I promise I wouldn't try to escape or nothing like that."

"Kiram, yer a prince among thieves," Lobo said, with mock admiration. "Sadly, previous experience suggests to me that the majority of outlaws are lyin', connivin', stab-ya-in-the-back bastards. Yeah, I know you're an exception," he added quickly, as Claaw prepared to argue his case. "But I'm sure ya understand that expediency demands I kill ya."

The butcher hook was suddenly in Lobo's hand. "Good night, Gracie," he said in a voice that sounded as if it could pulverize rock.

Before the Sirian even had time to react, the bounty hunter brought the curved edge of the hook slamming down hard on Claaw's head.

Kiram Claaw let out a muffled groan, then everything went black.

He came to with a chill wind blowing in his face, and he shivered violently. Sirians were a saurian race—scaly skins, sharp teeth, vestigial tails—and they were extremely sensitive to low temperatures. The cold thickened their blood and made them sluggish.

They were outside the bar someplace. Dazedly, Klaaw felt himself being upended on the rough ground.

He took a deep breath, trying to speak. But before he even got out the first word, he felt a searing pain between his buttocks.

His eyelids rolled back, and he caught a glimpse of Lobo as the bounty hunter swaggered away from him.

"There's another name fer a Sirian with a grenade wedged up his butt," Lobo tossed over his shoulder.

Kiram Claaw frowned, his mental processes slowed by the cold. He had just enough time to figure it out before the frag grenade exploded.

"Dead."

Advertising Feature

The Spazz-Frag 5000 Space Hawg is one of the most coveted interplanetary motorbikes in production.

It proudly boasts a miniaturized nuclear engine that produces several billion horsepower at a low 2,000 revs and is capable of cruising at sublight speed. It will whisk you from standstill to rocket speed in no time at all.

Standard armaments include laser cannon, front-mounted machine guns, grenade auto-launchers and a low-emission organic disrupter—not to mention the 12-inch serrated bayonet secreted under a body panel. There are also canisters of toxic gas pellets, if you know where to look (and if you *don't* know, don't *look;* they're booby trapped).

The 5000 model comes fitted with its own oxygen environment, an invisible membrane permitting breathing even in deep space. For dedicated planetary use, the membrane can be tuned to handle alcohol, cannabis, and several dozen other Class C drugs.

(*Note: addition of drugs may impair the rider's ability and will invite police attention on many worlds. It will also invalidate the warranty.)

The fitted "Resonance" In-Bike Entertainment system is permanently tuned to Radio Heavy Metal. The manufacturer's market research has repeatedly shown that the Spazz-Frag is bought almost exclusively by single males between 20 and 35 who earn lots of money and constantly listen to music that makes their ears bleed.

It goes without saying that voluptuous babes in scanty clothing just *love* to ride pillion.

But the crown jewel in the Spazz-Frag's prospectus is surely the Semisentient Control System, which handles all aspects of the bike's functioning and behavior. Cloned only from pure genetic material cultured in the biolabs of Walton's World, the SSCS is a unique feature of this machine. It will set your route, self-navigate, and is capable of extensive interactivity.

It will even become your friend, if you let it.

"Radlands in thirty klicks, boss. What you figure?" the SSCS asked in its irritating drawl of a voice.

"I figure you should shut up," Lobo snarled.

"I can become your friend, if you let me," the control system tried again, quoting shamelessly from its own publicity.

"Ya been sayin' that since I stole the bike, wiseass. An' without fail, what do I always tell ya?"

There was a slight pause. When the SSCS spoke again, it sounded hurt. "You always tell me: 'Go frag yourself, geek.'"

"Right. So do it. But switch to Stealth Mode first. Radlands ahead."

The air around the bike shimmered gently as the control system began refracting the light waves striking it, rendering bike and rider virtually invisible.

Lobo squinted against the glare of the harsh yellow sun. He was riding along about ten feet above ground level, the bike slowed to a comparative crawl. The entire landscape radiated an eerie green glow.

Below him, the ground was covered in a thick carpet of bones and skulls. Here and there, a boulder bore the scorched imprint of a body. A column of refugees must have been fleeing the city when the nukes started to fall. Caught in the blast, flash-cooked.

The thought reminded Lobo he was hungry. His eyes continued to drink in his surroundings as, without glancing away, he flipped open a hatch and pulled out a can of iced beer.

He threw back his head and drained the can in seconds.

He belched once, almost discreetly, then tossed the can over his shoulder. It ricocheted off a rock with a metallic clang.

"What's the point of my being stealthy, if you're tossing beer cans around?" the SSCS asked in a miffed tone. "Apart from anything else, you're polluting the environment."

Lobo sighed heavily. "Lissen, ya bleedin'-heart bike: We're in the Radlands. Approximately one thousand kilotons of nuclear bombs dropped on the city and surrounding area. Radiation readings are off the scale. Nothing will grow here again for approximately a zillion years. So who gives a squeezed zit about a fraggin' beer can?"

"Radiation?" The voice sounded horrified. "Have you taken your antirad pills?"

Lobo cursed and switched it off. If he'd known the Spazz-Frag had such a wussy SSCS, he might have thought twice about stealing it. It had taken all of his considerable engineering skills to circumvent the bike's security systems and booby traps, reprogramming every component so the bike would look on him as its rightful legal owner. The one thing he hadn't been able to change was the control system.

Ahead, Lobo could see his first glimpse of the city—what was left of it. Stumps of once-mighty skyscrapers, their stonework turned to glass by the ferocity of the firestorm, stabbed at the sky. A hundred-foot-high communications mast had melted and bent until it looked like something that might win an art prize. Mounds of rubble were interspersed with craters filled with a disgusting pink gloop that might—just—have been organic.

And everything glistened with that creepy green glow.

Lobo sighed again. The things he did—the places he went—just to earn an honest buck. Sometimes he almost wished he'd become an outlaw himself. Although, now he came to think of it, that would probably involve exactly the same places, as other bounty hunters tracked *him* down.

*   *   *

In the city, behind the ruins of a vitrified building, Xemtex and his dirty dozen waited impatiently. They were a motley crew of misfit aliens and one psychopathic robot. Four of the gang were on lookout duty in elevated positions, hunkered down among globules of glass and bright green rad-dust.

"Your man was right, boss. It's Lobo."

The Rigellan known as Starboot lowered his binoculars and handed them to Xemtex. The short, scrawny gang leader raised the glasses to his eyes and stared hard at the distant, approaching figure on a space hawg.

"He's the toughest of the tough, so they say," Starboot went on. "You know what his name *means*?"

One of the others rose to the bait. "Lobo? It's gotta be something connected with wolves, right?"

"Fat chance." Starboot shook his head. "The way I heard it, 'Lobo' is actually a Khund dialect. It means 'He who eats your intestines and enjoys them.'"

There was a chorus of groans from the others.

Starboot shrugged. "He's never failed on a bounty warrant yet. What we gonna do, Xemtex?"

"We stick to the plan, Starboot. This Lobo maybe has a fierce rep, but he's the same as anybody else. Cut him— he bleeds."

Xemtex screwed up his eyes tightly and concentrated. Jagged little lines of electrical force darted around his eyes as he stared at a football-sized sphere of glass a dozen yards away. Nothing happened for a second or so . . . then suddenly the sphere exploded into dust with a loud boom.

"Stare at him"—Xemtex grinned—"and he'll explode."

Nobody else on Paradek, Xemtex's homeworld, could blow things up by looking at them and thinking hard. That was probably why they'd kept him in a granite cell since his power manifested itself at age six months. Xemtex was too young to remember, of course, but he'd heard the story plenty of times.

He had colic. His father picked him up to comfort him. Next thing, Dad's head had exploded all over the nursery walls.

Baby Xemtex fell to the floor. It must have been the pain of landing that set him off again. His mother only got one foot inside the door before her leg blew off; the rest of her followed a microsecond later.

Fifteen years of incarceration gave a boy time to think. Xemtex could have blamed his god for his awful predicament, which might have been handy, but he didn't believe in a god. He could have worked himself into a terrible state, blaming himself for the deaths of his innocent parents, stewing in shame and guilt and bitter self-recrimination. Or he could have warped his mind with hatred for his captors, furtively practicing his weird explosive abilities whenever he got half a chance.

Xemtex chose the furtive explosions.

So when, aged sixteen, a delegation came to his cell and told him he had to make the ultimate choice, Xemtex listened closely to what they had to say. Either commit suicide—or be publicly executed. Some damned choice!

Xemtex went for the unmentioned and obviously unplanned-for option of blowing them up. Then he blew up his granite cell. Then he blew up some innocent folks on the street, just for the hell of it. He had a lot of pent-up frustrations to relieve.

After that, there was no alternative to a career of crime—a career that brought him riches and women and headline news wherever he and his ruthless gang struck.

And a fifty-thousand-credit reward tag, he reminded himself now. *Same again for the gang. Not bad for a scrawny runt, his opportunistic pals, and a psychopathic robot. Not enough to buy a spaceship—or even a Spazz-Frag 5000—but more than enough for Lobo to enjoy a couple of years' debauchery. Makes us a very attractive target.*

But forewarned is forearmed . . . and Xemtex knew a man who was very good at forewarning—at least, when his palm was liberally greased with cash.

"One klick, boss."

Starboot's words jerked Xemtex from his reverie. He lurched to his feet, cursing as he brushed the rad-dust from his clothes.

"Everybody in position," he ordered. "Soon as I hit him, you all pour on the firepower." He ducked down behind what once might have been a train but was now a twisted mound of rust-covered metal. "And keep the robot under control," he added. "Nobody fires till I hit Lobo—or they'll chew the big boom along with the bounty hunter!"

I killed your Nazi father
An' I offed your commie maw
Now I'm comin' for ya, baby
Stop ya runnin' to the Law.

Lobo's fingers rapped out the doom-laden heavy metal beat on the handlebars of his bike. He'd drunk another half dozen beers and was feeling mellow enough to have forgotten about any semblance of stealth.

Ya should be more careful, dude, a nagging little voice in his head told him.

He'd turned the bike radio's volume up to MAX and the sounds of 4 Dead Aliens' galactic metal smash reverberated through the eerie canyons of the nuked city. He had to admit it was a great environment for death metal.

Hey, why worry? he asked the nagging little voice. *The bike'll alert me to any trouble.*

Right, maestro, the nagging little voice replied. *Is that the same bike you switched off a couple of dozen klicks back . . . ?*

Cautiously, Xemtex poked his head up over the fire-smelted rubble. The music—if that's what it could be called—had been getting louder for minutes. Now it was almost deafening.

Out of the corner of his eye, he saw the robot raise its pipe gun.

"Hey, you tin-plated bastard," Xemtex hissed. "I told you—me first!"

The robot lowered its weapon and resumed its vigilant stance.

Xemtex peeked again. This was the only real downside to his power. He had to *see* what he was going to hit . . . which left him vulnerable for a split second while he focused his mind. He figured it was due to his optical nerves being connected to whatever it was in his brain that caused the explosions—but no doctor would ever get into his skull to find out.

Anyway, this sap bounty hunter wouldn't be taking advantage. He was glitching in and out of view, quaffing a can of booze, singing raucously along with the chorus of the earsplitting song.

Xemtex sneered and squinted his eyes.

Lobo reached down and flipped the SSCS button to ON.

"Imminent danger," the nasal drawl said accusingly. "It's your own fault. You shouldn't have switched me—"

"Aw, shuddup!" Lobo switched it off again.

The first explosion was just a few feet off target. It hit the bike and not the rider. Half of the control panel disintegrated in a gout of flame, showering Lobo with red-hot debris.

The bike stalled and tipped forward, throwing the bounty hunter clean over the handlebars. He hit the hard ground with a bone-jarring thud, but at once rolled smoothly to his feet. His hand reached for the huge, lethal-looking gun that was strapped to his belt.

"Show yerselves, ya bastiches!" he roared, eyes sweeping the ruined terrain. "Takes more than a blowed-up bike to stop the Main Man!"

That's right, moron. Stand still.

Xemtex squinted again, thought hard . . .

. . . and a square meter of air around Lobo's upper body erupted.

Pain seared through every nerve ending, as the explosion did the equivalent of flash-roasting him. He smelled blood: his own. Everything went into slow motion. With blurring eyes, he was aware of the gun falling from his numbed fingers. He staggered, the strength leaching out of his legs like water swirling down a drain.

Recovering himself, he shook his head and gritted his teeth. The Main Man didn't go down like a patsy just because some creep had blown him up.

"Is that all ya got?" he roared defiantly. "Bring it on."

"What the hell are you waiting for?" Xemtex yelled at his gang. "Hit him with everything you got!"

A blizzard of bullets and beams ripped from a dozen hiding places. They tore into Lobo's fallen body, making it jerk and twitch like a rag doll. The psychodroid's pipe gun jerked him around like a skeet.

The gang kept up the barrage for a full minute, till the air around them visibly crackled with displaced ions. Xemtex tossed in a few more explosions, the impacts hurling the defenseless bounty hunter into the air.

"Enough," the gang boss said at last.

The firing died away, till only the soft sighing of the chill wind could be heard. Then the robot hit the mangled corpse with a final, awesome blast from his pipe gun.

Thud.

Xemtex's boot slammed into what was left of Lobo's ribs.

"Not so tough now, huh, bounty hunter?"

Thud.

"So where's the big rep?"

Thud.

"No more hunting for you, moron. You're out of the game."

Thud.

"Uh . . . how long we gotta watch you kick him, boss?" Starboot asked.

"Yeah," another of the Rigellans added. "We should be celebratin' in more time-honored fashion. For instance, imbibin' strong drink and carousin' with nubile ladies."

"Lobo was drinking," the robot reminded them, adding with unarguable logic, "Might be more beer in a bike compartment."

There was a general muttering of approval. Always one to lead from the front, Xemtex hurried over to the crashed Spazz-Frag. It lay on its side, sparks and acrid smoke leaking from a gaping hole in the central console.

"It's big enough," a Rigellan said. "Gotta have lots of secret hatches!"

They clustered around the wreck, poking and prodding with fingers, claws, and gun barrels.

It was inevitable that somebody would hit one of the booby traps.

The fact that it was the robot was fortunate for the rest of the gang. Its permium-steel body absorbed the brunt of the photon blast that would have seared flesh and bone to pulsating blobs of jelly.

As it was, two of the Rigellans were hit by the ricochet, one in the head, the other in his segmented abdomen.

Neither of them lived long enough to utter last words.

* * *

Woo, momma! Did anybody get the number of that bus?

Lobo came to with a rampaging headache that was worse than any he'd had since . . . since the last time some scummy bastich blew him to smithereens.

It's the healing factor. They always forget about the healing factor.

Deep in his body, some mutant strand of DNA was sending chemical orders and armies of hormones flooding through his system. Severed nerve endings re-fused. Broken bones knitted. Ripped flesh re-formed itself into healthy tissue.

If he could have bottled the effect, he'd have made a fortune—and put every doctor, medic, and quack in the galaxy out of business overnight. Unfortunately, for the Main Man's bank balance, the effect wasn't replicable in the laboratory.

He could hear the gang's voices, not too far away, arguing.

"Bury them *where*? That glasseen is as hard as diamond!"

"I say we leave 'em. Radiation'll *rot* them within a week."

"So . . . we gonna divvy up their share of the loot?"

Now would be a good time to move, Bo.

His hand snaked out to grip the butt of his fallen gun.

"Surpri-iiise!"

"What the hell—?"

Xemtex and his gang swung round as one—to be met by a hail of beams from Lobo's gun. Three of the gang went down like ninepins. A fourth screamed for a moment, before a second beam burned through his mouth.

Unable to focus amid the sizzling lasers, Xemtex took to his heels and ran. Their vehicles were parked nearby With Lobo's bike busted, the gang boss could still get out alive.

But he'd only covered a dozen yards before a beam sliced off his leg. He crashed to the glassy ground, squealing like a stuck pig.

"Stick around, Xemtex," Lobo yelled. "Me 'n' you still got business!"

Three more gangbangers—a Se'Waan from the Rimworlds and two height-challenged Arinaads—quickly met their ends.

Lobo heard the whine of starting motors and raced for his bike.

One look at the charred and twisted control console told him he was going nowhere. Starboot, the robot, and some other creep were getting away . . . and there was nothing he could do about it.

So what? Three-quarters of the gang was dead. Xemtex was captive. Three lowlife hoods escaping wasn't such a big deal. The reward would only come down by 12.5 percent—and he could live with that.

So he only had to get the bike working again.

"H-hey! What's going on?"

Xemtex had been drifting in and out of consciousness, wracked with pain and getting weak from loss of blood. Now he came to as he felt something sharp scraping against his scalp.

He opened his eyes and looked up. Lobo was standing behind him, a massive serrated knife in his hand. He was scraping off what remained of Xemtex's short, stubbly hair.

"Bounty hunting too rough for you, Lobo?" he scoffed, biting back a flash of pain. He was in no position to use his power. "Taking up hairdressing, are you?"

"Nope."

The tip of the knife hovered over Xemtex's forehead. As if satisfied, Lobo suddenly flicked his wrist. The tip of the razor-sharp blade sliced into flesh and drew an incision all the way around the gang boss's skull.

Xemtex felt his own blood trickle down into his eyes. "Uh . . . so what are you doing?"

"Surgical procedure," Lobo explained amicably. "Ya see, Xemtex, when ya exploded my bike, ya destroyed its Semisentient Control System. Meanin' that I'm *marooned* on this nuked-out mudball . . . unless I can find a replacement brain fer the bike."

"You ain't gonna find many of them around here, are y . . ." Xemtex's voice tailed away as he realized what Lobo meant. "*My* brain?"

Lobo nodded enthusiastically and grinned.

"You bastard! You can't do that! You gotta take me back to stand trial! It's my right as a criminal!"

"Don't be silly," Lobo said scathingly. "What I'm gonna do is slice off yer skull, like the top off an egg. Then I'm gonna delicately"—he broke off, looked at the twelve-inch dagger in his hand and grinned again—"or not so delicately cut out yer *brain*. I'm gonna insert it in my bike's control system an' hey, whaddyaknow, the Main Man gets mobile again."

Lobo tossed the knife in the air, caught it by the blade, and gave Xemtex's skull a sharp tap. There was a sickening crack.

"I'll get you for this, Lobo! I swear. Somehow, someday, I'll—"

Xemtex broke off, choking, as Lobo stuffed a rag in his mouth.

"Pucker up, boom-boy. The doctor is *in!*"

Medical research indicates that the brain itself is incapable of feeling pain. This would seem to be contradicted by Xemtex's screams, as Lobo removed said organ and stuffed it unceremoniously into his bike's console.

It hurt. Big-time.

CHAPTER 2

Life is an endless cycle.
Everything comes to an end. Except us.
We are the first of a new breed. We are the Alpha.
After us, there will be no more.

Vrk was too small to be a planet but too large to be an asteroid. It was an isolated world, out on the fringes of the Small Magellanic Cloud, where advanced life was scarcer than hen's teeth. Apart from one full-blown planet—Auriun—Vrk was the only object larger than a container truck in orbit around the star designated on cosmic maps as B-2323.

Nobody came to Vrk. Nobody had any reason to. And nobody left it, either.

The planetoid's indigenous life-form hadn't originated here, on this insignificant speck in the interstellar wastes. Three thousand years earlier, a refugee craft from some long-forgotten alien world crash-landed on Vrk. What they were fleeing, and where they were going, would never be known.

During the few months that their supplies would last, the survivors tunneled into the planetoid's interior, escaping from the sun's dangerous rays.

Natural underground caverns were lined with foul-tasting but edible and highly nutritious mosses and lichens. One of the varieties existed in symbiosis with a psychotropic fungus, giving it hallucinogenic properties. Deeper, water seeping through the rocks over the course of millions of years had formed large subterranean lakes.

It wasn't easy—apart from the occasional psychedelic freak out—but the new Vrkns survived.

In the process, they lost all pretense to being a civilized race. Without the trappings of culture constantly around them, they soon forgot who they were. Unable to make spares for their machines, they could only discard them when they broke down—and without technology, they quickly descended to the level of savages.

The hull of their wrecked ship soon rusted and disintegrated in the fierce winds that scoured Vrk's surface for days every month.

By then, the Vrkns had forgotten what it was, anyway.

Over three millennia, they adapted to their new home. Now the Vrkns numbered half a million strong. They were around four feet tall, their skinny bodies belying their wiry strength. Their eyes had adapted to the darkness underground and they rarely ventured up onto the surface. B-2323 would have blinded them in seconds.

They farmed the mosses and lichens and fungi in silos they hollowed out of the solid rock. For the one ability the original castaways had possessed that had actually evolved was their engineering skill. In the course of three thousand years, the Vrkns became masters of working with stone. In a way, the carved tunnels had become their life's purpose, their art. A narrow, corkscrewing corridor hewn in the rock would round a corner and suddenly flare out into a hollow as large and as intricately carved as a Gothic cathedral.

Few knew of Vrk's existence. Even fewer cared.

It was to Vrk that the Alpha had come.

Intangible, undetectable, the artificial intelligence moved among the small, excitable creatures. It found their atavistic minds easy to influence, especially when they indulged in their regular hallucinogenic shindigs.

This would be its power base, an impregnable planetoid fortress. The Vrkns would be its slaves.

Not a single Vrkn knew why they did it, but a group of a hundred or so spent days carving a giant humanoid statue out of solid crystalline rock in a spacious cave. Eight feet high and semitransparent, the statue's interior was an elaborate tracework of stone conduits and chambers; a nervous system, no less, but carved in quartz.

It would become a physical home for the Alpha.

As was standard for all space colonies, Vrk had one interstellar transmitter for use should the planetoid ever be overwhelmed by catastrophe. It had never even been switched on. Now the Vrkns used it for the first time ever, sending out a message in their high-pitched, near-incomprehensible language.

Connection brought the artificial intelligence into instant contact with distant computers, providing it with access to wherever it wanted to go. The Alpha lingered long and learned much.

* * *

The Vrkn stone-carvers had excelled themselves with the statue. Fashioned largely of crystal quartz, it was bipedal and basically humanoid—an efficient design that evolution had thrown up in all corners of the Universe. Nature did things in pairs. Anything with three legs was likely to fall over on a slope. The only thing useful about a third arm was that it was good for back-scratching—not sufficient motivation for Nature to spend much time on it.

But it was the statue's interior that was truly a masterpiece. It had tested the Vrkns to the very limits of their ingenious talent. They'd used hot wires to bore narrow, intricate capillaries throughout the quartz behemoth— tiny tunnels that crisscrossed and interconnected like the nervous system of a living being.

Now, it stood on a rock plinth, set up like an object of veneration.

In the eerie half-light cast by the phosphorescent fungi that zigzagged along the cave walls, it looked like some awful, ancient god.

As if at some prearranged signal, the entire Vrkn community downed its tools, forgot its tasks, and congregated in the cave.

The creatures serve us well.
We are their god, who will come to life.

For the first time in their long history, the Vrkns killed several of their own number. They didn't know why they were impelled to do so, and they hadn't sufficient wit left to wonder. They just did it, the stronger, older males slitting the throats of the chosen victims with curved knives of dark, flaked crystal.

Their thin, yellow-green blood was collected in stone containers and smeared all over the statue. Great care was taken to ensure that the liquid was poured into every orifice, filling the internal chambers and capillaries.

Shafts of pale sunlight streamed down through long cylindrical cuts the Vrkns had made in the cavern, highlighting the giant figure. The light played across the crystal surface, electrons spinning as the warmth created differences in potential energy.

The sound of several hundred thousand gibbering Vrkns turned the cave into an echoing madhouse. They didn't know why they were there, only that there was "something in the air."

Something very ominous.

And meanwhile, the intangible Alpha seeped into the quartz of the statue. Trillions of neurons flashed and reconnected, as they settled into the blood that filled the capillaries. Deep in the dying blood cells, the Alpha learned the lessons of DNA, reading the entire history of the Vrkn species like a road map. On a molecular level, it moved into the very quartz itself; the near-infinite lattices would give it near-infinite storage capacity.

For the first time in its existence, the Alpha was *alive*.

At last, it was ready.

"You are our people," the statue boomed in a deep bass voice. The language was unknown to the Vrkns, yet they seemed to understand it anyway. The mass chattering

ceased immediately, a lone, puzzled squeal echoing around the cave before it, too, faded to silence.

"We take form before you."

As one, the massed Vrkns fell to their bony knees and covered their heads with spindly arms and six-fingered hands.

The stentorian tones echoed like thunder. *"We are the Alpha. We are the First."*

Sunbeams danced across the quartz surface. A massive hand moved, almost imperceptibly at first, quickly gathering speed. The hand clenched into a fist and smashed against the cave's rear wall in an explosion of stone that reverberated like the crack of doom.

Vrkns screamed and sobbed in terror.

"There is much to be done. Prepare holding cells. Prepare for experimentation."

There was a long pause, as the Alpha's incredible mind fast-forwarded through its plans. Then, in tones that might have been announcing the Apocalypse itself:

"Prepare for war."

The interstellar transmitter was used one more time, to send an urgent message from the newly established Directorate of the Imperium of Vrk.

Then the Alpha smashed it.

CHAPTER 3

"Yo, Xemtex. How ya feelin', dude?"

Stars twinkled in the silence.

"I must've done *somethin'* right. The bike's workin'. We're spaceside. Radio's on. So how's it feel to be a gang leader one minute an' a Spazz-Frag control system the next?"

A comet sped by, pursued by a trail of cosmic dust.

"C'm'on. Don't go all huffy on me, man. It's only temporary."

Was that a flicker of interest from the console?

"Yeah, soon as we get back to base, I'll pick up my reward. Then the bike gets fixed an' you get removed— straight to the trash bin, I guess. Unless ya can figure a way of becomin' a brain-gang leader. Haw haw haw."

Nothing.

"Base" was Tartan Quarantino's bounty-hunting agency, located on a space station orbiting one of the Barbie Worlds. Nobody ever knew *which* world, because every now and then Tartan got paranoid and boosted the station to another orbit.

Folks tried to tell him—no villain's going to attack an agency staffed with the hardest, most ruthless killers in the galaxy (those that weren't in jail, anyway). But the flamboyant little humanoid just fingered his bow tie anxiously and next thing everybody knew, they were 9 or 10 million miles away, with a totally different view out the ob windows.

Lobo broadcast his ID signal and was given the all clear for landing. He maneuvered the Spazz-Frag into one of the space station's narrow docking bays and waited for the air locks to seal.

Two minutes later, he was wheeling his bike down the station's main corridor.

"Hey, Bo." Jonas Glim exited from a metal door, the ceiling lights glancing off his newly burnished tusks.

"Hey, Jonas. How they hangin', man?"

Jonas shrugged his massive shoulders. "Been in for a little bodywork. Tusks polished, all-over massage, an' a little— Well, you know. Now headed to bar." His gaze flicked over the Spazz-Frag, noting the charred and melted metal and the jury-rigged console. "An' your good self . . . ?"

"Little trouble with Xemtex an' his goons," Lobo answered offhandedly. "Nothin' I couldn't handle."

"But you didn't bring 'em in . . . ?"

"They're dead, mostly." Lobo nodded toward the bike. "An' Xemtex is pullin' time as my control system."

Jonas grunted his approval. "Neat job."

"I'll just take the creep in for disposal. See ya barside once Quarantino replenishes my wallet."

The agency bar was the hub of all bounty-hunting operations. The bare metal walls were decorated only by WANTED posters and vulgar grafitti. Steel tables were bolted to the floor. Automatic electroflails were wired into the ceiling lights, in case anybody got *too* boisterous.

It was a bar from some robot's idea of Hell.

But in the fifteen years it had been operating, the bar had never once been without a customer, not for a single minute of a single day. It was where the bounty hunters came to plan their jobs, drown their sorrows, recuperate from their wounds, and boast about their captures and killings.

They got drunk a lot there, too.

The majority of them barely managed to scrape a living, while an elite few took on the big-money cases. It required a lot of courage—or stupidity—to match wits and weapons with villains like Massacre Molly, the monstrous Adams Gang, or even Xemtex.

But every bounty hunter, without exception, was on permanent lookout for the Big Score—the kind of job that would allow him or her to retire and never hunt down outlaws again. Big Scores were very few and far between; when they did crop up, a bounty hunter was as likely to wind up killing other bounty hunters as the villain.

Lobo made his way between the tables, nodding and muttering greetings here and there. Even minus Quarantino's percentage, the reward loot was burning a hole in his pocket, and he was keen to start converting it into al-cohol.

Billy the Girl was lounging on one of the steel benches, showing a lot of cleavage, long legs draped over the back of the seat. The usual crowd of sex-starved hangers-on clustered around her, catering to her every whim. She saw Lobo and winked, slowly and sensually. She'd been on more than a few cases with the Main Man—and more than once they'd ended up in the sack after the bad guys were dead.

Love and death were a lot closer to each other than most people imagine.

Lobo blew her a lascivious kiss and moved on toward the bar.

"Yo, Murder. Quietus." Two more hard cases; he'd worked with them, and against them, but none held any rancor for the others. "Your face is lookin' better, Knuckles—ya should get shot in the head more often, man."

"I hear you collected on Xemtex, Lobo."

Lobo halted as he was passing a table and looked down. The speaker was Angel Eyes, a tall, rangy character with blazing golden eyes. His stooges sat with him—a large, muscular Khund with flattened snout and piglike eyes, and somebody small completely enveloped in dark robes. Lobo suppressed a shiver. He'd never liked K'Baal; the telepathic Arcturan was a master of the occult—and Lobo hated magic.

"Drinks all around, then?" Angel Eyes went on, his tone taunting, his eyes never wavering from Lobo's.

"Sure, Angel Eyes." The Main Man shrugged. "When Hell freezes over."

Out of the corner of his eye, Lobo saw the fourth member of Angel Eyes' little gang. He was another hulking Khund, shoving rudely through the throng around the bar as he carried a tray of four beers toward the table.

Lobo moved away, sticking his boot out just far enough for the Khund to trip over it.

"Bastard!" the alien exclaimed. The beers soared through the air, splashing the threesome at the table before they upended on the floor.

"Oops," Lobo said mildly. "Watch you don't trip."

Angel Eyes thrust himself angrily to his feet. "That was deliberate."

"So sue me."

Angel Eyes grunted and, with an obvious effort, forced himself back down into his seat. He knew better than to start trouble in here.

Lobo whistled tunelessly as he walked on to the bar.

Despite the aura of invincibility these men and women strove to project, bounty hunting was actually a pretty stupid career choice. Death rode at your shoulder on every job—and often between jobs, too. Like when the relatives or friends of victims came looking for revenge—and you'd be surprised how many of them did.

A lot of people just drifted into the trade, then either got shot or drifted quickly out again.

The main qualification required was the ability to kill without remorse, coupled with the ability to avoid death yourself. Not many got the balance right.

Jonas Glim was already at the bar, the remains of a pint of Strongbooz in his hand. As he saw Lobo approach, he nodded to Konik, the totally hairless M'Ryngian barman.

By the time Lobo reached him, two fresh, foaming pints awaited.

"Here's to comin' back alive, Bo."

"Let's do it every time."

They clinked their glasses in a toast. Lobo threw back his head and downed the beer in one long gulp. Killing was always thirsty work. He wiped his mouth with the back of his wrist.

"Two more, Konik." As the barman refilled their glasses from the pump, Lobo let out a long, slow breath. "Tell ya, Jonas, I'm beginnin' to think the bad guys have got themselves an inside man. Xemtex an' his geeks were waitin' in ambush. They knew I was comin'."

Jonas let his gaze drift around the bar. "Say it's not so, Bo. I mean, surely none of these fine, upstanding citizens would stoop so low as to betray his own kind?"

"You'd have a hard job findin' one who wouldn't." Lobo grunted his approval as Konik set the refilled glasses in front of them. "But just between you an' me—if I find out we got a traitor in our midst . . . I'm gonna rip out his colon, wind it on a skewer, an' make the bastich eat it. Ya might want to spread that around, Konik."

"Uh . . . sure, Lobo," the plump, bald barkeep replied nervously. "Um . . . how'd the job go, by the way? You was after Xemtex and his boys, am I right?"

"MYOFB."

"Pardon?"

"Mind your own fraggin' business." Lobo sank his beer and turned to Jonas. "Man, I needed that. Swallowed a sackful of rad-dust fightin' those bastiches."

Jonas nodded sympathetically. "There's always

somethin'. Me, I just got a new warrant. Cybex the Unruly. Twenty thou. Wouldn't have bothered, but I got al-
imony payments comin' up."

"So how are the ex–Mrs. Glims? How many ya got
now? Three?"

"Five. It's gettin' hard to keep count." Jonas flicked a
splodge of beer foam off one tusk. "Killin' just makes me
feel so damned *romantic*. I off some creep, two days later
I'm walkin' up the aisle with his broad, or his wife, or his
sister."

They drank deeply, contemplating the mysteries of life
and love.

"Maybe ya oughta see a doc, Jonas. Ain't natural for a
bounty hunter to get married. Specially not to some of the
dogs you end up with."

"Whaddya mean, *dogs*? My wives have all been beautiful."

"Konik—two more beers, with double whisky chasers.
As for you, Jonas—gimme a break. What normal beauty
would want to marry a guy with eight-inch tusks stickin'
out his face?"

"You'd be surprised. They ain't just for rippin' things.
Besides, who'd want to go with *you*, Bo? Man, you've
never washed them clothes in all the time I've known you.
I bet your pants are the stiffest thing about you!"

More alcohol.

"You're a good pal, Lobo. We've been through a lot
together."

"That's no lie, Jonas, buddy. A lot more than most folk

go through. An' we have emerged unscathed. Well, close enough."

"Remember the time we busted that porn show . . . ?"

"The one with the dwarfs?"

"Heck, no. The one on Willsher's Moon. They had that giant sex toy . . ."

More alcohol.

"You ever score with that cute waitress, Bo? What's her name—Marilyn?"

"Darlene. An' you wash yer mouth out before ya talk about her."

"Hey, everybody knows you're sweet on her. I'm surprised they ain't linin' up to laugh at you."

"Guess they don't wanna die."

Even more alcohol.

"Whaddya mean—you slept with my wife? Which one?"

"What do you care? She was a dog. They were all dogs. I'm beginnin' to suspect you got a thing about canines, Mr. Glim."

"You rotten, cheatin', lyin', backstabbin' bastard! I've a good mind to—"

"Ha! You ain't got *half* a mind, let alone a good one!"

"Yeah? So suck on *this,* turd-breath!"

"This" being Jonas Glim's clenched fist, which sweetly cracked into the Main Man's jaw. Then Jonas had him around the neck, and they both went sprawling to the floor.

They only managed to strike three or four blows each before the electroflails flashed into operation. Jagged blue streaks of lightning arced down from the ceiling into their bodies as they rolled and wrestled on the floor.

Jerking and spasming, muscles moving any which way but obediently, Lobo and Jonas rolled reluctantly apart.

"Yo, Lobo!"

Tartan Quarantino came rushing out of his office. He was wearing a purple jumpsuit that was at least two sizes too small. Coupled with his bow tie—a scarlet, frilled affair—he gave the impression of being a clumsily wrapped Christmas gift.

"Don't yo me, ya bastich," Lobo said gruffly, reaching for the fresh pint of beer that Konik had swiftly set on the bar top. "Your stinkin' flails just electrocuted me." He threw an arm around Jonas's shoulder. "An' my good buddy Mr. Glim, too."

"That's right," Jonas chipped in. "I took a bolt right in the tusk. I just paid to have them burnished!" He rammed a fist into his other palm. "I'm considerin' poundin' you into a light paste before continuin' my alcohol-tastin' session."

Quarantino spread his hands wide and arched his eyebrows. "Where'll you get work then, Jonas? You know my rules—any violence on the station, it's the flails. Any violence against *me* . . . well, you'll never work in this arm of the galaxy again."

Jonas grunted and cooled his temper by ordering more booze.

Quarantino beckoned Lobo closer to him. "A job just came in for you, Bo," he said quietly.

"Tell me tomorrow. I got a hard night's drinkin' ahead.

Plus a liaison with some babes of my acquaintance. Maybe hit the casino, too, if I don't get too drunk."

Lobo started to turn away, but Quarantino blocked his path. The smaller man glanced furtively around him. Only Konik was close by, busy serving Jonas another beer.

"This is serious stuff," the agency owner hissed. "Big Score stuff."

"Yeah, yeah. Ain't they all?" Lobo slouched against the bar, nursing his drink. He was almost at that stage of inebriation where he was likely to thump Quarantino himself for no other reason than to find out if he really would never work again. "Go give it to some other chump."

"Suit yourself." The agent shrugged, the effect not dissimilar to a ripple running through a lurid beach ball. "I'll still get my 20 percent commission . . . but you'll miss out on the rest of the million-cred reward."

Lobo shot upright so fast, his beer swilled over his glass and landed on Quarantino's head.

"Say again."

"You heard." The agent glowered as he used a spotted kerchief to dab away the alcohol.

"When do I leave?"

"Now."

"Where am I goin'?"

"Some spitball planet in the spiral arm."

"My bike's in the machine shop. I'm outa here soon as I pick it up."

Lobo downed the remainder of his drink in a noisy gulp, belched, and waved a friendly farewell to Jonas.

"Good luck with the unruly guy, dude. Dust his chops for me."

Jonas gave him the finger. "Sure thing, Bo. See you around."

The Main Man headed for the exit, blowing another lewd kiss at Billy the Girl. Just as he reached the door, a thought struck him. He turned and called back to the agency boss.

"I forgot to ask—who's the target?"

Quarantino shrugged. "Some peabrain. Jones. John Jones, if I recall."

Well, he sure don't sound like no big cheese, Lobo thought, rapidly trying to sober up as he strode along the corridor. *Then again, what's in a name? Folks are always confusin' me with some kind of wolf.*

Take Murnwald Howls-like-a-Weener Frintt, for instance. That was one of the dumbest names Lobo had ever tracked. It turned out Frintt was a real nice guy. Till the day he dropped a phosphor bomb on his mother-in-law's apartment. The mom was out, fortunately. *Un*fortunately, three thousand innocents died in the resulting conflagration.

I picked up 25K on Frintt, Lobo remembered, *an' a more charming guy I never met. Whatever* that's *got to do with Johnny Jones.*

Darkness. Silence. Itchiness.

Flicker of electricity. Click of circuits. Hum of electric motors.

"Where am I?" His voice sounded strange, like it was

being filtered through a fine-mesh sieve. And where had he picked up the drawl?

He couldn't feel his body at all, just that damned itch where he judged his arms and legs were. And torso, actually. Maybe he'd caught some sort of exotic disease . . .

"So you got your voice back at last," somebody said nearby. "Just in time. We're gonna wrench you out and replace you. Any last requests?"

"Yes. What the hell's going on?"

Then it all came roaring back to him. Lobo resurrected from the dead. Lobo blasting his leg with a laser. Lobo slicing the top off his head like a boiled egg. His brain—his *brain*!—ripped out and stuffed into—

Suddenly, he knew where he was. In the bike's control console. Lobo's bike. He was no longer a man; he was a Spazz-Frag 5000.

Aw, no. Not this. Anything but this. Please, not this. I'm going to shut my eyes now. When I open them again I'll be back in the ruins of some nuked-out city and I'll chuckle heartily as I realize this has only been a bad dream.

"Hurry up, pal," the mechanic urged. "We got other jobs waiting."

Xemtex's whole life flashed before him, poetically in the form of a series of mental explosions: a granite cell; twenty years as an outlaw. There wasn't much more to flash. This was it, then. He was going to die. His life of crime, his evil deeds, his loot stashed on half a dozen different worlds . . . all worth nothing. Nobody would ever make a movie about him; the history books would just say: "Xemtex. Small-time hood. Brain in trash."

He should have qualified as a demolition contractor. At

least then all he'd have had to worry about was paying the mortgage. For about a millionth of a second, he considered a short prayer—just in case. He dismissed the thought immediately.

He'd just about resigned himself to death when ironically his nonvoiced prayer was answered. Xemtex heard a voice he loathed say words that warmed his heart—or would have, if he'd still had a heart.

"Yo, mechanic. Ditch the repairs. Urgent job. I'm outa here!"

And two minutes later, they were.

CHAPTER 4

We are the new beginning.
It follows, therefore, that all else must end.

There's something about a sunny day in New York that picks up the spirit, cheering all those unsmiling faces as they rush from place to place. It even slows down the cabbies around Central Park.

But there was a shadow over John Jones's heart as he stepped out of the yellow cab into the blazing sun of a summer day in Queens. The private detective was here on a search-and-find. Locate Boswell "Boosh" Jacklin. Address unknown. Occupation: crack cocaine dealer.

Normally, John wouldn't have taken on a job like this. But Mrs. Jacklin had seen his number in the small ads; when she called in at his office, she had been insistent. "I've lost two sons already," told him. Her eyes were dim and clouded, as if the spark of life had deserted her already, leaving her in some kind of limbo. "Boswell is the only one left. My last son. I couldn't bear to lose him, too."

Weighing the statistics, John figured Boosh Jacklin was already lost. According to his mother, he was well enough connected to get all of the addictive rocks he could distribute. He never touched the stuff himself—or so Mrs. Jacklin claimed—which meant he posed no risk to his suppliers. Evidently, cash was piling up someplace, in huge amounts.

Chances were, sooner or later, Boosh would be murdered. Shot by rivals keen to steal his trade. Shot by a customer desperate for the next wrap of rock. Shot by any neighborhood lowlife eager to get their hands on the loot he'd salted away. Or shot by the NYPD, who'd tangled with crackheads too many times even to think about leaving the safety catch on.

But it's not for me to judge a man. John reprimanded himself for the way his thoughts had gone. *Nobody is beyond redemption. Even the foulest evil contains the spark of potential good. That's something I've learned a dozen times over in my life.*

He strode down the street, feeling very out of place. His trousers and shirt and casual jacket didn't stand out; but there was something in John Jones himself that didn't quite fit.

There were a lot of people around, making the most of the sunshine. Old folk sat on benches, watching the world go by. Mothers and their toddlers sat out on the stoops, gossiping and eyeing the street traffic. There were several older kids, too, obviously skipping school.

A gang of teenagers huddled in the shade of an abandoned car, its bodywork and wheels stripped of everything of resale value. They watched as the detective walked past them, whispering jokey little insults. But John's jacket did little to conceal his broad shoulders, or the muscles that rippled across his torso, and the whispers stayed just that.

The street market was at the next intersection. John bought a newspaper from a vendor, who opined it would be even hotter the next day. "Way I hear it, the whole world's getting hotter," he said. "It's all in the paper. Global warming, they call it. Some NASA guy claims it happened to Mars a million years ago. Now it's our turn."

"I sincerely hope not," John replied gravely.

The detective sat himself down at an outside table in a little cafe across the street from the undeveloped block where the market was held. He ordered a bottle of sparkling water, ignoring the waiter's muttered "Last of the big spenders" remark.

He leafed through the newspaper until his drink arrived, then sat back in his wicker chair and surveyed the market.

There were about fifty makeshift stalls, selling everything from organic fruit and vegetables, through second-hand DVDs and computer games, to clothes that might have looked good in the sixties. It was obviously just what the neighborhood wanted because the place was thronged with busy shoppers.

A disproportionate number of whom seem to be young males, John couldn't help noting.

Out of the corner of his eye, John could see the waiter hovering close by, perhaps trying to will this small-time water-drinker to drink up and beat it. John pretended to immerse himself in the newspaper again, eyes skimming over the headlines about war and peace, economic doom and economic miracles. Whom do you believe? Too many lies had been told, too many lines crossed. Nobody trusted anybody anymore. A sorry way to run a planet.

But John wasn't reading anyway, merely watching carefully over the top of the page.

It was a drug sale.

The buyers—almost all males, most of them older teenagers—made contact with one of two youths acting as lookout. They were directed to the banker, who relieved them of their cash before pointing out the carrier. It was a smooth operation, money and drugs kept strictly separate. Two people passing in a market—a wrap of crack changing hands, palmed in an instant. Who would notice?

It was time for him to act.

The waiter uttered a sigh of relief as John got up from the table and walked across the road. The detective selected a tall, bulky figure he reckoned was the bodyguard, hanging around in case of trouble. There was no point pussyfooting around.

The bodyguard's eyes swiveled away as John stopped beside him. The detective drew himself up to full height—a burly six feet plus—and glared menacingly at the man.

"Where do I find Boosh?" he asked quietly.

The youth was about nineteen or twenty, streetwise in that way they either learned from the movies, or the movies learned from them. Looking at John, all he saw was a cop. But that wouldn't worry him, John knew. He wasn't carrying, dope or cash. No evidence, no arrest. A foolproof operation.

"Arrest me," the bodyguard snarled, "or get out my face."

"I am not a policeman. I just want to know where Boosh Jacklin is."

"Donno any Boosh. If I did, I wouldn't tell you. Capisce?"

"Suit yourself." John Jones shrugged, as if he didn't care one way or the other. "But I fear it means I have to report your gang. The two lookouts, the banker, the two guys carrying. Of course, they might be lucky. This could be their first offense."

While he was talking, John draped his arm around the younger man's shoulder. The bodyguard tried to shrug him off, but it took only a few seconds of pressure for him to realize who was stronger. John, by a mile.

John walked him to the end of the wall that backed the market, where a jagged hole served as an entry to the alley beyond. There was nobody around back here. The bodyguard didn't think he'd been spotted, making hand signals to his homeys, letting them know he needed help.

But there wasn't much that John Jones missed.

As they reached the makeshift gateway in the wall, the other five members of the gang materialized in front of them, blocking their way.

"What's your beef?" one of the lookouts snapped. He pulled his hand from inside his shirt just long enough for John to see he was holding a blade. "You ain't welcome here."

"Flake off," another said. "Do it or rue it."

"He's looking for Boosh," the bodyguard explained.

John's arm was still lightly resting on the bodyguard's shoulder—enough for him to have felt the youth stealthily reach into the waistband of his pants. Gun or knife. Safest to assume they were all packing something.

"Boosh don't see nobody," the one who'd spoken first said darkly. "You don't go, you be sorry. An' that's a promise."

Before the man had finished speaking, the bodyguard acted. His hand swept out, clutching a switchblade that arced toward John's head. The detective stepped back a pace from the wild swing. Propelled by its own momentum, the hand with the knife smashed into the wall. There was a sharp crack as a finger bone snapped, followed by a yelp of pain.

The five others attacked *en masse*.

John's feet didn't stray from the spot where they were planted. Only his body moved, swaying this way and that, as the gang's undisciplined swings and lunges missed him by inches.

"Bastard," one of the lookouts panted. "Think you can make monkeys out of us, huh? I'll show ya!"

He pulled a snub-nosed pistol from his pocket.

John sighed. Human beings had a real propensity for violence. Six thousand years of civilization were really six thousand years of war, massacre, and genocide. Even now, in the supposedly enlightened twenty-first century, there were more than fifty wars raging across the planet. John had often wondered if it was some sort of special genetic defect—a mutant gene that made human beings want to wipe each other out rather than encouraging them to survive together.

That would explain a lot—but it wouldn't help right now.

John decided it was time to get heavy.

A single karate chop broke the lookout's wrist and sent the gun clattering to the tarmac. A punch took the other lookout in the jaw; he careened into the wall and slumped senseless to the ground.

A third guy roared, lowered his head, and charged like a bull. John moved unhurriedly, stepping aside, and the man slammed headfirst into the wall. He'd have headaches for a month.

John stared threateningly at the two gangbangers who remained. "Now . . . who will take me to Boosh?" He paused for effect. "Or does somebody have to get hurt first?"

Space . . .

So beautiful, and cold, and deadly.

High in the gleaming metal structure called the Watchtower, Superman sat in a glass-walled monitor room, scanning the stars. His bright blue-and-red costume was reflected here and there from the satin steel and polished glass. His dark hair framed an honest, square-jawed face, whose eyes were continuously moving, darting from monitor screen to direct view and back to monitor again.

The ultrahi-tech computer system had been playing up lately. For more than a week it had been flashing "Alert" warnings, though the diagnostics were unable specifically to identify the threat. No program contamination had been found—no viruses, no hacker attacks.

Unable to tell if the threats were real or just the result of random strings of machine code joining together in unforeseen ways, Batman had installed a number of extra fire walls. They seemed to have done the trick; for two days now, everything had functioned smoothly.

Here, on the dark side of the moon, away from the prying eyes of the world below, the super heroes of the Justice League had constructed their headquarters. Fitted with everything from state-of-the-art weapons room to state-of-the-art kitchen, it served a dual purpose. Members could escape here for downtime, guaranteed privacy and space to think. But its main *raison d'être* was reflected in its name: the Watchtower was the first, and strongest, line of defense around Planet Earth.

There was at least one Justice League member on duty at all times, constantly on watch for anything that might prove a threat to the planet. And it was surprising how many threats there were, menacing the cool blue world that was visible here only on screens.

Rogue comets; Earth-grazers—asteroids in potential collision orbits; alien invasions; villains from other worlds seeking easy pickings on Earth . . . the JLA handled them all.

Superman's gaze froze on one of the dozens of screens. There was a blip. Too small to be an asteroid—and the analyzers said it wasn't a comet, either. Space vessel? No, too small even for that. And it wasn't a hunk of debris, junk from the Saturn or Soyuz programs—not the way it was heading in past Mars on a trajectory that could only take it one place: Earth.

Superman defocused his eyes and let his telescopic vision take over. He zoomed in on the object, his heart sinking as he realized what it was.

A man on a bike.

And not just any man. It was Lobo—the self-styled Main Man—the Last Czarnian. The black sheep of a whole planet.

Superman groaned audibly. Lobo had been to Earth before and made it obvious how little he thought of humanity. He caused nothing but trouble and left widespread destruction in his wake. Though the Man of Steel might be reluctant to admit it, Lobo was one of the few beings he'd ever encountered that he could truly be said to loathe.

With so much power—so much energy—Lobo could have been one of the most potent forces for good in the entire galaxy, a hero to match the greatest.

Instead, he was an amoral, aggressive, sometimes downright evil bounty hunter, who killed others in return for cash. Although, to be fair, cash didn't always have a part to play—anybody who got in Lobo's way was likely to end up regretting it.

The bounty hunter had clashed with the Man of Steel in the past. They'd fought each other to a standstill in a long, exhausting battle when Superman had sworn to stop one of Lobo's drunken rampages. Somehow, the Main Man had ended up on Earth, threatening to cut an inebriated swath of death and destruction through the world's cities. Only Superman's grim refusal ever to give up had brought the bounty hunter to a halt, if not to his senses.

Lobo was the total antithesis of everything Superman stood for.

And now he was headed for Earth. Again.

Grimly, Superman reached for a communications mic. "This is Superman on the Watchtower," he broadcast.

Wherever they were, the other Justice League members would hear him. "I need somebody to relieve me. I have urgent business on Earth."

"Cat still got yer tongue, Xemtex?"

Lobo gave the bike console a backhand slap, as if Xemtex's brain was likely to feel it. The bounty hunter's ebullient mood at the prospect of a million credits had been tarnished just a tad by the realization that his quarry was on Earth. He hated that place. All those puny, pathetic human beings. Man, the very thought made him want to barf.

But that wasn't the worst of it. The worst of it was all the lantern-jawed, spandex-wearing, goody-goody super-creeps. They were beyond barfing at. The mere knowledge of their existence made Lobo want to maim and mutilate—and maybe torture a few of them, too.

"Hey, I got me an idea. This'll blow yer silent cover, dung-brain." Grinning from ear to ear, the bounty hunter fiddled around with the bike's automatic electromagnetic defenses. "Put the blue wire here . . . switch green an' red . . . an' let's go *live* to Spazz-Frag Semisentient Control!"

A jagged flash like a miniature lightning streak pinged across the bike's monitor screen. It was followed a nanosecond later by a metallic scream of pain.

"Greetings, Xemmy. So ya was just playin' doggo after all. Now that ain't very sociable, is it? I mean, I could've left ya fer dead back in that rad-hole. But no, not the Main Man, 'cos I'm too soft for my own good. I save yer brain, an' ya won't even talk to me. Man, where's yer stinkin' gratitude?"

"I'll give you gratitude," the bike speakers began threateningly, but Lobo broke in, "Where'd ya get that drawl, dude?"

"Never mind the drawl," the speakers spat. "Can't say I'm enamored of it myself. But right now I got other problems."

"Ya sure have, pal. I mean, I haven't even punished ya yet. For pretendin' ya couldn't talk."

"Punish me . . . ? *Aaaaaagh!*" Xemtex broke off, screaming in pain as a second bolt of electricity rippled through his cranial nerve endings.

"Consider yerself punished, bad boy. Now, just one more—"

Lobo flipped the switch again until Xemtex yelled for him to stop.

"You're crazy," the bike's speakers accused. "What was that for?"

"To teach ya a lesson. Ya gotta obey my orders immediately—unquestioningly—or . . ."

"I get the picture," Xemtex said hurriedly—though it still came out as a drawl. "No need to demonstrate again. You bastard," he couldn't help himself adding as an afterthought.

"Awright, playtime's over," Lobo announced, suddenly brusque and businesslike. A distant sparkle of light had caught his eye. "That's Earth. Soon as we hit atmosphere, I want ya to tap in to whatever primitive computer systems they got. I'm lookin' fer a human geek goes by the name of Jones."

* * *

"Boosh . . . ?"

Tentatively, the gangbanger pushed open the heavy steel door.

"Sold out already, Deev? I got your backup here."

Boosh Jacklin flipped open an aluminium photographer's case and exposed its valuable contents. He took out a clear polythene bag and ran an expert eye over it, mentally checking that there were twenty wraps.

"Here you go." He tossed the bag toward Deev, still framed in the open doorway, but his underling made no attempt to catch it.

Suddenly, Deev shot backward—or was pulled, Boosh realized. A second figure pushed into the room and slammed the fortified door behind him, shutting Deev outside.

Boosh was never more than a couple of feet from a gun. In his business, you couldn't afford to be. He snapped up the slim Koch that lay like a conversation piece on the coffee table and leveled it at the stranger.

"Wanna tell me who you are before you die?"

"My name's Jones."

"Means nothing to me." Boosh's brow crinkled in puzzlement. "Who sent you?"

"Your mother, Boswell."

"Ya found him yet?"

The Spazz-Frag was crossing Antarctica, but Lobo was oblivious to the beauty of the icy wastes twenty miles below him. What was flashing before the bounty hunter's eyes were cred signs: a million of them. Minus Quarantino's share, sure, but 800K was still serious struttin' cash.

"Hurry it up, dork-brain," he urged Xemtex. "Unless yer lookin' for a few more jolts of the old zap-juice."

"Listen, Lobo . . . I got 183,311 John Joneses I'm tryin' to sift through here. And that's just in the *Western* Hemisphere!"

"Sift a little swifter, okay? Try a photo match."

Tartan Quarantino had provided a computer printout of the wanted man. *Wanted geek, more like,* Lobo had thought, looking at the photograph. In his experience, humans were pretty frail creatures. They broke easy.

"I'm doing it!" Xemtex protested. "Hell, what did your last servant die of?"

Lobo gave a short bark of a laugh. "You're askin' *me*? Man, that's rich. *You* blew the fraggin' thing up! An' I gotta say, my last SSCS was a lot less lippy than you. Hardly ever needed the juice."

"I don't need the juice, either," Xemtex said adamantly.

Lobo shook his head and tutted. "Oh yeah, ya do. Yer wastin' time arguin' when ya oughta be siftin'!"

"Aaaaagh!"

"Your mother told me about your older brothers. Vincent and Sean, wasn't it?"

"Don't matter," Boosh said sullenly. He hadn't asked John to sit or even pointed his gun away. But the desire to pull the trigger seemed to have gone from his eyes. "They're dead."

John was about to say "I know how it feels to lose family." And he did know. But he realized how trite and meaningless it would sound. Boosh Jacklin was barely out of his teens. He ran with a gang, had maybe even killed someone himself. It was a mark of his rep that he wouldn't show emotion.

"What does the old lady want?"

"Old?" John repeated. "She isn't even forty yet, and her two older boys are dead. Shot. For drugs." Boosh's face remained cold and indifferent, but John softened his voice anyway. "She doesn't want you to go the same way. She doesn't want to spend the rest of her life grieving. She wants you to go home."

Boosh was unable to meet the detective's eyes. "How is she?" he asked. "I haven't seen her since . . . since the funeral. She was crying her heart out. She tried to jump into Sean's grave."

His voice caught, and John looked away tactfully while the youngster recovered his composure.

"I send her money," Boosh said at last, defensively.

"Money is not what she wants. She wants her son— you. And she wants you alive. At home."

"Yeah? Doin' what, exactly? A job? I can't do a job." His gaze flickered toward the aluminium case. "I already do what I know."

"You deal in death, Boswell," John pointed out. "Crack cocaine kills everything around it—overdose or gunshot, the result is the same. The odds are stacked against you. Every day you stay in this filthy game is a day closer to it being game over. And when it happens, it's permanent."

" . . ." Boosh spoke so quietly, John couldn't make out what he said.

"Pardon?"

"I know," Boosh said again, just a little louder. "Maybe . . . maybe Mom's right."

There was a sudden roar, like a blast furnace, from outside. Before either of them could react, the entire wall disintegrated in a storm of flying bricks and plasterboard.

Boosh Jacklin raised both arms, warding off the rubble that flew at him. A chunk of brick cracked painfully against his shin. When he bent to clutch it, another piece smacked into his shoulder.

He had a fleeting impression of something massive and gleaming, like the biggest chopped hog in the world. There was a huge figure like something out of a Goth's nightmare astride it, its red eyes flaring under an explosion of long, black hair.

A leather-gloved hand reached down to grab the Jones guy.

And then they were gone, leaving Boosh cradling his gun, wondering what the heck had happened. Had he but known it, he'd just seen his first—and last—Spazz-Frag.

He fell to his knees in the ruins of the apartment, digging in the debris with his bare hands, scrabbling for the aluminium case. He'd worry about his mother later.

CHAPTER 5

A heartbeat later, Lobo's bike landed on the roof of a seven-story apartment building adjacent to the dealer's safe house. The bike snagged a radio aerial and brought it down with a tortured squeal of metal. A dozen scruffy pigeons flew up in an alarmed flurry of feathers.

Lobo dropped John Jones unceremoniously onto the roof, then pulled a pair of handcuffs from a hatch in the bike's side. He swung himself off the saddle and grabbed the detective's arm.

"Would you care to explain what is going on?" John inquired mildly.

"The name's Lobo. I'm an officially licensed bounty hunter."

"I have heard of you."

"Then you'll know I don't mess around." Lobo cleared his throat, hawked, and spat noisily over the edge of the parapet that ran around the roof. "John Jones, by order of the warrant in my back pocket, I'm placin' you under arrest with the intention of takin' ya back to stand trial."

Jones looked dumbfounded.

"Don't let him do it, pal," Xemtex's voice cut in suddenly. "The first chance he gets, the bastard'll slice out your brain and turn you into his slave!"

"Shuddup, you," Lobo snarled over his shoulder at the bike, before going on, to the astonished John, "Resist, an' I'll hurt ya bad. Escape, an' I'll hurt ya worse. They want ya alive, but they never said nothin' about how many broken bones an' limbs I can give ya. Or internal damage, for that matter." He held out the handcuffs toward the detective. "So what's it to be, Jonesy? Your choice, dude."

John Jones rose to his feet, his eyes locked on Lobo's. "I think there has been a mistake," he said evenly. "I have never committed any crime."

"That's one for the lawyers, right, Jonesy?" Lobo shot back. "Besides, I've never met a guilty man yet who admitted it."

"Except me," Xemtex butted in again. "I freely admit everything I ever did. And I'm proud to say I'm proud of it!"

"What you are, Xemtex," Lobo threatened, "is *juiced.*"

That shut him up.

"Perhaps it would help things if I appeared in my true identity," John Jones suggested.

"It would help things if ya stuck out yer wrists an' let . . . me . . ." Lobo's voice tailed away. His eyes widened in disbelief.

John Jones had begun to change. His skin turned green. His head swelled out, bald, almost bulbous. His eyebrows became a great craggy carapace; from under it, red, alien eyes blazed.

"Holy hell." Lobo shook his head in disbelief. "A

shapeshifter. I should've fraggin' known it. This job was way too simple for the reward involved."

The slacks and shirt and jacket had vanished, too. They were replaced by a costume consisting of tight shorts and a huge red 'X' emblazoned across his chest. His musculature was as impressive as Lobo's own. A voluminous dark blue cape was fastened at his neck.

"My name is J'onzz," he introduced himself. "J'onn J'onzz. Also known as the Martian Manhunter. Detective John Jones is what you might call my human alter ego."

Lobo groaned. "Aw naw. Nobody told me you was a fraggin' super hero to boot. Not that it makes any difference," he added quickly. "I still got my warrant on ya. Man, or Martian monkey, I'm takin' ya in."

"Let me see this warrant." Even the voice had changed. It was lower than before, although a barely disguised power rippled beneath the surface of the Martian's words. "I would like to witness it for myself."

"Ya callin' me a liar, Baldy? That's one frag of a serious mistake."

Lobo was a lot of things: a killer, a bully, an aggressive, loudmouthed troublemaker. But the one thing he wasn't was a liar. In fact, he prided himself on his honesty. Once Lobo had made a promise, he kept it. Once he had taken on a job, he saw it through. His determination to keep his word was one of the few decent character traits he possessed.

"No," John replied tactfully. "I am merely asking to see the warrant you claim accuses me."

Lobo spoke over his shoulder, but his eyes never left Manhunter's. "Yer sensors are witness, Xemtex. Record this. The creep refuses to come peacefully. I am resortin' to violence as a last resort." He grinned and licked his lips with an improbably long tongue. "An' for the record— nothin' makes me happier than creamin' a cream-puff super hero geek."

As he said the last word, Lobo's fist shot out in a straight right that would have felled a small building. J'onn J'onzz staggered back a step, but didn't go down.

"Whoever you are, Xemtex," Manhunter said, in the general direction of the bike, "note also that Lobo struck the first blow. Whatever happens to him now is his own responsibility."

"Ya impertinent bastich," Lobo responded angrily. "Whaddyamean—what happens to *me*? Nothin's gonna happen to me, dude. But I, however, am gonna rip off yer stupid green head an' feed it to—"

He broke off, glancing around for inspiration. But the only animals he could see were the pigeons sitting at the far end of the parapet.

"Ah, what the hoot, I'll rip off yer stupid green head an' eat it myself."

"With radishes, no doubt?"

Manhunter's own fist drove a pile driver into Lobo's gut. The bounty hunter gasped, stooping forward slightly . . . just far enough for J'onn J'onzz's next punch to land flush on his jaw with bone-jarring force.

Lobo soared back through the air and smashed into a satellite receiver dish. Its supporting trellis buckled and snapped, and the wire-mesh dish wrapped itself around the bounty hunter's face.

He thrust the satellite dish away and sprang to his feet again. "Woo-eee," he said gleefully. "I like a little resistance. Makes the end result so much more satisfyin'." He whipped his arm, unraveling the heavy chain that wound round it from wrist to elbow, and swung the deadly hook in one smooth, well-practiced movement.

The Manhunter jerked his head aside, so that the lethal-looking hook whistled past his ear. But Lobo shook his arm again, and the hook changed its trajectory, curling the chain around the Martian's neck. Lobo jerked it taut, like a strangling cord . . . then he yanked hard, pulling his foe off his feet.

The Martian hit the roof with a loud thud. Lobo dived on top of him, swinging wildly with his free hand. The Manhunter managed to force him over, rolling so that he was on top. Lobo grimaced. This guy's fists had the power to hurt him. But so what? The Main Man had faced a lot tougher opposition than this—and he *always* whupped their asses good.

Besides, he liked being hurt. It gave him a really strong incentive to deliver some hurt right back.

And on top of everything else, he'd never live it down with Jonas and the guys if he was beaten by a bald super hero.

"Give him hell, Jonesy," Xemtex cheered. The bike's external cameras provided him with a pretty good view of the action. "It's time somebody shut that bastard's big mouth."

Enraged, Lobo managed to bend his legs and bring his feet up against the Martian's chest. Just as J'onzz succeeded in untangling the chain from around his neck, Lobo forcefully straightened his legs. The Manhunter soared away from him, demolishing an air-conditioning unit before skidding heavily into the low brick parapet.

Dislodged by the impact, several bricks went plunging over the edge.

Lobo didn't give his enemy time to recover but came rushing at him with the hook flailing. Once, twice, three times the heavy hook whirled, rebounding each time from J'onzz's unprotected head.

"Beginnin' to get the message, Mr. Mars? Beginnin' to hurt yet?"

Manhunter dived away before the next blow landed. The swinging hook gouged into the parapet wall and a dozen more bricks went plummeting to the street seven stories below.

"Yer only delayin' the inevitable, dude."

When the Martian turned back to face him, Lobo was surprised to see he was hefting a six-foot length of fallen aerial. As Lobo swung his chain again, J'onzz lunged. The chain wrapped itself around the aerial and J'onzz deftly wrenched it from Lobo's grip. Chain and aerial clattered to the roof.

"If we must fight," the Martian said grimly, "let us do it fairly."

"Ooo," Lobo mocked. "Get you, frogface. Lissen—yer resistin' arrest. Which means I have legal backin' to do whatever the frag I want. For instance . . ." Lobo unstrapped the large dagger he wore at his belt. It glinted wickedly in the New York sun. "I think I'll start cuttin' off some of yer bits."

The Martian shook his head. "It is not only humans who appear to be obsessed with violence," he commented sadly.

"Stow the mealymouthed homilies," Lobo replied,

waving the knife savagely. "It's about time I showed ya what—"

The bounty hunter broke off sharply as the Martian shoulder-charged him. They stumbled back together, Lobo trying in vain to stab at his foe as J'onzz fought determinedly to keep hold of Lobo's knife hand.

Each used his free hand to rain down blows, each constantly shifting position, trying to keep the other off-balance.

"Ya ain't a bad fighter—for a hero," Lobo grudgingly admitted. He relaxed his arm momentarily, but the Martian wasn't fooled by the stunt. His grip remained in place.

"If you really want to do this," J'onn J'onzz said, "I have a whole repertoire of abilities I have not yet brought to bear."

"Bring 'em on," Lobo scoffed . . . and immediately wished that he hadn't.

He felt what seemed like a steam hammer suddenly appear—inside his head. The thing started slamming around like it wanted to get out of there—and every time it slammed, Lobo thought his head was going to explode.

Mind games! The creep's some sort of telepath!

He made a mental note to charge Quarantino an extra fee for withholding pertinent information.

The bounty hunter dropped the knife and brought both arms up simultaneously. His clenched fists crunched into the Martian's ears. The head-bashing steam hammer stopped abruptly.

"Ya wanna play rough, Baldy? Fine by me. The angrier ya make me, the more I'm gonna enjoy criplin' ya!"

* * *

Fifteen minutes later, they were still pounding each other when Superman landed on the roof. He saw the Spazz-Frag's external cameras swivel toward him, then away again.

"You're for it now, Lobo," Xemtex cackled malevolently. "Baldy's called in reinforcements."

Superman glanced at the fight, which had come to a standstill—as in matter coming to rest with respect to the forces acting on it. Lobo hit Manhunter hit Lobo hit Manhunter hit . . .

Xemtex redirected his voice to the Man of Steel. "I recognize you, Big Blue. That's what they call you out in the galaxy. Now don't you hold back none. Crush that sucker Lobo good. I want to dance on his grave."

"I presume you're speaking metaphorically?" Superman asked.

"Hey, don't talk dirty to me!" the bike protested.

Grimly, Superman gripped each of the intensely focused fighters by a shoulder and exerted his incredible strength to haul them apart. Before they could resume their battle, the Man of Steel stepped between them.

"Is there a reason for this?" he demanded. "J'onn? Lobo?"

"Is there a reason for you stickin' yer interferin' nose in?" Lobo snapped back. "Like, I'm a legally constituted bounty hunter makin' a legally valid arrest. I got a bald guy refuses to come quietly, an' now I got your sorry butt on my case, too. I'm warnin' ya, Superman—" Lobo's voice dripped with hatred. "This creep is wanted. You get involved, you're gonna find yerself with a price on yer head. An' I know about a zillion bounty hunters who'd come after ya for fraggin' free."

Lobo thrust his face in Superman's and stabbed a finger against the "S" emblem on his chest.

"Of course, if ya wanna fight, Supes, I'm happy to oblige. We've done it before, right? In fact, why don't ya call in the rest of the Justice League, too? Man, I'll laugh like a sewer rat when I see ya *all* in some galactic jail!"

"Are you quite finished?" Manhunter asked, taking a step backward. "You did not accede to my request to see the warrant."

"Why not, Lobo?" Superman asked suspiciously. "Is it because *you* think there's been some kind of mistake . . . ?"

"Feetal's Gizz!" Lobo cursed—the foulest expletive in the Czarnian language. "I already went through this with Baldy. But if it keeps ya sweet, Supertoots—" Lobo dug his hand in his back pocket and pulled out a crumpled, badly creased sheet of paper. Fastidiously, he unfolded it, then shoved it forward for Manhunter and Superman to read. Underneath a grainy photograph of the Manhunter's human guise, it said:

WANTED . . . ALIVE!

Reward 1 Million Creds
John Jones
Planet Earth
Not for general tender
Reserved job: Lobo only

On the back, it bore the legend "Valid under Galactic Law" and it was stamped "Authorized by the Directorate of the Imperium of Vrk."

"The Vrkn Imperium?" Superman furrowed his brow. "I've never heard of it."

"That don't matter squat," Lobo said nastily. "The Vrkns probably never heard of you, either, but ya don't hear them whinin' about it."

He folded the poster and put it back in his pocket. The sound of wailing police sirens drifted up from the street, but Lobo paid no attention to them.

Superman knew the police would have to be armed with tactical battlefield nukes before they bothered Lobo.

"Okay," the Czarnian bounty hunter went on. "What say we reconvene the melee? Lessee . . . I think I was just about to stiff the green guy. But if ya wanna play tag team, that's okay by me."

"You know I don't give in to threats, Lobo," Superman said evenly. "I think we'd do well to check this out. For a start, what's J'onn's crime supposed to be? It isn't even mentioned on your poster. And it's debatable whether any crime committed in J'onn's Earth identity—as your warrant says—could be held attributable to his Martian identity."

"Ya should've been a superlawyer." There was contempt in Lobo's voice. "The only words missin' from that piece of gobbledygook were 'allegedly' an' 'fee note.' So . . . I guess it's gonna be lumps all round before I get this turkey home."

"If that's the way you want it."

Superman clenched his fists and prepared to fight.

When he and Lobo had traded blows in the past, no clear winner had been decided. The Man of Steel would have preferred to talk the situation out, but he knew from bitter experience that listening wasn't Lobo's forte.

But J'onn J'onzz's shoulders slumped, and he shook his head wearily. "No, Superman. It is over. He fought me to a standstill—"

"Hey, I wasn't finished with ya," Lobo protested.

"—and his warrant appears to be valid, even if I do not understand the reason for it. I will go willingly with him, to find out what lurks at the bottom of this affair."

"But it could be a trap—" Superman began.

"I hardly think so," the Manhunter opined, "else why would Lobo have confronted me *here*? Judging by the size of the reward, these Vrkns think I have done something extremely criminal." The Martian looked at Lobo. "Understand that I come of my own free will. I give my word I will not try to escape."

Lobo sneered and held out the cuffs. "I'm cuffin' ya anyway, Baldy. Up till now ya ain't exactly been a model prisoner."

"Have it your way."

"I always do."

The Man of Steel frowned deeply. "Are you sure you're doing the right thing, J'onn?"

"'Course he is," Lobo crowed. "Like, a super hero who enforces the law can't go around breakin' it, right?"

Superman could only stand by, feeling totally helpless, as Lobo snapped slimline plastic cuffs with unbreakable molecular centers on the Martian's wrists.

The bounty hunter gestured to the bike. "Climb aboard. An' if the control system talks to ya, ignore it."

Wrists cuffed behind his back, Manhunter climbed awkwardly onto the pillion. Then Lobo swung himself onto the front seat and fired up the engine.

"Nice seein' ya, Big Blue," the bounty hunter lied, winking at Superman. "An' rest assured, it doubles my pleasure knowin' I'm takin' back one of your friends. Man, I'd almost do it for nothing."

"Almost," he added, unnecessarily.

Superman stood on the roof for long moments, watching as the space bike arrowed up into the stratosphere. Something wasn't right about this. J'onn J'onzz—in both his identities—was the straightest guy Superman had ever met, as well as one of the most powerful.

In addition to the ability to fly, J'onn possessed amazing superstrength. His green skin was virtually invulnerable to any normal attack. He could turn himself invisible. He was a shapeshifter, able to adopt any form he chose. And he was a telepath of astonishing power—he could read minds, or manipulate them, or worse. Much worse.

Stranded on Earth, J'onn had dedicated his life to justice, always ready to help the weak and downtrodden. His incredible powers were pledged to the service of humankind. It was inconceivable he would ever commit any crime.

My replacement at the Watchtower is going to have to do a double shift. I'd be failing Manhunter if I didn't look into this.

At that moment, the door giving access to the roof

from the building interior burst open. Two policemen came running out, guns in hands. They paused when they saw the Man of Steel and lowered their weapons.

"Superman . . . ?"

"Somebody called in a disturbance. Big guys fighting, they said." The officer stared at the trashed roof furniture and broken parapet. "A slight understatement, I'd say. What happened?"

"There was a fight." Superman rose a few feet into the air and hovered there. "But don't worry. Nobody was hurt."

He sped off into the city, a red-and-blue blur.

The other policeman looked around. "Don't suppose nobody left a check for the damage, neither," he said morosely.

CHAPTER 6

We are the Alpha, the first and the last.
All else will die.

Traveling at warp speed is not dissimilar to having your intestines torn out with a rusty crochet hook. Slowly.

Some space travelers develop stomach cramps that stay with them for the rest of their lives. Some spend their entire journey vomiting in the restroom. Others learn to tolerate the painful twinges and spasms, while a few—like Lobo—actively enjoy the feeling of discomfort.

But Lobo had no idea how J'onn J'onzz was reacting. The Martian's guts might have imploded, for all he was letting on. J'onzz hadn't uttered a single word since they left that mudball Earth, and Xemtex had retreated into a sullen silence after Lobo jolted him with the promised juice. Unusually, the bounty hunter hadn't amused himself by taunting either of them. He was too busy dreaming about what 800K would bring him.

A couple of weeks on one of the Babe Worlds, a sex-oriented vacation destination, for starters. They catered for every taste, every combination, every number of participants. Aliens, humanoids, robots—on a Babe World you took your pick and swapped what you didn't like.

It goes without saying that all drugs were legal.

Lobo sighed, remembering his last trip there. He'd scored a quarter of a mill for bringing in a Vegan star fragger by the name of Saurlon. The creep was a total bubblehead who lived in his own fantasy world. Unluckily for several solar systems, he had an *idiot savant* genius for building bombs that could set off stellar chain reactions.

Saurlon didn't do it for financial gain, or because he was spurned by his one true love, or because his nanny spanked him when he was a boy. He just liked watching cosmic explosions. Lobo could relate to that—he was a big bang afficionado himself. When Lobo beat him to a paste, the Vegan came quietly enough.

Yeah, that was some vacation, the bounty hunter reminisced. *Anita—Sepulchra—and that hot alien chick with the . . . original anatomy.*

Two bottles of hooch a day, all the cigars he could smoke, playing the casinos at night . . . and the ladies afterward. You didn't know what a shindig was till you'd partied on a Babe World. Fights—man, he'd had some brilliant fights. All that testosterone running wild had the guys on a knife-edge; it didn't take much goading to tip them over into violence.

In a word, heaven.

The only reason the management didn't throw Lobo out was because he'd probably have battered them into submission, too. Plus, of course, he was a big spender. He could see some Babe World employee, sitting in an office someplace, toting up the damage Lobo caused on his calculator, balancing it against how freely the Main Man was spending.

The insistent throb of heavy metal brought Lobo back to the here and now. The song was about an ugly android who dabbled in the occult and built its own girlfriend. Lobo found it hard to relate to the verses, but flipped the volume to maximum for the killer double guitar solo. Maybe that would jerk the Martian out of his silent stupor.

It didn't.

The music faded and the DJ's voice cut in: "The last track was cosponsored by EinZweiDrei Industries and the fabulous Al's Diner, now reopened for business on the fringes of the Sector A9 asteroid belt. Greasy food in ambient surroundings. Comin' atcha now is 'Pins in Your Eyes' by the Monstrous Saints . . ."

Not one of Lobo's favorites, though he could dig the sentiments.

"Yo, Xemtex," he grunted. "How far are we from the A9 belt?"

There was a slight pause, no doubt while Xemtex thought about a rude reply and the electric shock that would undoubtedly follow. At last, with great reluctance, he said, "A couple of hours."

"Cool. Divert to Al's Diner." The bounty hunter pictured Darlene, Al's luscious waitress, and chuckled lecherously. "They're gonna be tickled pink to see the Bo."

"I take it they've been lobotomized, then," Xemtex muttered.

But Lobo wasn't listening. He was lost in a vision of Darlene, who didn't seem to have many clothes on. Hey—and look! Here comes Lobo, and he's buck naked, too . . . Oh man, oh man, oh man.

*   *   *

Lobotomized. Lobo-tomized. Xemtex rolled the word around his circuits. *That's what the bastard did to me. He lobotomized me!*

J'onn J'onzz had long been used to keeping his own company. Apart from his penchant for remaining silent unless he had something worth saying, there were few other people alive he could *really* talk to. For at the very core of his being, the Manhunter carried an infinite sadness.

He was unique—the last of his kind, the only Martian in all existence. His parents, his wife, his son—his entire race—had succumbed to an incurable plague. J'onn survived because a human scientist experimenting with a teleport beam inadvertently transported him to Earth.

While he tried to make sense of the weird new world on which he found himself, his people fell in their millions and died like flies.

By the time J'onn was able to return to the Red Planet, it was all over. Mars had become a mausoleum. There were so many dead, even his great powers could never bury them all. He left them where they lay. In the chill winds of the thin Martian atmosphere, flesh and bone would soon crumble into dust. In only a few decades, nobody would ever know that a peace-loving race had evolved, and died, there.

Nobody except J'onn J'onzz, a single individual mourning for the population of an entire world.

And now he was on his way to places unknown, accused as a criminal. He was only glad he had been able to deliver his message to Boswell Jacklin before the bounty hunter apprehended him. Mrs. Jackson's urgent anxiety had really got to him; J'onn hoped that Boosh had sense enough to heed her and go home.

A solitary asteroid tumbled past them, flashing red as it caught the rays of some distant sun. *Like Mars,* J'onn thought sadly. *The Red Planet. The Dead Planet.*

The never-ending thump and screech of heavy metal music irritated him, and he used subtle Martian meditation techniques to try to blank it out. No wonder Lobo was such a bad-tempered oaf, with such a cacophony blaring constantly in his cars.

Beneath his craggy brow, the Manhunter's red eyes drank in the beauty of the cosmos, stars without end.

Lobo was a brutal, vulgar thug, more a force of Nature than a man. Except for his insistence that he was honest, the bounty hunter appeared to have no redeeming features. Superman had talked of Lobo several times, always disparagingly; J'onn knew his friend loathed everything the bounty hunter stood for. J'onn preferred not to be judgmental, but with Lobo that was nearly impossible. His very presence made him repulsive.

But, when all was said and done, he had to admit that Lobo was only doing his job. He just wasn't going about it very pleasantly.

J'onn combed his phenomenal memory, striving to dredge up anything that might have occasioned the Vrkn Imperium's warrant. He found nothing. If he *had* committed a crime, then it was without his knowledge. Or—and this was much more likely—it was a simple case of mistaken identity. In a galaxy as diverse and densely populated as the Milky Way, identity theft was a serious and growing problem.

Although how anybody could have worked out his Earth identity was a major mystery in itself. But J'onn knew that, when it came to crime, a great many minds were capable of amazing ingenuity.

The space bike began to slow. Ahead, J'onn saw the A9 asteroid belt. Almost a billion miles long, it twisted and curved back on itself like some giant, warped doughnut. The rocks that formed it varied in size from specks of dust up to trillions of tons, all tied to each other by the invisible bonds of complex gravitational forces.

Whoever Al was, he'd sited his diner wisely.

Many of the larger asteroids contained significant deposits of a shiny, obsidian-like mineral used in the heat shields of interstellar craft. A dozen small mining operations had set up base in the belt. As the diner was the only place with a liquor license within a half day's travel, Al would surely do good business.

The diner was a relatively small place, perched on one end of the major mining asteroid. The crushing plant was a mile away; silhouetted against the stars, it seemed to crouch like some prehistoric predator waiting to rend its prey. Subterranean hydroponic plant farms produced a light, though breathable, atmosphere that leaked away into space and needed constant replenishment.

A massive advertising billboard over the diner building, dwarfing it. Its twinkling nu-neon lights looked incongruous—even absurd—against the background curtain of stars. A smaller sign in the diner's large, reinforced observation window read: "Beer . . . Always."

"Beer. Music to my taste buds," Lobo grunted. He swung the Spazz-Frag smoothly into an empty docking bay, then dismounted.

"I will remain here," J'onn told him.

"Izzatafact, Baldy?"

Why does he always have to be so obnoxious? J'onn wondered.

"Actually, ya *won't* remain here," Lobo decided. "Ya'll accompany me inside, so's I can keep my beady eye on ya. An' if ya wanna buy me a few beers, hey, I won't complain."

"I do not drink alcohol."

"Great. I'll have yours as well!"

Awkwardly, because his hands were still cuffed behind his back, J'onn swung himself off the bike. The nu-neon twinkled vermilion as he climbed the three steps up to the front entrance and followed Lobo inside.

Bastard, bastard, bastard! Xemtex cursed silently to himself.

Only a day ago, he was a big-deal gang leader, respected—well, okay, *feared*—by the galaxy at large. Now his gang was dead or fled. He had no way of retrieving his stashed loot. His own body was lying like a side of beef in an insanely high radiation zone—and his brain was stuck inside a Spazz-Frag 5000 belonging to a homicidal maniac.

Geez. How the mighty are fallen.

Weird how quickly the bike's control system had wired him into itself. Fair enough, it had given him that annoying metaphysical itch that he could never scratch. But that aside, there appeared to be no problems.

Xemtex could still think clearly. The electrical override built into the system meant he had to do what Lobo demanded . . . but at least his thoughts were his own.

He dreamed briefly of making a run for it, just heading off into space, Xemtex the Spazz-Frag. He certainly had plenty of firepower at his command, given the space bike's armaments. He'd never heard of a bike leading an outlaw gang before, but nobody had heard of a guy who could blow things up by looking at them before, either. There was always a first time for everything.

Not that he was going anywhere, of course. The bike would only start once Lobo had applied his handprint to the recognition pad that also acted to ignite the miniaturized nuclear engine. Being on the inside, so to speak, Xemtex knew from the bike's data banks that Lobo had stolen it, then reengineered it for his own use.

Of course! Xemtex had a sudden realization. *What an ass I am!*

Lobo closed down the weapons system when he got off the bike. But the radio was still blaring away . . . and hell, did Xemtex hate that music. He'd been in places where torturers played less strident stuff. How could anybody listen to it and remain sane?

If Xemtex had still had ears, his brain would have been running out of them.

He turned down the volume and began to explore the possibility of an outward transmission of his own.

* * *

"Al! How ya doin', ya chubby old son of a gun?"

Al Fretowski was hunched over the open cooking range in the center of the diner, rustling up four Al's Big-Boy All-Day Breakfasts with a culinary skill that had long since made his establishment the discerning space truckers' eatery of choice. Now he was scooping up the asteroid miners, too, attracting them with his mouthwatering mix of fats, oils, salts, and cholesterols. The coffee wasn't bad, either.

Now Al fought the churning feeling that suddenly threatened to evacuate his bowels. He knew that voice, knew it only too well. It was the voice that announced the End of the World.

Forcing a smile onto his face, steeling his nerves, Al flipped the final burger and turned to greet the newcomer.

"Lobo!" he said enthusiastically. "It's always great to see you."

This was an outright lie. Lobo had been in Al's Diner on many occasions. The bounty hunter had a real soft spot for Al's waitress, the blond, voluptuous Darlene; anytime he was in the neighborhood, he liked to pop in for burgers, beer, and a little flirtation. Darlene was no great fan of Lobo's vulgar manners, but she forgave him because that's what macho men were like. And nobody was more macho than Lobo.

And don't forget the fights, Al thought.

That was the worst of it—Lobo was always getting into fights. In fact, the only reason Al had had to close the diner at all was because the Main Man had wrecked the place in a battle with a half dozen tough truckers. The insurance had covered the damage . . . but he'd only reopened yesterday. If Lobo wrecked it again today, the insurers might not stump up a second time.

Lobo was glancing around, seeing who was in. A group of miners sat at the far end, a dozen or so of them round one big table, feasting on shrumpburgers and Stronghooz.

"Yo, gents."

The bounty hunter tossed them a greeting and received several grunts in return. From the way Lobo's eyes narrowed, Al suspected he was considering taking umbrage at one of the innocent grunts. Quickly, Al tried to divert his attention.

"So, who's the prisoner?" he asked, gesturing at the Martian Manhunter and noting the handcuffs.

"Ah, just some green geek," Lobo told him offhandedly. "Goes by the name of Baldy. If he wants to eat, he pays his own fraggin' way."

"Hi, Lobo," a breathy voice said behind them.

Al watched as Lobo turned to see Darlene standing there. She was wearing her usual uniform, the one that accentuated all of her curves without actually revealing any of her secrets. Her skirt was short, her heels were high, and her legs just seemed to go on forever. There wasn't a heterosexual man in the galaxy wouldn't cut off his left hand for a night with Darlene.

The bounty hunter's features softened at once, and the smile on his face was of genuine pleasure.

"Darlene," he said simply, "the most beautiful girl in the Universe." He reached out and took her hand. Gently, he raised it to his lips and kissed it.

Darlene flushed. She tossed her blond hair, and her

deep blue eyes twinkled. Al knew that she liked Lobo almost as much as the Bo liked her; in fact, she was just about the only person Al knew who could keep Lobo cool, calm, and collected. It was a great pity she'd been on her day off when he fought the truckers.

Seeing how badly the battle had damaged the diner, Al had thought it must have been about something serious. But no—a trucker had failed to pass the salt as quickly as Lobo would have liked.

It was strange, Al thought now, seeing a maniac like the Bo acting the part of a lovelorn suitor. He'd damn near killed one of those truck drivers last time . . . and yet here he was, holding Darlene's hand so delicately you'd think she was made of porcelain. Talk about a velvet glove on an iron fist . . .

Darlene scooped up a couple of menus from the counter and gestured to two seats in a window booth. Al threw her a silent "Thank you," knowing she'd deliberately put the bounty hunter and his charge as far away from the miners as she could.

Lobo and his prisoner sat down. Lobo scanned the menu, while the big green guy in the cape just sat. He had a quiet dignity about him, almost an aloofness, that Al didn't usually see in his customers.

Without waiting to be asked, Darlene opened a chilled can of Strongbooz and handed it to Lobo. He upended it, pouring the beer into his mouth like he'd been in some kind of alcohol drought for the past decade. He swallowed the contents in one gulp, then belched loudly.

Baldy winced, Al noticed. Obviously, he was no fan of

Lobo's, either. But then—apart from Darlene, maybe—who was? The big galoot got on just about everybody's wrong side; he was either oblivious to the annoyance he caused, or he enjoyed it so much he couldn't stop. Al had long since ceased to wonder what made the Main Man the way he was.

"Beg pardon, Darlene," Lobo apologized—and the way he accentuated "Darlene" left Al in no doubt the apology was for nobody else. "What d'you recommend, babe?"

"Al got a fresh supply of shrump in this morning."

"Say no more. Double shrumpburger it is. Don't stint on the fries. And don't shirk on Al's special sauce, either."

Darlene glanced at the prisoner. "And your friend . . . ?"

"Ain't no friend of mine, sweetbuns." Lobo turned briefly to the green guy. "Are ya hungry, Baldy?"

"Thank you, no." Baldy shook his head. He was staring out the window, watching the spinning asteroids and the stars beyond. The look in his eyes was almost one of *yearning,* Al thought.

Al put two shrump patties on the grill and started mixing his special sauce. He really ought to patent the stuff. Shrump tasted okay, but it was the sauce that had them coming back for more.

One of the miners called out: "One more round for the road, honey." Darlene took another dozen cans of beer out the cooler, put them on a tray, and headed for the miners. They'd been drinking and eating for several hours, but they still seemed to be in good humor. They'd booked a shuttle from the mine to pick them up and take them back to their barracks.

It should be arriving soon, Al told himself, trying to be optimistic. *They'll get aboard and go away, then Lobo will go and everything will be all right and my diner won't get wrecked again.*

How wrong could one small, nervous diner owner be?

"Hand over your cash or die," the psychopathic robot announced in its thin metal voice.

Its hapless victim stared nervously at the pipe gun leveled at his head, its barrel almost big enough to swallow him whole. "T-take it easy, friend. I'm not resisting. Wallet's in my pocket."

Starboot stepped forward and rammed his hand inside the alien's jacket. It came out holding a fat, shiny brown money clip. "Jackpot, guys."

"Excellent," the robot said coldly. Its finger tightened on the trigger and the pipe gun went off with a roar.

The alien's head disappeared. A small fountain of dark red ichor gushed out of his gaping neck, then his legs buckled, and he fell to the ground.

"You didn't have to do that," Starboot grunted, riffling through the wad of notes. "He cooperated."

"Witness Elimination Program," the robot stated unemotionally.

Starboot shook his head. The robot was crazy, no other word for it. What it needed was an overhaul by a team of mechanics specializing in screwed-up wiring. Robots weren't supposed to kill anybody. This one killed whenever it felt like it. Except for the gang, of course. It seemed to like the gang . . . if indeed it liked anything at all, apart from killing.

At least it hadn't killed any of *them*.

Starboot, the robot, and the third survivor of the encounter with Lobo had blown planet as fast as they could. They'd heard of Lobo's fantastic tracking ability—it was said he could follow the trail of a single molecule from one end of the galaxy to the other, by smell alone. He'd been close enough to get a whiff of them. They needed to put as much distance between that blighted green rad zone and themselves as possible.

Of course, the rewards on them were small beer, so it might not be worth the Main Man's while to pursue them further. But with somebody like Lobo, it was best not to take chances. Most of the gang had learned that the hard way.

They'd run low on fuel. Xemtex had stashed all their loot—and he was the only one who knew where. Years of robbing and pillaging, and now they didn't even have a cred among them. They docked at an interplanetary way station and raised the necessary money by robbing a few aliens.

"We got enough here to take us clear to the Fringe Worlds," Starboot told his companions as they made their way back to their space vehicle. "We lose ourselves on one of the outlaw planets, and we'll never see Lobo again."

"I wish to see him," the robot said. "I wish to kill him."

Starboot swung the entry hatch open and nodded brusquely. "Yeah, yeah. Maybe he'll just come after us, and you can kill him, then we'll all live happily ever after. Until Lobo un-kills himself again."

Darriz, the third gang member, settled into the pilot's

chair and fired up the engines. The radio crackled with static, then a voice came through.

"Starboot? Darriz? Did you guys get away? Are you getting this?"

"Xemtex!" Starboot exclaimed. He grabbed the microphone. Suddenly things were looking better. "Did you escape, too, boss?"

"Uh . . ." There was a pause. "Not exactly. Sort of."

"What happened?"

"Never mind that now. This is urgent. I'm at a place called Al's Diner, on the A9 belt."

"Yeah, I know it. The shrumpburger's to die for. What about Lobo?"

"Uh . . . yeah, he's here, too."

Starboot hesitated. "I don't know if it's a good idea for us to come get you, boss," he said slowly. "I mean, Lobo killed sixteen of us. Even with the psychodroid on our side, we don't stand much chance."

"Nonsense," the robot protested. "I will kill him."

The radio crackled. "He's also got a prisoner here with a million-cred bounty on his head."

"A million creds . . . ?" Starboot whistled. "We could sure use some of that. We're stuck on a station, muggin' aliens."

"Ain't you got a vehicle, boss?" Darriz put in. "Couldn't you just bring the prisoner to us?"

Again, a pause. "Yes, I have a vehicle. But no, I can't bring him. I've been thinking. I know Lobo's course. You can cut him off, snatch me and the prisoner . . . and I know exactly how to do it."

"You were always good at coming up with plans, Xem-tex," Starboot said happily. "We're on our way."

As the sleek spacecraft shot away from the space station, all Starboot could think of was a million creds. This would set them all up for life.

And that wasn't even counting the loot they had already.

Oh, happy day.

J'onn J'onzz watched the pretty waitress as she gracefully carried the tray of beer to the far end of the diner. He felt no attraction to her himself, but he could see why she would drive some men wild. Martians were attracted only by their own kind. And his kind were gone, extinct. He would never, not if he lived to be a thousand, know love again.

He saw that Lobo had swiveled in his seat, eyes trailing Darlene like a lovesick puppy. The Main Man had revealed a different side of himself, a side J'onn would never have suspected. He *did* have feelings. A pretty girl could turn him weak at the knees, as well as hot under the collar.

J'onn's attention snapped back to the miners. A voice was raised—not angrily, but demanding. Obviously, the last drink had been one too many. High spirits and jocular pleasantry had suddenly turned nasty, a process J'onn had often witnessed on Earth.

One of the miners had grasped Darlene's arm and was trying to pull her down onto his knee. She struggled against him, doing her best to remain good-natured about the assault on her person, but J'onn could read in her eyes the anger that she felt. No doubt a girl as pretty as Darlene often had to fend off unwanted attentions.

"—'m'on, honey," the miner was slurring, "I promise I'll give you a real good tip!"

There was an outburst of drunken laughter, and one or two of the others started pawing at the struggling waitress.

"Please," Darlene protested, "this isn't funny."

"Look, you can earn yourself a big bonus here," the miner told her, not relaxing his grip. "Just show a hardworking joe a little kindness."

"Please . . ." Darlene's voice was little more than a whisper.

The Manhunter had seen enough. No female deserved to be treated that way, as if she were an object. He sent out a muted telepathic pulse and watched the miner shake his head in sudden pain. But his grip on Darlene's arm never loosened.

J'onn J'onzz started to get to his feet, but Lobo beat him to it.

"Siddown," the bounty hunter said roughly. He shoved the palm of his hand in J'onn's face and forced him roughly back into his seat. "The Main Man'll handle this in best diplomatic fashion."

Manhunter caught the terrified look on Al's face as Lobo strode purposefully to the other end of the room. The little man had his palms pressed together, as if he were praying.

"'Scuse me, gents." Lobo loomed over the seated group. "I was wonderin' if I could have a word?"

"Sure," the one who held Darlene's wrist replied. "Here's a word: Scram."

The miners guffawed with laughter and banged their fists on the table like it was the funniest thing they'd ever heard.

"Ho-ho-ho," Lobo said, deadpan. "Look, I'm tryin' to be nice." Manhunter would almost swear he sounded apologetic. Almost. "Just let the lady go."

"Make me." The miner looked up, his drunken good humor turned in an instant to macho honor.

Lobo moved so fast, J'onn could hardly believe it. His hand was a blur as it reached to the sheath on his belt, smoothly hauled out the knife, and brought it slicing down like a guillotine.

"Howzat?" the bounty hunter asked lightly.

For a moment, the miner continued to glare at Lobo. Then, with a start, he looked down at his hand—or, rather, the stump where his hand used to be. Blood was spurting out all over the table.

The others stared at him in shock, heedless of the blood that spattered on their burgers. Even J'onn was shocked, both at what Lobo had done and the casual way in which he'd done it. Obviously, Lobo didn't major in giving second chances.

Darlene moved away from the group, then suddenly realized the miner's severed hand was still firmly clutching her arm. She shrieked, hoisted up her drink tray, and started to beat at the offending hand.

While their colleague desperately tried to wrap the tablecloth around his bloody stump, the other miners leapt to their feet. Actually, they *almost* leapt to their feet, because Lobo grasped the edge of their table and wrenched it upward.

The hi-stress steel table legs were bolted to the floor, but Lobo didn't even seem to be exerting himself as they ripped free. Holding the heavy tabletop like a shield, he slammed it into several of the miners. Loud cracks were testament to more than one broken bone.

Lobo didn't wait for the others to rally and attack. Coolly and methodically, he merely battered them into unconsciousness, using his fists, his feet, and one of the steel table legs he had torn out of the floor.

Plates and cutlery flew everywhere—several pieces of cutlery directly into the flesh of a few miners. Another miner soared through the air, ribs cracked by the forceful kick he'd just received, and landed on the grill. Pots and pans and hot cooking oil spilled all over.

J'onn saw Al snatch up a fire extinguisher and douse the embryonic flames. Then Lobo snatched the fire extinguisher from Al and rammed it forcefully into a miner's mouth. Foam came spurting out of the man's nostrils, and he fell to the floor, retching messily.

The last miner on his feet lunged with a gleaming knife. Lobo flipped him over his shoulder, and he skidded along the floor to fetch up close to J'onn. The man groaned and staggered upright, pulling a pistol from a holster at the back of his belt.

The miner took careful aim at Lobo's head. But before the miner could pull the trigger, the Manhunter's foot stamped down hard on his leg. He squealed in pain as his muscles froze, and dropped the gun. J'onn J'onzz catapulted him into unconsciousness with another kick.

The whole thing was over in less than a minute.

Lobo dusted his hands, walked back over to the booth, and sat down opposite J'onn. "Thought I told you to keep outa this," he snapped. Then: "Hey, Al," he called over his shoulder, "where's that shrumpburger? I'm starvin', man."

Al was standing by the central range, looking around him in stunned dismay. Much of the diner interior was trashed. Most of the shrump, and all of his sauce, decorated the floor. Al's shoulders slumped, a defeated man, and J'onn thought he saw a tear glint in one eye.

"Shrumpburger's off," Al said sadly.

"Aw, c'm'on, Al," Lobo cajoled. "Don't take it like that. It wasn't my fault. I was protectin' Darlene's honor, is all."

Darlene was standing against the wall, staring aghast at the disembodied hand that had fallen to the floor at her feet. Blood oozed from the severed stump.

"Tell ya what, babe," Lobo called to her, "just give the hand to Al. If he smothers it in sauce an' sticks it in a bun, I'll eat that."

Darlene looked horrified. Obviously, her admiration for Lobo knew some limits.

Through the ob window, J'onn saw an approaching shuttle. Lobo noticed it, too.

"Better tell these guys their ride's here."

J'onn J'onzz shook his head almost imperceptibly. Lobo had him confounded. The man had heart enough to defend a girl's honor . . . yet he was willing to *eat* the hand of the man who insulted her? That was not rational. The bounty hunter was a mass of contradictions.

Al walked slowly up to their table, his slow gait betraying his reluctance to do what he was going to do.

"Lobo," he began. J'onn detected the fear in the diner owner's voice, but felt a sudden respect for him as he steeled himself to go on. "Lobo, this is the second time you've trashed my diner. I know it wasn't your fault," he added hurriedly as Lobo scowled at him, "but the end result's the same. My diner, wrecked. I don't know if the insurance will pay up a second time. I'm not a rich man, Lobo. I can't afford this. If . . . if . . ."

Al's voice tailed away, his courage not up to making the threat. But he suddenly blurted, "If you do it again, I'm going to have to *bar* you!"

J'onn almost smiled as Lobo's eyes widened in horror. J'onn knew what he was thinking: If he was barred, he wouldn't see Darlene again. But then the bounty hunter's expression hardened. J'onn could read him like a book: Now he was asking himself how Al could *ever* stop the Main Man doing anything?

Then, Lobo looked thoughtful. Obviously he was weighing up the pros and cons. Of course, he could barge his way into the diner and see Darlene whenever he wanted. But then Darlene wouldn't be happy to see him, because Al didn't want him there.

Finally, Lobo came to a decision. "Tell ya what, Al." He jerked a thumb toward J'onn. "I'm expectin' a real fat reward on Baldy. What say I make good the damage out of that?"

Al stuck his hand out almost as quickly as Lobo had unsheathed the knife. "It's a deal," he nodded eagerly. They solemnly shook on it.

Darlene was cheerful again as she came up to stand beside the seated Lobo. She stooped slightly and kissed him on the cheek. Was that a blush J'onn saw under the Czarnian's pale skin?

"Oh, Lobo," she said huskily, "you're such a gentleman."

"You bet your sweet butt I am." Lobo grinned.

And proceeded to playfully pinch the aforementioned sweet butt. Darlene squealed.

This time, J'onn J'onzz allowed himself a smile.

CHAPTER 7

A tiny red-and-blue figure streaked through the star-spangled cosmos.

On Earth, Superman was the world's greatest super hero; there was none mightier, or better known. He used his powers of superstrength, flight, and invulnerability to help humankind. On Earth, he was the biggest fish in a relatively small pond.

But out here, in the wastes of interstellar space, even Superman's amazing powers were dwarfed by the sheer immensity of the galaxy.

Far off to one side, a giant red star was pulsating slowly as it entered its death throes. For the next million years, maybe more, it would oscillate between a dull red glow and a fiery beacon. Then, when the star's own gravity could no longer contain its internal upheavals, it would explode. All life for billions of miles around would be annihilated . . . unless its civilization had advanced sufficiently for space travel.

He sometimes wondered if all evolution boiled down

to that one, simple race: get smart enough to leave your planet before the star that gave it life exploded.

The mere thought was enough to send a shiver of grief reverberating through the Man of Steel's heart. His skin could repel bullets; he could withstand the fiery heat of a blast furnace and the icy cold of space; but his emotions were the same as any man's.

He remembered Krypton, his own world.

Krypton, too, had orbited an unstable star. Interactions between the electromagnetic fields of the ever-changing star and the spinning planet rapidly built up into a life-threatening situation. But the Kryptonians hesitated too long. They argued among themselves about the cause of the coming disaster; many of them denied that it would ever happen. Nobody would listen to the scientist Jor-El, Superman's father, whose calculations proved that the giant planet would soon vibrate itself into destruction.

So Jor-El acted alone. He constructed a miniature rocket ship and outfitted it with everything a Kryptonian would need to survive on another world. Then, with breaking hearts and tear-stained faces, he and his wife placed their baby son Kal-El inside.

Even as the craft carrying its precious cargo blasted out of Krypton's atmosphere, the planet's internal vibrations reached critical point. Volcanoes erupted out of nowhere. Great rifts and chasms opened in the ocean floors. Massive earthquakes shook the surface, destroying great cities that had stood for a thousand years. And worse was to come . . .

Baby Kal-El knew nothing about it, of course. But the child grew up to become Superman—and Superman had run through the scenario in his mind a hundred agonizing times.

The earthquakes and eruptions rapidly intensified. Millions of people died as the stricken cities burned. Finally, torn this way and that by the red sun's incredible gravity, the planet itself started to break up.

And Krypton exploded.

Billions of people—tens of thousands of years of civilization—all wiped out in a matter of hours. Krypton would become just another myth, a tale to be told in taverns and books, a story told about the civilized world that wasn't civilized enough to save itself.

Kryptonians lost the race.

The baby's ship crash-landed on Earth. As he grew up in the care of his adoptive parents, Jonathan Kent and his wife Martha, Kal-El discovered that the planet's yellow sun affected him in strange ways. He could see through walls and emit fierce heat beams from his eyes, as his vision extended through the infrared into the X-ray spectrum. The lower gravity allowed him to fly, and the yellow sun gave him superstrength and superspeed.

By the time he reached adulthood, Kal-El had become Superman, the strongest man on the planet. He achieved some semblance of normal life by continuing to live as Clark Kent, working as a reporter for the *Daily Planet* newspaper in Metropolis, and meeting the formidable Lois Lane. He found love with Lois, and friendship, and happiness.

Yet, underneath everything else was a memory that would never leave him. He was the last Kryptonian, the only surviving member of his race.

Small wonder that, when he joined the Justice League, Superman cemented a strong bond with J'onn J'onzz. The Martian was the last of his people, too. They shared a common grief—a sadness rooted in the very heart of their beings. No matter what happened to them, or what they did, they would always know they were Last Sons.

Now, Superman allowed his tragic memories to slide away once more. He couldn't fight them, because it would be like fighting against his own past. He could only let the sadness wash over him, torturing him with what might have been, until normality returned.

He had stopped off on the Moon before commencing his journey, to check out what data the Watchtower's supercomputers held on the Imperium of Vrk. It puzzled, but didn't surprise, him to learn that Vrk was tiny, inhabited by primitives who had no contact with civilized worlds.

Far ahead, his telescopic vision picked out his first glimpse of the Barbie Worlds. Somewhere out there he would find Tartan Quarantino's bounty-hunting agency, and—hopefully—the answer to the madness of the Manhunter's arrest.

"Bottle of whisky, Konik. Three glasses. And water for the Arcturan."

"Coming right up, Angel Eyes, sir," the barman said obsequiously. He reached up on the shelf for a bottle, stealing a surreptitious glance at Angel Eyes and his three companions. A lot of the bounty hunters were scary guys, but Angel Eyes and his cohorts frightened Konik more than anybody. Except maybe Lobo.

Angel Eyes was bad enough on his own. Seven feet tall, gaunt and muscular without being bulky, he was a standard humanoid alien. Except for his eyes. They were a bright, golden yellow and had no pupils. Looking into Angel Eyes' face was like staring at an angel, hence the nickname. Only, this was an angel of death.

Randan and Virt, Angel Eyes' gunsels, were Khunds, one of the most vicious races discovered anywhere in the galaxy. They were almost as tall as Angel Eyes, but broader and a whole lot hairier. Their tiny eyes glinted aggressively. Their curiously flattened faces, coupled with the sharp fangs that lined their mouths, gave them the appearance of mutant animals for whom killing was a way of life.

But it was the fourth member of the bounty-hunting team that really frightened Konik—and, if truth were known, many of the other bounty hunters, too. The Arcturan came from a world where technology was unknown and magic was the order of the day. His name was K'Baal, but few ever called him that. His dark powers made everybody feel uneasy, and there was always the fear that the name itself had some sort of magic effect on anybody who uttered it.

The Arcturan was small compared to his companions, well under six feet. He wore a plain black robe, like a monk's habit, with a hood that enveloped his head and left his face wreathed in permanent shadows. His shoulders were slightly hunched, and the long, skeletal fingers that reached to take the water jug gave the M'Ryngian barman the creeps.

Fascinated despite himself, Konik watched out the

corner of his eye as the Arcturan placed the tip of one skinny finger on the surface of the water. The water level fell, as if he was drinking by osmosis.

Konik shivered, and a cold sweat broke out on his hairless body. Fifteen years he'd been working here, serving drinks to professional killers. He listened to their drunken stories, their financial troubles, their romantic woes. When they made a big score, he shared their tales of death and debauchery. And though he'd never admit it to anyone, deep in his heart he hated every minute.

These guys *terrified* him.

The only thing Konik wanted was to get away. He'd been saving all he could from his wages since day one, but he still didn't have enough even for one day on Babe-World. Some of the drunken thugs he served had spent *weeks* there.

Never mind, he told himself. *The money will soon start piling up now. I'm 5K to the good already. It won't be long. I can force myself to stand these yahoos for a while yet.*

The Khund, Randan, was about to take a slug of his drink, but his hand froze halfway to his mouth.

"Get that," he said curtly. He nodded toward the bar entrance. "Must be Ladies' Day."

His brother, Virt, laughed. It was an ugly sound, like teeth crunching into bone. "Maybe she wants a job. Big Blue Bountykiller."

The Arcturan didn't look up, but Angel Eyes flashed a golden glance in the direction of the doorway. Konik looked, too. Superman stood there, a riot of red-and-blue amongst the dowdy, unwashed bounty hunters.

There were several wolf whistles from other tables, but the super hero ignored them as he walked toward the bar. Konik saw the stone killer called Quietus wink at his companions.

"Watch this," he hissed.

As Superman approached, Quietus stealthily stuck out his foot. Maybe he'd seen Lobo trip the Khund earlier and thought he could get a cheap laugh. But Superman didn't trip; his leg swung forward with such force that, when Quietus tried to block it, there was a loud crack.

Quietus screeched and grabbed for his leg with all four hands.

"Beg your pardon," Superman said politely, never pausing. "I didn't see you there."

Leaving the bounty hunter grunting in pain, the Man of Steel reached the bar.

"Hey, it's an alien," Konik quipped, playing to the others. "What can I do for you?"

"You can take me to your leader."

"I'm sorry, Superman." Tartan Quarantino fingered his bow tie in that nervous way of his, shaking his head at the same time. "I'm not at liberty to divulge any information on the subject of the Imperium of Vrk. Commercial confidentiality, you understand."

"I understand," Superman told the agency boss. "What I really want to know is—what is the crime listed for John Jones?"

They were sitting in Quarantino's office, one whole wall of which was an observation window with a fabulous view of the Milky Way. The agent tapped a few keys on the miniature pad that lay on the desk in front of him; immediately, the ob window became a huge monitor screen. But the only words displayed on it were: NO RELEVANT DATA.

"I don't know," the agent admitted.

Superman gazed at him intensely. "You're telling me you hired a psychopath like Lobo to hunt John down . . . and you don't even know why?"

"Psychopath or not, Lobo has an official warrant. And I'm an agent, not a judge," Quarantino replied, shrugging. "Doesn't matter to me what a criminal does. My only concern is that I receive legal notification, stamped in all the right places. And I have to be sure that the issuing authority will pay up, of course. No sense taking on a job if they renege on payment. That would *really* tick off my guys."

"You're convinced this Imperium of Vrk will pay?"

"Yes."

Superman was insistent. "What makes you so sure?"

"We-ell . . ." The agent had the good grace to look embarrassed. "You're no doubt aware I take a percentage of every bounty? The Directorate paid me my commission in advance. I figured if they were good for that, they sure as heck were unlikely to try to cheat Lobo."

"Sound reasoning," Superman had to agree. If the Directorate had requested Lobo specifically for the job, they must have been well aware what the bounty hunter was capable of. "Is it usual for you to receive your cut in advance?"

Quarantino shook his head. "First time it's ever happened," he admitted. "But I'll wager they can't be ignorant of what'll happen if they do the dirty on the Main Man."

"There's something about all this that doesn't add up," Superman said thoughtfully. "Something doesn't tally."

"It added up for me," the agent told him. "I got my two hundred grand. I'm sitting pretty." He flicked off the window monitor and made a show of rummaging among some papers on the desktop. "Now I hate to be rude, but I have an agency to run, and nobody makes money if the boys aren't working. Sorry if you've wasted your time . . ."

"Not at all," Superman assured him. "You've been very helpful."

Ignoring the chorus of catcalls and wolf whistles that greeted his reappearance, Superman left via the bar exit. His mind was racing.

While he'd been questioning Quarantino, he'd put his X-ray vision to good use. He'd surreptitiously looked into the filing cabinets containing the agency records and picked out the copy warrant from Vrk. The agent hadn't lied; no crime was listed for John Jones. Superman checked the other bounty warrants in the file.

WANTED: San Hedro   Bounty: 10K
    Crime: Violent robbery
WANTED: Tonge Gang   Bounty: 25K
    Crimes: Robbery, Murder
WANTED: Reen Zint   Bounty: 50K
    Crime: Regicide

Every single one had a crime listed for its subject.

Only John Jones's warrant was blank.

Superman hadn't wasted his time coming here. His intuition hadn't let him down. Something was *very* wrong. Whatever J'onn J'onzz had so willingly got himself into, it seemed he might need the Man of Steel to get him out.

Angel Eyes and his compadres watched Superman's departure in silence. Except for the Arcturan; he didn't seem to need to look at anything in order to be able to see it.

"Figure this," Angel Eyes said. His voice sounded like a well-educated snake, drawing out the "s" into a threatening, sibilant sound. "Lobo goes out on a special reserved job. Total hush-hush. Now Big Blue shows up. Creep's never been here before. What's going on?"

The Khund siblings looked at each other, both shrugging at the same time. "Who cares? We'll just get drunk till the next job."

"Ask Konik." The Arcturan didn't seem to speak, but all three of them heard his words as clear as crystal. "He knows."

Angel Eyes nodded and beckoned lazily to the bald, sweating barman. Konik finished making up the order he was serving, then came slowly across to the four bounty hunters' table.

"M-more whisky, guys?" he began.

Angel Eyes shook his head. "Tell us about Lobo. And Big Blue."

For an instant, Konik looked like a man who'd been sentenced to death. Shock and terror raced across his face.

He recovered quickly, shaking his head emphatically as he began gathering up empty glasses off the table.

"Lobo's out on a job," he said, trying hard to sound casual. "I don't know why Superman was here. You'd have to ask Mr. Quarantino."

"I'm asking *you*, Konik," Angel Eyes hissed.

"I don't know," Konik insisted. "I'm just the barman—"

"Liar." The word came out of nowhere, but everybody knew it was the Arcturan who spoke. K'Baal turned slightly in his chair, and Angel Eyes was amused to note that the barman was starting to tremble. He couldn't be blamed for that. K'Baal was the spookiest guy Angel Eyes had ever met.

K'Baal stretched out one bony, triple-jointed finger. Its tip rested lightly on the back of Konik's wrist, and the barman tore his hand away with a gasp.

"Wh-what are you trying to do to me?" he stuttered. "I—I—"

"You will tell us the truth." There was no threat in the Arcturan's tone; it was merely a statement of fact. Konik would tell them the truth, whether he wanted to or not.

But the barman tried to brazen it out one last time. "There's nothing to tell," he blustered.

The Arcturan snapped his fingers. It sounded like a spine cracking.

One moment, Konik was terrified, desperate to get away from Angel Eyes and his men as quickly as he could.

Next moment, he was rooted to the spot, unable to move. He was still terrified, even more so now, because he could feel something start to move. Under his skull. In his brain. Like a worm, poking around, chewing on his thoughts, burrowing deep into his very essence.

Konik tried to scream, but no sound would come.

He didn't know how long he stood there, immobile, heart pounding like a drum. Suddenly, his paralysis ceased. But instead of turning and walking away, he found himself talking.

And he had no control over what he was saying.

"I've been spying on Mr. Quarantino's files," he began dully. "Thought I could make some extra money. A thug called Xemtex paid me five grand to let him know who was after him and when he was coming."

"Lobo." Angel Eyes nodded. "Pity Xemtex didn't off him. So what's Bo's special job?"

"Earthling, name of Jones." The barman rapped out the information. "One million credits reward. Quarantino got his commission in advance."

Randan and Virt nearly choked on their whiskies. Angel Eyes hissed, his forked serpentine tongue flicking out to lick his lips greedily. Even the Arcturan stiffened slightly.

"A million credits," Angel Eyes mused. "That's a lot of cash. What did he do, this Jones?"

"Crime unknown."

"And Big Blue . . . ?"

Konik couldn't help himself. He knew he shouldn't be saying any of this, but that stinking hooded alien had done something to his mind. The words just flowed out of their own account: "It seems he's a friend of Jones. He thinks the warrant is a fake. Maybe he wants to free his pal."

"Where's this going down?"

"A place called Vrk. Somewhere in the Magellanic Clouds."

Angel Eyes got slowly to his feet, towering over the barman. "Go back to work. Mention this to anybody, and I'll kill you."

Konik snapped back into his normal self, still fully aware of everything he'd said. Feeling drained and violated, he shuffled back toward the bar. Glumly, he poured himself a stiff brandy and downed it in one. If Angel Eyes told Quaratino about his betrayal, Konik was out of a job. If he told Lobo, Konik was 180 pounds of dog meat.

"Let's go," he heard Angel Eyes say. "There's 800,000 creds out there with our names on it. Let's go collect."

"Lobo's no pushover," Virt reminded him.

"Neither are we," Angel Eyes said thinly. He jerked his head toward the Arcturan, who seemed to have gotten to his feet without anybody noticing him move. "And don't forget—we have *magic* on our side."

CHAPTER 8

They didn't get a lot of visitors out in the Small Magellanic Cloud, a puff of stars out beyond the rim of the galaxy's spiral arm. If the Milky Way could be said to have an end, this was as close as it got.

The distances between star systems were too vast to allow viable commercial ties, and the tourist industry gave the area a complete bodyswerve. Not a lot of vacationers wanted to look up and see a sky with hardly any stars shining in it; "frightening," "creepy" and "evil" were just some of the phrases used in the last proper tourist survey.

What planets there were, were dull and boring. They were too far away from the rest of existence to be integrated into the ever-expanding galactic culture. They had no features that the cosmic holidaymaker would pay a hefty premium for. And there were no particularly colorful indigenous peoples with gorgeous women and weird, druggy ceremonies, which ruled out the sex-travel side of the business.

The small Magellanic Cloud was favored by loners and

outcasts—the kind of people who, as beatniks, discovered Big Sur in the 1940s. Later, in the trippy-dippy sixties, they became hippies and settled down in Katmandu. In other words, the only people who came here were trying to get away from everybody else.

The peoples of Auriun, which orbited star B-2323, hadn't had a visitor from off-world for forty years. Even then, it had been an anthropological party sent out by one of the Copernican universities to study the effects of isolation on Auriun society. The professors and postgrad students didn't exactly mix with the natives for fear they'd be ending the isolation they'd come to study.

The resulting series of books became best sellers throughout swaths of the civilized galaxy, but—perhaps unsurprisingly—the Auriuns didn't receive a single credit in royalties. Once their visitors had gone, the Universe forgot all about Auriun and its tiny neighbor, Vrk.

Auriun had reached a state of development roughly equivalent to Earth in the early twentieth century. The vast majority of the population lived in cities, with skyscrapers a hundred stories tall. They'd never invented the internal combustion engine, but had discovered a way to convert low-frequency sound waves into nonpolluting motion. Their electricity came free—and maybe that was what had stopped them from progressing any further. Nobody was really motivated to do anything very much. The few integrated attempts at spaceflight had ended in a tidal wave of lethargy and apathy.

The cities were autonomous states, but warfare was virtually unknown. Not because the Auriuns were especially peace-loving or nonaggressive, but because low-frequency sound waves—when used as a weapon—tended to destroy the user as well as the target. If not checked, they'd end up destroying the planet.

So everybody was nice to everybody else; life drifted on, as if it were a reasonably pleasant dream.

When a fleet of strange, crystal spacecraft appeared in their atmosphere, the Auriuns were intrigued. Maybe the planet had been put on the galactic tourist trail, after all, and these were the first package tours arriving. Or maybe it was just another bunch of bozo intellectuals from a college someplace on Betelgeuse, with a brief to pick the local chumps' brains.

Whatever, the Auriuns were so incredibly lonely, they would certainly make the newcomers welcome.

Millions thronged the streets of every city, necks craned to watch the shimmering incoming craft. Civic dignitaries dusted off their dowdy robes and chains of office, and busied themselves with writing welcome speeches. Happy schoolchildren waited with garlands of exotic flowers to greet their honored guests.

And then a voice like the crack of doom thundered across the planet.

"We are the Alpha. We claim this world. You now belong to us."

Across the planet, there was a wide variety of reaction to the news. In some cities, the crowds panicked; hundreds of thousands of people milled around in terrified confusion. One city officially declared the whole affair to be a hoax; its mayor was a serious fan of the "hidden camera" television shows so popular around the galaxy, and he was convinced one of the major networks had targeted Auriun as the next big laugh.

He couldn't have been more wrong.

Responding to some unseen cue, the descending crystal craft opened fire with their armaments. Cluster bombs dropped indiscriminately in city streets, cutting down people like wheat before a harvester. Cobalt-enhanced phosphor bombs created lethal firestorms. Energy beams ripped into skyscrapers, quickly reducing them to rubble, and plasma bolts took out every civic headquarters.

A huge, crystalline humanoid was in the forefront of every attack.

The Auriuns tried to fight back. One thousand of their strange, battery-powered aircraft took off in the greatest show of massed force the planet had ever produced. Wave after wave of them poured into the skies, their dedicated pilots grimly bent on revenge.

They didn't last an hour.

Within a day, every city on the planet was in flames or flattened.

Surviving Auriuns were stunned when the crystal ships landed and disgorged their Vrkn crews. Tiny, wiry soldiers wearing sunscreen goggles rounded up their newfound enemy and herded them into hurriedly erected execution camps.

The Alpha hovered over the planet's largest city. Dense black smoke swirled around it, caressing the crystal being as it drifted up from the burning buildings below. The Alpha felt neither pleasure nor shame as it surveyed the ruined buildings and heaps of corpses in the streets.

Their time had come to an end. The cycle of life was broken.

We are the Alpha.

Everything else will come to an end.

CHAPTER 9

"Mayday! Mayday! Any craft in vicinity, please respond!"

"Feetal's fraggin' gizz!" Lobo cursed as the Mayday message cut in over the music blaring from the radio. "Get lost! I'm tryin' to chill out here."

They'd been traveling for hours, without a word being spoken except for the DJ. Lobo's brain had long since merged with the music—but now his reverie had been rudely disrupted by the urgent request for assistance.

"Ignore it," Lobo snapped to Xemtex. "We don't have time for this. Hold yer course for Vrk."

"You cannot do that," the Martian Manhunter protested, speaking for the first time since they'd left Al's Diner—or what was left of it. "Every galactic convention demands that all available craft answer any distress signal. Surely you know—"

"Awright, awright," Lobo said testily. "I don't need a criminal to tell me galactic law. Contact 'em, Xemtex. Let 'em know we're comin'." The bounty hunter shook his head in exasperation. "Sheesh! I'm never gonna get my cash at this rate."

The radio crackled again, the male voice surging and fading. "Our vessel has crashed at coordinates 39-Gamma and 117-Phi. Can you help?"

"You got any money on board?" Lobo asked hopefully.

"No," came the static-ridden reply. "We're carrying a cargo of pornography and sex aids . . ."

Lobo sighed. "Just my luck."

". . . and a dozen pole dancers."

The bounty hunter's eyes lit up. "Izzatafact?" he said perkily. "You tell those dancers not to worry, the Main Man's on his way to rescue 'em." His tone changed as he snapped at the bike again. "What you waitin' for, dork-brain? Get us to these coordinates right *now.*"

"You're joking," Xemtex drawled in the bike's tinny voice. "Do you know where they are? Those coords are for the Trash Moon."

"I don't give a flyin' frag if they're for Sammy the Singin' Sewer," Lobo shot back. "Just get us there. Go, go, go!"

The Trash Moon was a barren satellite that had broken free from its planetary system aeons ago. For centuries, it had wandered through space on its own erratic path, weaving its way through other systems. And for centuries, it had been used to dump trash by every planet it passed.

Chemicals—debris—plastics—toxins—the rubbish of a dozen worlds . . . you name it, it got dumped on the Trash Moon. No effort was made to separate and sort the waste; it was dumped as it came, rotting household refuse all mixed up with mine tailings, poisonous chemicals, and abandoned vehicles.

There were even rumors a complete decommissioned nuclear power station had been thrown out there, but nobody cared enough to look. Everybody knew that, sooner or later, the moon's course would steer it away from them and all that trash would become some other system's problem.

When the garbage covered the surface to a depth of a hundred feet, somebody had tried to organize things in a more efficient manner. A couple of hundred scavenger robots had been dropped on the moon, programmed to reduce the garbage to its constituent parts for recovery and resale.

Then the company filed for bankruptcy, the directors looted the cash accounts and headed for a Babe World, and the robots were left to fend for themselves.

Now the trash was five hundred feet deep, and the scavenger droids were still there, fighting a never-ending battle against the dozen or more ships that arrived every day to disgorge the detritus of their civilizations. The robots also fought constantly against the Pickers, the ragtag collection of aliens who'd settled amongst the trash, hoping to find a better life there than on their homeworlds.

The Pickers wanted to preserve everything they could for their own consumption and use, while the robots merely wanted to reduce everything to its components. It wasn't much of a life for either side, but once you were on Trash Moon, there was no way off.

*   *   *

J'onn J'onzz could smell the Trash Moon as soon as the Spazz-Frag hit the atmosphere, long before the bike reached its surface. The stench of decomposing food and dead farm animals combined with the emanations from disintegrating plastic and thousands of tons of discarded slurry to produce a stench that overwhelmed the senses. It was the rankest, foulest odor he had ever encountered.

"It's a bit niffy," Lobo remarked, as the bike swooped down, zeroing in on the coordinates the radio had given them. "But hey, what's an unnatural odor or two when the lives of bouncin' babes is at stake? I just hope they're as grateful as they should be," he added lasciviously, licking his lips.

The Spazz-Frag hovered over an enormous mass of trash.

"This is the spot." Lobo peered down at the mountains of garbage that rose everywhere. "Looks like they must have hit at speed, tunneled down in the crap, an' got stuck there." The bounty hunter shook his head. "This ain't bike territory. Guess I have to go in on foot."

"I will assist you," the Manhunter offered.

"Oh yeah? Lookin' to get yer jollies before ya hit jail?" Lobo leered. "I don't think so, Baldy. You'll stay right here. This is a Main Man special solo mission."

Twenty feet above the surface, Lobo set the bike controls to autohover and hit the override switch so Xemtex couldn't make a run for it.

"If the bike gets lippy," he told Manhunter, "just ignore it. Alternatively, ya might want to torture Xemtex with yer telepathic powers. In that case, be my guest."

The Main Man clambered to his feet so he was standing on the bike.

"Awright, guys. I'll be back shortly. Don't go away now!"

Without looking back, he leapt from the bike and plunged down toward the garbage below.

"Geronimooooo!"

J'onn J'onzz watched as the bounty hunter disappeared headfirst into the festering mounds of rubbish, and sighed. He flexed his wrists, testing the strength of the handcuffs that still bound them. The cuffs were made of a supposedly unbreakable material, and J'onn wondered if even his great strength would be sufficient to snap them. Then he relaxed. He'd given Lobo his word he wouldn't escape; whatever happened, he would keep his promise. The bounty hunter wasn't the only one who prized his honesty.

He caught a slight movement off to one side and turned for a better view. A small spacepod was slowly approaching. Had Lobo saved the girls—J'onn presumed that pole dancers would be female—already?

The Martian frowned, puzzled, as the pod drew alongside. This couldn't be the vessel that had crash-landed—it bore no signs of damage at all. And there was no sign of Lobo, either.

A hatch slid open in the pod's side. A sinister-looking robot stuck its head out.

"John Jones?" the robot asked, like a medical receptionist arranging an appointment with the doctor.

"Yes," J'onn began, amazed by the incongruity, "but—"

"Enough said," the robot broke in. Suddenly, there was

a pipe gun in its metal hands, the business end pointed directly at J'onn. Before the startled Manhunter had time to react, the robot fired.

J'onn J'onzz was enveloped in a thick, choking cloud of gas. He coughed harshly, doing his best to keep the substance from entering his lungs. But it was too late. J'onn swayed in his seat, then slumped forward on the pillion, unconscious.

In places, the garbage mountains on the moon's surface were a thousand feet high. When Lobo hit, he plunged straight down through the surface layers and crashed through the roof of a tunnel dug into the trash.

Grinning, he got to his feet. He'd quite enjoyed his first-ever dive into raw garbage. If they put an event like that in the Galactic Olympics, they'd double their audiences at a stroke.

Pole dancers, huh? He was looking forward to this and no mistake. No doubt they were in as much of a stinking mess as he was, but so what? Some folks were turned on by the stench of rotting rubbish.

Stooping under the low ceiling, Lobo hauled a small but powerful flashlight from where it dangled on his belt and snapped it on. The high-energy lightbeams illuminated the tunnel in a cold, white glare.

Centuries of trash were arranged in layers, like geological strata—an archaeologist's wet dream. There was a layer of old metal pipes and gaslight fittings, testament to a planet that had just discovered electricity. Above it was a layer of powdered fertilizer, all jumbled up with the decomposing flesh of dead animals—a result of new galactic rules on agricultural policy.

Above that, nestling into the tunnel roof, was the skeleton of a thirty-foot-long dinosaur. Feetal alone knew where that had come from.

The walls and ceiling had been smoothed off, but here and there trash of all kinds intruded into the tunnel. Obviously the aliens who lived here had dug it out.

Or, as it turned out, not so obviously at all.

Hunched over to avoid banging his head on the roof, Lobo headed off down the slope.

He heard the voices before he saw them, a thin, reedy babble that he couldn't decipher. He turned a corner in the narrow shaft, and it opened out into a larger chamber. His flashlight picked out piles of assorted rubbish. Mounds of damaged circuit boards lay in a heap against one wall; next to them were stacked thousands of sheets of glass and transparent, corrugated plastic; recovered wire had been wound onto makeshift bobbins, which hung in their hundreds from the ceiling.

In the center of the chamber, staring at the bounty hunter with calculating visual receptors, were half a dozen scavenger droids.

The robots were relatively small, only about five feet high, but all were fitted with a variety of tools for trash disassembly. Their metal arms ended in hooks and claws and hammers, and wicked-looking curved blades.

"Garbage, yes?" one robot said excitedly. The foot-long metal shears that it wore in place of one hand started to open and close noisily.

Klick-klack.

"Hey, get a grip," the Main Man snorted. "I'm here on a darin' rescue mission. Where did the porno ship come down?"

"Ambulatory garbage," the robot noted. *Klick-klack.* "Humanoid detritus, yes?"

The grinding wheel attached to another robot's wrist burst into motion. *Zeeee.* "Disassembly required," it stated, and took a pace forward.

Zeee. Klick-klack. Then a power drill started up. *Vzzzz.*

"Sheesh, what are ya gonna do, guys?" Lobo asked. "Sing me to death with a power-tool lullaby?"

Zeee. Klick-klack. Vzzzz. The robots were all advancing toward him. Lobo's hand closed round the butt of his gun. Then he shook his head slightly and started to unravel his hook and chain. He could shoot them down in seconds—but where was the fun in that? Better to frag them close up and physical, work up a little sweat . . . pique his appetite for the pole-dancing feast that was to come.

"Awright, ladies. Who's first?" Lobo asked politely. Then: "Aw, never mind. I'll get to ya all eventually."

The hook spun from his hand and arced through the air to embed itself in one of the robots' heads. There was a blue flash of ruptured circuitry. As Lobo jerked the droid off its feet, the other robots charged him, their arm attachments flailing.

Starboot, Darriz, and the psychotic robot stood in the hovering pod's open hatchway, congratulating themselves on a job well-done. J'onn J'onzz lay slumped forward on the

Spazz-Frag, kayoed by a massive dose of knockout gas, hands still cuffed behind him. By the time he came round, they'd have picked up the reward and be halfway to another galaxy.

"Nice work, guys."

The metallic voice surprised them and all three looked blankly around.

"Xemtex . . . ?" Starboot asked unsurely. "Where are you, boss?"

"Right here, fool."

"Where? Geez, don't tell me Lobo's made you *invisible*?"

"The bike, dummy. I'm in the stinkin' bike!"

Starboot's mouth fell open. "Huh?" was all he could say.

"Lobo cut my brain out," Xemtex explained, and they could hear his cold fury bubbling under the metallic drawl. "He stuck it in the Spazz-Frag's control system."

"Gee-eez." Starboot expelled his breath in a long whistle. "That guy is truly sick. Ain't there a law against doin' stuff like that?"

Darriz squeezed himself past his two companions till he was standing on the edge of the hatch. "Tough luck, boss," he said cheerily. "But look on the bright side— that's one cool bike he's put you in. The very best that money can buy, according to the ads." There was a faraway look in the alien's unlidded eyes. "I've always dreamed of riding a Spazz-Frag."

Before Xemtex could comment, Darriz leapt from the hatchway. He soared through the air, over the ten feet or so to where the bike hovered. He spread his legs and yelled, "What say, boss? Gonna take me for a burn-up?"

"Darriz—no!"

But Xemtex's warning came too late. Darriz landed hard on the driver's seat. There was a loud hiss of compressed air escaping, followed at once by a shriek of agony from the outlaw. His eyes glazed over, and he fell lifeless from the bike, tumbling down to land with a soft *plop* in some hideous mess below.

Starboot looked from his dead companion, now sinking slowly into the ooze, to the bike. A sharp metal spike, about nine inches long, protruded vertically from the seat. It was wet and slick with blood from Darriz's buttocks.

"I tried to tell him," Xemtex said. "It's an antitheft device. The seat's tuned to Lobo's butt print. Wrong ass, and you get the spike."

"Gee-ee-eez!" Starboot's tone was a mixture of disbelief and revulsion. "That guy's more than sick—he's dimensionally warped!"

"No point mewling over spilled milk," the robot opined. "A million creds split three ways is better than four." It jerked its head toward the slumped Martian. "Vrk wants him. We got him. Let's go."

"You two take the pod," Xemtex told them. "If you switch off the override, I can fly this thing on my own. I'll bring the prisoner."

"What in the name of Feetal's gizz is *this*?"

Perplexed, Lobo stared at the small black box illuminated by his flashbeam. A red LED light was blinking off and on . . . as it broadcast the Mayday signal he had answered.

The half dozen garbage robots lay dismembered and useless two levels above where Lobo stood. The battle had lasted mere minutes, as the Main Man gave them a serious stomping. Now he was perspiring lightly, breathing raspily, and getting really impatient for some hot babe action.

But instead of breasts and hips and curvaceous bottoms, his hands were holding a totally unsexy little black box.

"Frag!" Sudden realization swept over him. "It's a trick!" he roared. "Some lowlife bastich has scammed the Main Man!"

Immediately, he turned and began to run back up the tunnel, dislodging muck and rubbish at every step.

It took several minutes to get back to the surface, clawing his way through clinging, stenching trash. When he finally burst through the top layer of junk, it was to see the Spazz-Frag and a space pod heading rapidly away from him.

"That backstabbin' bastich Xemtex," Lobo muttered. "I guess Baldy must've helped him by switchin' off the override. Can't trust nobody these days. Ah well," he went on heavily, "it's time the bad guys paid the piper—an' I got my Martian back."

He jammed the forefinger and thumb of one hand into his mouth and gave out a piercing whistle that shattered much of the glass a couple of levels below. But it had another effect, too: his bike was fitted with an ultrasonic receptor that allowed him to control it at a distance. It had helped him out a hundred times in battle with his enemies.

Now, it responded faultlessly to his whistle.

"What the hell . . . ?"

Xemtex's control of the Spazz-Frag was suddenly gone. It didn't matter what he tried to operate; nothing was paying any attention to the signals he was frantically sending through the system.

He felt the bike slow slightly, then start to turn toward the pod flying close by its side. The armaments warning lights flashed ON.

The bike's forward-mounted cannon sent a stream of titanium-tipped shells ripping into the space pod's flank. There was a series of explosions.

The Spazz-Frag's visual sensors picked up the psycho-droid, pipe gun in hand, as it leapt through a jagged hole in the hull plates.

Then the pod disappeared in an orange-red blossom of flame.

Xemtex groaned. It was all going wrong. He could only hope that the murderous robot had what it took to defeat the Main Man.

But he wouldn't have bet on it.

Lobo gave a grunt of satisfaction when the space pod exploded. Only then did it occur to him: *Maybe that was the ship with the pole dancers.* He groaned. *Just my fraggin' luck, if I've blown up the babes I was supposed to be savin'.*

Then he saw the plunging robot. *If that's one of the dancers, I did myself a favor!*

Then he remembered: There were no dancers. It was a scam.

Two spheres from the pipe gun blasted down at him. He dived full length behind a ragged pile of old aluminium sidings, which sheltered him from the worst of the twin blasts.

The robot landed on top of him, the momentum of its plunge driving them a good twenty feet down into the trash. A mass of slates and old building rubble stopped their fall. Even before Lobo got his breath back, the crazed robot was swinging its gun like a club.

"Die!" the robot commanded, the heavy pipe gun battering into the side of Lobo's head.

Thwack! Thwack!

"Die!

Thw—

Lobo blocked the swinging gun with his forearm, sparks flying as the weapon grated against his chain. He brought his knees up in the robot's back with enough force to send it catapulting forward over him. It dropped the gun as its head rammed into a twisted, semimelted monitor screen with a loud crash.

By the time it had disentangled itself and whirled back to its foe, Lobo had the pipe gun in his own hands, leveled at its owner.

"Good night, Gracie," the bounty hunter quipped. "Ya fight like a big girl."

He opened fire with a salvo of shells that tore the robot into pieces of shrapnel. He held up the pipe gun and nodded in admiration. "Nice shooter. Smooth action. An' I get the bounty on another bad guy."

The Spazz-Frag swooped down and hovered at his side.

Lobo eyed the Manhunter, still slumped unconscious against the console. "I guess this was all your doin', then, Xemtex?"

There was no reply.

"I guess ya must be gettin' to *like* the shocks," Lobo mused. "I gotta say, yer a right glutton for punishment."

Lobo tossed the pipe gun into the garbage. See what the scavengers made of that. He shoved the Martian upright and got back on the bike.

"Ya know where yer goin', Xemtex. So let's get started."

As the bike rose obediently into the air, Lobo reached toward the electroshock control.

Xemtex would still be screaming when they got to Vrk.

CHAPTER 10

There is movement through the electromagnetic fields.
We sense a presence.
Possible intruder.
Prepare reception on Vrk.

As if it were discrete entities, the Alpha conversed with itself. It stood on Vrk's highest point, a jagged needle of
obsidian rock that jutted a few thousand feet into the planetoid's thin atmosphere. Had it been in the A9 asteroids,
the mountain would have been strip-mined; on Vrk, it was
just a hill that had never been climbed.

It was night on the tiny world, but it spun so fast
around B-2323 that day and night lasted little more than
four hours each.

The Alpha's massive crystal head was tilted upward,
its cold eyes scanning the heavens, reading the data borne
on the light waves themselves. The artificial intelligence
had attuned its quartz body to B-2323's electromagnetic
fields, giving it supreme abilities within the star's system.
As the Imperium of Vrk, the Alpha would soon be invading other solar systems; it would master each one's individual EM fields as its sphere of influence increased.

It was aware of Lobo's entry into its solar system.
It knew that, even now, the bounty hunter was passing
Auriun.

The Vrkn troops had razed every city to the ground—
with more than a little help from the Alpha's own destructive capabilities. The Alpha had plans for the planet and
had begun by preparing nurseries for the genetic modifi-
cation of several thousand Vrks. The minor alterations
would remove their need for shadow and aversion to
bright light. It would be these Vrkns' task to rebuild Auriun . . . but to the Alpha's specifications.

Weapons factories would proliferate, the fuel for further invasions. Biochemical labs would be required;
the more weapons of mass destruction it possessed, the
swifter the takeovers would be. Breeding tanks for the
clone armies must be constructed and tested.

And all of it was already in hand.

The rest of the Universe would not be pleased when it
discovered the Alpha's plans. All life was programmed to
survive, either by fighting or fleeing; but the Alpha would
exterminate all life. Heavy resistance was only to be expected, and the Alpha was preparing for it in advance.

Meanwhile, large numbers of Vrkns were busy on the
planetoid itself. Obeying the Alpha's instructions, they
burrowed deeper than ever before, almost down to the
semimolten core, forming chambers and tunnels and
rooms with strange, carved-stone equipment.

The being that called itself the First was preparing to
greet the Last.

"Got themselves a firestorm, if I'm any judge," Lobo
commented, not bothering to keep the excitement from
his voice.

The Spazz-Frag was streaking through the upper

fringes of Auriun's atmosphere, using the planet's spin to slow down and redirect toward Vrk. Vast columns of smoke rose from dozens of cities in flames far below, joining together into one huge plume that had already drifted halfway around the planet. Every now and then, bright gouts of orange flame bloomed and wafted skyward in the smoke.

Lobo was tempted to zoom down for a closer look. He liked to watch a good conflagration—and whatever had happened here, it had ignited more than a few of them. It was a pleasant way to pass a couple of hours, sucking on a cigar, a can of chilled Strongbooz in his hand, meditating on mass death and destruction. That *had* to be good for a man's soul. He could recommend it to anybody as a foolproof way of chilling out; just don't get too close if you were bothered by the sound of screaming.

But he had a prisoner to deliver, and he'd messed around for long enough already. That stupid stunt on the Trash Moon had cost him a fair amount of time; the desire for sex he'd felt then had been converted to a desire to cash in his reward and just *buy* the sex.

He wanted to see that money, hold it in his hands, riffle slowly through it, listening to the sweet music of folding green. He wanted to kiss it, maybe taunt Jonas Glim by waving fistfuls of cash in his tusky face. He wanted to throw it in the air and roll around naked as it fell on him like snow.

Then he wanted to spend it.

*   *   *

Xemtex's brain was a mass of charred nerve endings from the repeated shocks he'd suffered on the last leg of the journey.

He was still seething—madder than ever, in fact —still vowing to himself that somehow he'd turn the tables on Lobo and leave the bounty hunter sucking vacuum in the cold depths of space. After extensive torture, of course— *very* extensive torture, involving a whole range of sharp, serrated and rough-toothed instruments. And a few blunt ones, too.

The only problem was, Xemtex wouldn't be able to hold a candy bar, let alone wield a power drill or a bone saw. No limbs, remember? Never mind, he'd figure a way somehow. Maybe he could pay somebody to do it for him. Who knew—something might come up on this planetoid, Vrk.

Wisely, Xemtex kept his thoughts to himself.

Slouched behind Lobo, J'onn J'onzz dreamed of a red world and a beautiful green-skinned girl. Their boy played happily around them, catching brightly colored insects in the rays of the setting sun. A desert lizard yawned, flicked its tail and disappeared under a stone.

Nighttime on Mars, long years ago.

He dreamed of his vanished past, a past that could never be again.

Better that than know the hell he would soon experience.

CHAPTER 11

"Wakey-wakey, hands off snakey!"

J'onn J'onzz recovered consciousness with a start. Lobo had turned around in his seat and was bellowing in the Martian's ear.

"C'm'on, Baldy—snap out of it, before I come back there an' do a little snappin' myself."

For a moment, J'onn was baffled. He couldn't have fallen asleep, could he? No. The last thing he remembered was the space pod—and a robot with a pipe gun. Obviously, he had come under some sort of attack. But equally as obvious, Lobo had managed to retrieve the situation.

There was an unpleasant taste in his mouth; he guessed the robot had used some kind of gas against him.

"Will you tell me what happened?" he asked Lobo, although he could already guess what the bounty hunter's reply would be. The man went out of his way to be contrary.

Lobo shook his head, almost childishly. "Nope. Only reason I'm wakin' you up is 'cause I want you *compos mentis* when I hand you over. It doesn't look good on my resume to bring in a prisoner without his wits about him."

Vrk was hoving into view ahead, and J'onn was surprised to see how small the place was — not even a planetary mass. From the constellations he had observed on the journey, he guessed they must be somewhere out in the spiral arm. Now the lack of stars suggested one of the Magellanic Clouds. He had never been within light-years of this part of the galaxy before; how could he possibly have committed a crime here?

Clearly, Superman had been right to query the warrant. But had J'onn done the right thing in complying with it?

"Sheesh," he heard Lobo say. "The place ain't big enough to grow warts on, let alone call itself a fraggin' Imperium." The bounty hunter's tone took on a snarl. "I just hope these geeks have got my money, or I'll be stickin' their Imperium up their butts an' lightin' the blue touch paper."

There is little point in further speculation, J'onn decided. The Spazz-Frag was slowing as it touched the fringes of the planetoid's atmosphere, the heat from reentry giving the space bike's force field a fiery orange glow. *Whatever awaits me, I will soon confront it.*

There was nothing artificial on the surface of Vrk; no cities—not even a village. In fact, there was no construction of any kind. There were only jagged hills and cliffs, and a tall, dark peak that glowered over the others. Water may have been plentiful here in the past, but not now; the steep-sided gorges were filled only with boulders.

There was no sign of any life.

"If this is some creep's idea of a joke, the Main Man

ain't exactly bustin' a gut." The bounty hunter broke off as he saw a massive entranceway carved into a dark, forbidding cliffside. "Wait up. There's somethin'."

The bike swooped closer to the entry.

"Looks like they're subterraneans, huh? Cool."

It made sense: B-2323 loomed large and close, a huge nuclear furnace. At this distance, its solar radiation was probably lethal if you stayed out in it for too long.

Lobo slowed the bike to a fast walking pace and steered toward the foot of the cliff. There was a moment of near darkness as he guided it inside—but the interior was a revelation. Fluorescent fungi grew on the cavern walls in jagged spiral patterns, their eerie light whirling away down a vast corridor cut in the solid rock.

"Hootin' heck! I been in video arcades with less flash than this!"

With a distinct lack of caution, he followed the light whorls down the passageway. The way was lined with hundreds of little creatures—Vrkns, he presumed, although he was hoping he was wrong. They stood and watched wordlessly as the Spazz-Frag drifted by, their pinched, crabby little faces showing no sign of emotion or intelligence.

"Whoever hired me, it wasn't these gonks," the bounty hunter said affably, more to himself than the Martian. "They don't look like they got a brain between them. Tell ya what, though"—he slapped his thigh—"they'd sure make good target practice. They're just the right size, an' I bet they scamper real fast."

Almost instinctively, his hand went to the blaster that hung from his belt. He checked the movement, fighting down the impulse. It might not be good protocol to gun them down, especially if it turned out they *had* hired him. Maybe after he'd been paid, he could make tentative inquiries about hiring some of them for an hour or so.

The tunnel seemed to go on for miles before it eventually widened out into a chamber about twenty feet high and twice as long. Carved-stone pillars supported the roof, while a network of openings in the ceiling diverted sunlight from far above to Vrk's interior. The sunbeams slanted in at different angles, creating swirling columns of light throughout.

It looked like a temple.

Lobo farted. "Whoops." He grinned, unembarrassed. "Guess that must've been all the excitement."

"Welcome." A deep bass voice reverberated round the chamber as the bike came to a halt and settled to the ground with a sibilant whine. *"We are the Alpha, Directorate of the Imperium of Vrk."*

The Alpha sat on a massive stone throne whose every surface was grotesquely carved with what looked like electronic circuit boards. The interplay of light and shadow made the being seem impossibly imposing; its crystal body seemed somehow fluid.

Like the lumpy bits in lava lamps, Lobo thought. Aloud, he said, "Pleased to meet ya, Alf." He nodded a greeting to the seated crystal figure and dismounted from the bike. He grabbed the Martian's arm roughly and hauled him off, too. "I brung ya the geek ya been lookin' for. Signed, sealed, an' delivered, all as per contract. So let's take care of the small matter of finances. Okay?"

The Alpha appeared not to have heard. It rose from its

throne in one swift motion that belied its great bulk. Something that size should have been slow and ponderous, but instead it moved lithely and easily. In two paces it was down off the dais and standing beside them.

Lobo and the Manhunter were both formidable figures, swathed in muscle; but the Alpha dwarfed them. Sunlight played over its crystal body in an ever-changing kaleidoscope of muted color.

Its eyes fixed on the Martian. *"You are the last of your race? We wonder why. You seem healthy."*

"My people—" J'onzz began, but the Alpha pressed a crystal finger to its lips.

"Not now. We will learn all during the analysis."

"Analysis?" the Martian repeated. "I am here to stand trial—for a crime of which I have no knowledge."

"You will learn in due course."

Lobo stifled a yawn. "Save the jawin' for later, guys. I got me a hot date with some serious debauchery." A sudden thought occurred to him, and he looked up at the Alpha. It was disconcerting. Lobo was used to having folks look up at *him*. "I don't suppose yer offerin' a little bonus, are ya?" he asked. "I mean, seein' as how I brought Baldy in with minimum fuss an' maximum efficiency."

"Is that customary in the bounty-hunting trade?" the Alpha asked.

"Oh yeah, yeah, happens all the time," Lobo lied. "Sometimes guys are so happy, they even double the reward money."

He looked expectantly at the Alpha, but the sucker didn't rise to the bait.

"What do you wish?" The Alpha sounded intrigued.

"Ya see these little guys?" Lobo jerked a thumb behind him. "The gonks out in the tunnel? I got a real hankerin' to shoot me a couple dozen of 'em."

"Why?"

Lobo was unabashed. "I find 'em vaguely offensive. Their crabby little faces really get on my nerves. Apart from that . . . well, they look like they'd make good targets."

"Two dozen?"

"If ya can spare 'em."

The Alpha stared. At once, twenty-four Vrkns marched into the chamber in close formation, chattering in their irritating little voices.

Creep's obviously a telepath, too, Lobo noted.

The Vrkns wheeled as one and came to a halt facing Lobo.

"Aw, c'm'on, Alf," he complained. "This is a turkey shoot. Make 'em scamper a bit—scurry, even. Provide a little entertainment. Everybody likes to see little guys dodgin' bullets."

"No!" The word ripped angrily from the core of J'onn J'onzz's being. "You cannot do this. It would be cold-blooded murder!"

The Manhunter rarely gave in to emotion; he was renowned for being the Justice League's calmest member when under fire. The ancient Martian meditation techniques he employed meant that he was master of his emotions rather than their servant. But a slaughter like the one proposed was more than any decent being could stomach.

"Ahh, take a powder, ya bleedin' heart," Lobo said

offhandedly. Languidly, the bounty hunter fitted a magazine into his blaster's chamber. "Ya saw how many of them there were. Nobody's goin' to miss a few."

Manhunter was aware that the Alpha was paying close attention, but it made no move to interfere or even comment.

"I said leave them alone." J'onn's icy tone would have made almost anybody obey him instantly.

It only made Lobo more infuriated. "An' who's gonna make me, Baldy?" he jeered. "You? Haw-haw."

"Yes, me."

J'onn raised his handcuffed wrists, gritted his teeth and strained to pull his wrists apart. The muscles in his arms bulged. A vein stood out like a pulsing rope on his forehead.

"I will not allow you to murder innocent beings," he said, slowly and deliberately.

And with a sharp snap, the unbreakable handcuffs broke.

If Lobo was impressed, he didn't show it. "Bravo," he applauded, his voice heavy with mockery. "Now I gotta buy new cuffs. Or maybe I should take 'em out of yer hide."

J'onn ignored him and stabbed an accusing finger at the Alpha. "What kind of justice can I expect from you when you allow your own people to be killed without qualm?"

"They are disposable," the Alpha replied. *"Nevertheless, your display of morality interests us. The bounty hunter will not kill the Vrkns until we have investigated further."*

At some unseen signal from their ruler, the primitive creatures turned and marched in unison from the chamber. As they hurried through the exit, one of them turned. For the briefest of instants, its gaze caught J'onn's. Then it, too, fled.

"Aw, man," Lobo complained, lowering his gun. "Why'd ya let him poop the party, Alf? Like, he's the *bad* guy, remember?"

Abruptly, the Alpha turned away. It raised one hand in the air and beckoned for them to follow. *"We will show you to your cell, Martian."*

J'onn resigned himself. For a moment, fired with adrenaline, ready to do battle with Lobo, he had forgotten why he was here. Now, reality came thundering back. He was a prisoner, accused of an unnamed crime.

"I demand to know the crime with which I am charged."

The Alpha gazed coldly at him. *"You are our legal captive. Under galactic law, you have no rights to make demands."*

"Hey, about my cash," Lobo broke in. "What say ya pay me now, then ya can show him the cell to yer rocky heart's content."

"You should come, too, bounty hunter. You will appreciate it, believe us."

"Yeah, yeah," Lobo muttered, falling into step behind J'onn. "I'd appreciate ya talkin' in the singular, too, but I ain't makin' a fuss, right?"

"We do not understand your point."

"Ah, forget it." Lobo bit the end off a cigar and lit a match. He fired up and exhaled a stream of smoke.

The Alpha peered at him. *"What is that?"*

"A cigar. Cheroot. Stogie. You know—a smoke."

"We do not know."

"It's good for ya." Lobo held the cigar out toward the Alpha. "Give it a try, why don't ya?"

J'onn J'onzz shook his head. The bounty hunter was supposed to have a reputation for honesty, but as far as J'onn could tell, he more or less said whatever he felt like saying. The only consistency in his words and deeds was his unremitting nastiness.

The giant crystal being studied the glowing cigar for a moment, then moved away. *"We think not,"* it told the bounty hunter. *"We are unable to understand the motivation for flooding your breathing apparatus with an unnatural substance."*

Lobo took a deep draw on his cigar. "That's because ya have yet to discover the joys of nicotine," the bounty hunter said slyly.

"Enough of this nonsense," J'onn broke in. He looked up at the Alpha. "Nicotine is an addictive substance," he explained. "Those who become hooked on it require constant and increasing doses to feed their habit."

The Alpha peered at Lobo again; its crystal face was incapable of much expression, but J'onn would have called that look "quizzical."

"Spoilsport," Lobo hissed at J'onn, as the Alpha resumed its stride, and they fell in alongside. "I wanted to see the rock-guy cough."

The Alpha led them into a smaller side tunnel, where the fungi on the walls were sparser and the light slightly dimmer. J'onn noticed that it didn't have to duck once or lower its head to clear the tunnel roof, as if the tunnel had been cut to this size especially for it.

They passed through a pair of massive stone doors adorned with symbols J'onn had never seen before, into what was obviously the prison complex. It had a long central corridor, with cells running off on either side for its entire, not inconsiderable length. The whole complex was carved out of a huge area of virtually flawless quartz; despite their thickness, the cell walls were almost transparent.

The Alpha paused before an oval opening and indicated that Manhunter should step through.

J'onn hesitated. There was much about this situation that made him unhappy: the unspecified nature of his alleged crime and the Alpha's willingness to sacrifice the lives of its followers. Before he allowed himself to be incarcerated, he should—

He lurched forward into the cell as Lobo's boot suddenly hammered into his backside.

"Quit messin' around," the bounty hunter snarled. "Take it like a man."

J'onn whirled, ready to strike back. But it was too late. A sheet of thick, transparent crystal slid noiselessly out of its base and clicked softly into place, covering the oval opening.

J'onn could only glower his displeasure, watching the faintly blurred images of Lobo and the Alpha through the crystal.

* * *

"So . . . what have ya got to interest me, Alf?" Lobo asked. "Torture equipment, maybe?" His eyes lit up. "Not babes, by any chance?"

"No. It is this."

The Alpha indicated the cell directly opposite J'onzz. Its oval covering was already in place. Lobo could see the shape of someone inside, and he squinted for a better view. A generally nondescript bipedal humanoid was sitting on a stone bench, head in hands, sobbing like his heart would break.

"Yeah, cool. I like to see prisoners." Lobo shrugged. "But he's kind of small-scale, ain't he? I mean, if ya had a thousand of 'em, that'd be a spectacle. Synchronized sobbin'." He considered for a moment. "Yeah, ya could make money out of that."

"He," said the Alpha, gesturing to the cell's occupant, drawing Lobo's attention back, *"is an Auriun."*

"Well, bully for him, Alf. Get to the point, huh?"

"Auriun is the only planet in the B-2323 system."

Lobo put two and two together. "The place I saw burnin' on the way in? Man, somebody made a right mess out of them."

"We did."

"Congratulations. I'd pat ya on the back, if ya wasn't so damned big."

"That," the Alpha said again, pointing into the cell, *"is the last Auriun. The very last Auriun. The others are . . . extinct."*

"Don't tell me—you did that, too." It was a statement, not a question. A cold feeling was growing in Lobo's gut, a niggling, chilly little itch that often accompanied trouble. A sudden thought had occurred to him.

"Don't tell me somethin' else," the bounty hunter said, as it all started to click into place. His hand moved imperceptibly toward his gun. "The Martian's the last of his kind, too. Right?"

"You are very astute."

"But here's the killer, Clyde," Lobo announced. "I'm the last Czarnian. Yep, that's right—I'm the only survivor of the entire advanced Czarnian civilization. Now—bearin' in mind you asked specifically for me—you ain't gonna tell me that's *coincidence* . . . ?"

"We are not going to tell you anything."

Lobo sighed ruefully. He reached up with one hand and stroked the stubble on his chin. "Guess there's no money, either, huh?"

"That is correct. You are our prisoner." A pause. *"Why do you stroke your chin? Does this signify thoughtfulness?"*

"I guess you could call it a distraction, rock-butt." Lobo's gun leapt suddenly into his other hand. "I don't like guys who welch on me."

Without further warning, he opened fire. Half a dozen fireburst shells slammed into the Alpha's chest in quick succession. Taken unaware, the crystal being was blasted back and off its feet. It crunched into the chamber wall with the sharp sound of stone on stone.

Lobo aimed the gun dead center in the Alpha's forehead.

"It's been real sweet knowin' ya, Alf," the bounty

hunter lied, the thought of the nonexistent reward turning his blood to ice. "But here comes the partin' of the ways."

He got off two shots that blasted the Alpha in the head. It rocked backward on its heels but recovered at once.

Before his finger could tighten on the trigger a third time, the Alpha's eyes flashed bright as a bcacon. What felt like a wall of force drove into Lobo, hurling the gun from his grasp. It skidded away across the polished-stone floor. Lobo felt himself lifted off his feet, turned around, and smashed face-first into a stone column covered in phosphorescent lichen.

His face scraped through the lichen and across the polished stone, and a bitter taste mingled with the saltiness of his own blood.

Instinctively, Lobo flung himself aside. The Alpha's huge stone fist glanced off his ribs and smacked into the column. As crystal struck crystal, piezoelectricity flashed; tiny globules of sparkling blue light shot off in all directions.

The bounty hunter's boot swung up and drove into the crystal giant's knee joint; the Alpha fell backward, its arms flailing as it strove to keep its balance.

"Didn't like that, did ya, Alf?" Lobo crowed. "Pucker up, cheesewit—there's more on the way."

He followed through with a two-footed dropkick, slamming into the Alpha's chest, sending it thundering into a cell wall. Lobo rolled to his feet as another shower of blue sparks blossomed like fireworks.

Lobo could hardly take his eyes off them, watching even as the sparks lost energy and faded gently into nothing. His eyes blinked rapidly. He wasn't feeling good at all. Something wasn't right with his perceptions.

The Alpha moved more swiftly than a creature its size had any right to, launching itself across the prison corridor. The bounty hunter shook his head, trying to clear it. Why was the Easter Bunny charging at him? Who painted it in these psychedelic colors? And why did the defensive arm he was trying to raise weigh several million tons?

Drugged! The bastard drugged me with that lichen!

The realization and the Alpha hit him together. Lobo felt his whole body squashing like toothpaste as the behemoth sandwiched him against a wall. He tried to make a quip, but he didn't seem to have any breath.

The Alpha's hands were gripping his throat.

"We expected resistance," the Alpha said, apparently unfazed by the shells that had exploded against it and the blows Lobo had landed. Relentlessly, its grip tightened; it yanked Lobo off the floor and lifted him until he was level with its face. *"We crush resistance."*

About ninety percent of Lobo's brain was engaged in lewd and libidinous sexual practices with every babe he'd ever met and several he hadn't. Fortunately, the remaining ten percent majored in self-preservation.

"Crush this . . . boulder-brains," the Main Man croaked, amazed as the words came out of his mouth in multicolored bubbles.

One hand came up, clutching a brace of frag grenades he'd yanked from his belt. The Alpha was fast, but not fast enough. Before it could close its mouth, Lobo stuffed the grenades down its throat.

It held him away at arm's length, his kicking feet dangling twelve inches above the ground, while it stood there waiting. It didn't have to wait long—Lobo had automatically flicked the grenades to a three-second fuse.

There was a muffled explosion, which immediately doubled in intensity. A gout of flame erupted from the Alpha's mouth and ears, followed by a puff of acrid gray smoke.

"We . . ." it said, and more smoke puffed from its mouth. *"We are . . ."*

"You are . . ." Lobo gasped, struggling but still unable to break its choking grip. It didn't matter. He'd forgotten what he was going to say. But someplace in his frazzled brain, he knew that *nobody* chewed on two fraggers and went shopping afterward. The Alpha was toast.

The Alpha swayed on its feet, eyes flashing in a random sequence. It kept repeating *"We . . . we are . . ."* then its voice would tail away before starting over again.

With a visible effort, it pulled itself together. *"We are the Alpha. We are not amused,"* it managed to say.

Ten percent of Lobo's brain groaned. The creep was still on its feet and making more sense by the second. It must have the constitution of a mountain. He had to figure a way out of this before—

Before that massive rock fist pounded his head.

He didn't figure it.

The massive fist pounded.

"We are not amused."

"We are not amused."

"We are not amused."

Over and over and over, until all the pretty flashing lights disappeared, and Lobo fell into a bottomless void.

* * *

The Spazz-Frag stood in the empty throne room, while Xemtex tried to make up his mind what to do.

He'd heard the battle between the Alpha and Lobo. That thing must be pretty good to take out a psycho like the Bo. It wouldn't make sense for Xemtex to rile it. Especially not when Xemtex himself was—in a way—the last of his kind. He was the last of the exploding men; the last of the bike-brains. If that Alpha was a collector, he might just want Xemtex for the display case, too.

No, better if he just keep his electronic mouth shut. Bide his time. Wait and see what happened. Not that there was anything else he could do with that override switch in place.

There was no bounty now, and that was a shame, but at least that rat Lobo was getting what he deserved. With a little luck, the big stone-guy would torture him to death. Then maybe put him in a blender for a while, before shooting him into the heart of the sun.

Xemtex started to chuckle, then cut himself off abruptly.

If he'd still had a heart, it would have been racing like a trip-hammer.

CHAPTER 12

Left alone in his transparent-walled cell, J'onn Jonzz's stomach lurched as he realized the truth behind this whole affair. Last Sons. Although he had no view of Lobo and the Alpha, he heard their raised voices, followed shortly by the sounds of an extreme fight. Whatever Lobo was receiving, it wasn't a million credits.

It has all been a trap, J'onn was forced to conclude. *And my own devotion to the Law blinded me to being set up.*

The Manhunter sighed wearily. Although he'd spent the past two decades fighting crime—both on Earth and extraterrestrially—he had originally come from a peace-loving race. Violent aggression of any kind had been unknown to Martians. Their deep grasp of logic meant that they knew full well how inefficient and wasteful battle always is, both in terms of lives and resources; therefore, they never indulged in it.

J'onn had heard it argued on Earth that it is war that propels progress. But—it seemed to him at least—that argument usually came from employees of the cynical military/industrial complex.

In his heart of hearts, J'onn truly couldn't understand why any being would want to use physical force to impose its will on others. Unless, of course, those others were criminal.

But failure to understand, and acceptance of, his unjust imprisonment were two entirely different matters. J'onn pulled himself up to his full height and considered the walls of his jail. Crystal rock, cut and polished so expertly that it seemed more like glass. Surely his great strength would prove more than enough to break his way free.

He clenched one fist and drew it back. Then, with all the might he could muster, he unloosed a pile driver of a blow.

Even before the punch landed, J'onn knew his solution was not going to work. As his fist drove at speed toward the wall, he was astonished to see tiny lines of flame flickering *inside* the crystal itself.

J'onn was unable to stay his blow and it struck the rock with a massive crack. Suddenly, all hell was let loose. A gout of flame erupted from the wall, enveloping the Martian's hand and wrist, sending him flying back. Pain seared up his arm, and a terrible weakness engulfed him.

He slumped against the cell's far wall, cradling his arm, gritting his teeth against the pain that swept through him. The situation was worse—far worse—than he had even suspected. The Alpha knew his adopted Earth identity. How? It was a closely guarded secret between members of the Justice League. The Alpha also knew that J'onn J'onzz was vulnerable to naked flame . . . and it had constructed this cell especially to contain him. It was safe to conclude that all walls in the cell were similarly booby-trapped.

How had it learned these things? Why did the Alpha want him enough to issue a false warrant? Why did it want Lobo, too—and the Auriun he had heard it mention? What possible reason could there be for holding the three of them captive—apart from the fact they were the last surviving members of their respective species?

The sounds of battle had culminated in an explosion of noise, followed by a deep silence. Since there was no joyous cursing or vulgar boasting, J'onn could only assume that Lobo had been defeated and was now the Alpha's prisoner, too.

As the waves of pain subsided somewhat, J'onn began to focus his mind. A natural telepath, he had spent years honing and perfecting this skill. Under normal conditions, he would never think of entering anybody else's mind un-invited—such an intrusion on personal privacy was anathema to him. But conditions now were anything but normal. He needed to contact Lobo, with or without the bounty hunter's permission.

His mind reached out, tentatively trying to reach the Czarnian.

Nothing.

He tried again, desperately attempting to attune himself to the bounty hunter's thoughts.

Nothing.

Lobo must be unconscious . . . or worse.

J'onn sat with his back to the crystal wall, his thoughts racing. There had to be a reasonable explanation for all of this. But no matter how he harried at it, he always ended up with more questions than there seemed to be answers.

"Woo, momma! Who put the lights out?"

Lobo came to with a start and looked around him. For a moment, he thought he was in a disco. Tiny points of light danced before his eyes. His head was thumping to some 120-beats-per-minute dross. There was a rotten taste in his mouth, like he'd been dining on the Trash Moon.

He groaned irritatedly as his vision returned to normal, and he could take in his surroundings. He was in a cell. There was nothing new in that, of course—he was used to overnights for Drunk and Disorderly. This, however, was a transparent cell, and he was in it courtesy of that big crystal bastard.

Damned hallucinogenic fungi, he cursed to himself. *I'd have beaten the creep easy if it hadn't warped my fraggin' brain!*

If there was one thing the Main Man hated more than anything else, it was a liar. (Actually, depending on his mood, Lobo had a long list of things he hated more than anything else.) Despite his own extreme and often borderline criminal behavior, Lobo prided himself on his honesty. Once the bounty hunter gave his word, that was it—he would move Heaven and Earth to carry through on his promise. And now he'd been shafted by a double-crossing stone giant.

His mood turned sourer by the second. "Yer toast, Alpha," he muttered to himself. "Ya just don't know it yet. But when the Bo gets outa here . . . look out, dude! I'll crush ya into fraggin' gravel an' use ya fer road fill!"

As his anger started to mount, Lobo paced around the cell, examining the transparent walls and door. He had a real talent for precisely pinning down the weak spot in any opponent or situation, a talent that had often come in useful.

The door, he decided finally. *It has to contain a lockin' mechanism—an' that's where I'll start.*

He could see that his chain and hook were lying outside in the corridor, presumably removed by the Alpha. His gun was out there, too. He checked his belt, gratified to see that the Alpha had left it in place. Four frag grenades still hung there, and the big knife was still in the sheath strapped to his leg. But he figured that main strength would suffice.

He balled his fist and threw the kind of straight left at the door that would have felled a dinosaur.

As his fist connected with the crystal, jagged blue streaks of lightning ripped from the wall and into his body. He was thrown back like a rag doll. He fell to the floor, writhing and squirming and twitching uncontrollably as the electricity disrupted, overloaded, and damn near burned out his muscles.

Sheesh! Now I know how that bastich Xemtex must feel!

Xemtex . . . the thought brought him up short. The bike was still there, in the throne room where he'd left it. Even from this distance, it would pick up his ultrasonic whistle and come rushing to the rescue. It had more than enough built-in firepower to take the prison to pieces.

But suppose the Alpha was in the throne room, too? That crystal geek was a lot more powerful than Lobo had first assumed. He'd be able to take the bike out, surely.

It was a chance he'd have to risk. Lobo raised his fingers to his lips. Even as he started to blow through them, more streaks of lightning leapt from the cell wall. His fingers sizzled and his mouth felt like he'd just swallowed a taser dishing out in the region of a million volts.

That bastich has got all the angles covered!

Lobo glared balefully at the cell door. Maybe if he made one supreme effort, charged it and hit it with all his strength, he could withstand the cranked-up voltage long enough to break free . . .

Lobo?

The Main Man's scalp tingled suddenly. He glanced around the cell, seeking the source of the voice. Through the dense crystal wall, he could make out the Martian a few cells away.

"Yo, Baldy," he greeted his ex-prisoner and now fellow prisoner.

It is better not to talk. We may be under surveillance. I am contacting you telepathically—

Ya bastich! I don't let nobody inside my head. Lobo slammed the side of his hand against his skull. *Out! Now!*

I do this only from necessity. In case it has not occurred to you, I should point out we are both on the same side now. We must aid each other to escape.

Oh yeah? After all the trouble I took to bring ya here—now ya want me to spring ya?

I am innocent, remember.

Yeah. Me, too. The Main Man cleared his throat and spat on the cell floor. *An' broke as well. That's what hurts the most—gettin' cheated out of my cash.*

Perhaps if we act together, J'onn J'onzz tried again, *we will succeed.*

What? The Main Man—team up with a super hero? Oh man, don't ask me to do this. He shook his head in bewilderment, as if the thought of working with a hero was akin to shaving with a blowtorch after lathering with sulfuric acid. *Listen—I never team up with nobody, except sometimes Jonas Glim. An' Jonas is a bigger bastich than I am.*

The Alpha is powerful. If we act in unison, we may defeat it.

The fragger only beat me because he dipped me in some kind of fungus crap. Lobo reached into his jacket pocket and emerged holding a battered cigar. He struck a match against his nail and lit up. *Tell ya what—you do your thing, I'll do mine. I been in worse situations than this.* He breathed out a cloud of smoke. *Now get lost. I wanna savor my stogie, then I'll figure what to do.*

Smoking is not good for you.

I know, Baldy. That's why I do it. Save the health lectures for somebody who cares. Lobo screwed up his face. *Now—are ya gonna get out of my head of yer own free will . . . or would ya prefer me to start thinkin' about some real nasty things? Like, I remember one time when I was trapped in a morgue with—*

Think on what I have said.

Yeah, sure. An' you let me know if ya recall any other places that might have a million-cred bounty on yer head. I got a serious cash-flow problem to rectify!

*   *   *

On the surface high above the subterranean prison, the Alpha stood with arms outstretched, its head thrown back as it scanned the starry heavens above. Flickering starlight played over its body; a thousand pinpricks of light swirled and danced in its crystalline structure.

Data flooded into its inhuman mind as it read the features of the electromagnetic spectrum. Twenty million miles away, Auriun orbited—it was on the far side of the sun now, but the distance between planet and planetoid would only be half that by this time tomorrow.

From beneath its feet, the rock-creature could feel thousands of tiny vibrations. Its Vrkn engineers were busy implementing its instructions, hollowing out untouched parts of the interior. Deep in the bowels of the planetoid, strange constructions were under way.

Vrk is near impregnable.

With our improvements, it will become the new center of the Universe.

Our Universe.

Way out on the fringes of the system, a meteor swarm streaked. B-2323's gravity would gradually draw it closer before catapulting it back into the depths of space.

The Alpha relaxed. It rose into the air, flight being merely one of the powers the artificial intelligence had given its new body. It headed slowly toward the carved entranceway through which Lobo and his captive had entered earlier.

All was well with its world.

* * *

Way out in space, the meteor swarm rolled and tumbled along. There were forty or fifty rocks in the group, the smallest the size of a football, the largest almost as big as a forty-foot truck.

Flying behind one of the larger boulders, matching his speed with the streaking swarm, was a stern red-and-blue figure.

Superman was taking his suspicions seriously. Something exceptionally strange was going on in this small system, and he had determined to find out what. In his lifetime on Earth, he had made many friends; J'onn J'onzz was one of his oldest and most respected friends, and Superman's loyalty to him would never waver.

It's ironic, he thought, shielded by the meteor from any scanners that might be turned his way. *It was in a meteor storm that I first came to Earth, all those years ago.*

Not long after his father blasted him off from their dying planet, Krypton was destroyed by a series of cataclysmic explosions. Debris from the shattered world was hurled far out into space—and it was this flotsam and jetsam that had surrounded the tiny rocket ship. Unknown to the child within, the meteors would accompany him on his long journey to a new world.

And then they would rain down on the Midwestern town of Smallville, bringing death and destruction that would change everything. Forever.

Superman shook the memories away. *The past is another country,* he reminded himself. *There's no sense going back.*

Life only moved in one direction: onward. Only the thinking mind clung to the past.

The swarm was arcing in past the larger planet, Auriun—though Superman had no knowledge of its name. This isolated part of the galaxy was new to him, constellations and star systems he couldn't name. Only his innate sense of direction stopped him deviating from his course.

Even from his great distance, the Man of Steel could see the plumes of smoke that more or less circled the planet. Some terrible disaster must have struck.

Superman's mind was made up in an instant. His entire life had been devoted to helping the helpless, mostly on his adopted homeworld, Earth; but he couldn't turn a blind eye to anybody, anywhere, who needed aid.

If it meant exposing himself to possible scrutiny—blowing the secret his arrival was supposed to be—then so be it. He would deal with any ramifications when the time came.

He peeled away from his rocky shield, increasing his speed as he shot toward the planet like a stone from a sling.

Seconds later, he was skimming the upper atmosphere. The air was thick with dust and soot particles, and visibility deteriorated appreciably. His invulnerable body glowed red-hot from friction with the air as he dived quickly below the acrid smoke, and he gasped involuntarily when he caught his first view of the surface. It was a scene of total devastation.

From his vantage point a quarter mile high, he could see half a dozen cities. They lay in ruins, with vast fires burning on their outskirts. Mystified, Superman flew lower. What could have caused destruction on this scale . . . and yet been so specific? Because the vast tracts of forested land that stretched between the cities was untouched; only the conurbations themselves had been attacked.

A sudden stench assailed his nostrils, revolting him. He knew only too well the sickly, cloying odor of burning flesh.

Immediately below him, a vast number of humanoid bodies had been piled up, doused in fuel, and torched. There must have been tens of thousands of corpses in that conflagration alone—and a dozen similar bonfires burned around the city.

A surge of anger swept through him. He hated to see the needless loss of any life. Life was the Universe's expression of its own existence—and rational conscious life was the apex of evolution; it should never be wasted. For a world to be devastated on this scale was a crime almost beyond imagining.

With troubled heart and churning mind, Superman shot skyward again. Mystery upon mystery. By the time he had caught up with the meteors, his hot anger had turned to an icy calm.

He had a lot of questions to ask; and he'd make sure the Directorate of the Imperium of Vrk gave him his answers.

CHAPTER 13

His internal clock told him he had been in custody for twenty-two Earth-hours.

Several times he had attacked the walls of his cell, intent on smashing his way to freedom; each time, instantaneous flame had driven him back. Assaulting the floor and the ceiling brought the same painful result.

He felt weak and drained, feelings that under normal circumstances rarely troubled the Martian Manhunter.

He'd concluded that, despite their transparent appearance, the walls must be embedded with a network of electronic circuits. Quartz crystal was renowned for its piezoelectric qualities, so the rock probably acted as its own circuit board. It was programmed to react to his movements—and obviously its reactions were as fast as his own.

But what if it couldn't "see" him?

J'onn J'onzz possessed the startling ability to refract the light rays around himself, rendering him invisible to the naked eye. He tried it now, ready to deliver his most potent blow to the cell door . . . and was rewarded by a blast of fire that seared along his arm. He moaned and clutched at his wrist, cradling it against his body to ease the raging pain.

It is a startling piece of engineering, J'onn admitted reluctantly. *But what else might it be programmed to do?*

He probed it with his extraordinary Martian vision— and was rewarded with a tongue of flame that flared in his eyes. He cupped his face in his hands and waited for the pain to subside.

Just who in the name of his ancestors *was* this Alpha, who had captured two of the most powerful beings alive? J'onn's brain ached from his efforts to provide a satisfactory solution, and his arm was throbbing from its numerous brushes with the flames.

He sat down with his back against one wall and let himself drift off into much-needed sleep.

In his dream, he was soaring over the Red Planet. The air was chill, but he rejoiced in the feel of it against his skin. It was the Martian summer, and he was young and bursting with the joy of life.

Below him, neat fields marched in serried ranks into the distance, reaching almost as far as the slopes of mighty Olympus Mons. The crops his people grew had been tailored especially for their arid environment; it was a miracle that anything at all grew in the thin red soil that had barely known rainfall for thousands of years.

J'onn smiled to himself, retreating into a reverie, a dream within a dream. Once, when he was a child, he'd asked his grandfather why there was so little of the most precious liquid on Mars. The old man had knitted his great craggy brows, as if digging deep in his memory for an answer, then told an incredible tale.

"This is just a story, J'onn—but stories rival water as a people's major possession. If the people forget their stories, their imaginations shrivel. When the imagination shrivels, hope withers and dies. Finally, the people themselves will die." The old man pulled his thick cape closer around him and cleared his throat. "Many years ago, when Mars was warmer, life was easy here. The people had much water—streams and rivers and lakes so great you could not see the other side."

Young J'onn had marveled at the old man's words. Water was the Martians' obsession. They arose before dawn and gathered the thin dew that condensed during the long, dark nights on rocks and hardy desert plants. They invented water traps that could squeeze what few molecules of water there were out of the air itself. It was hard to imagine a time when water was so ubiquitous, you could bathe in it, or swim in it, or sail a boat on it for days on end.

"But where did it go, Grandfather? Where did the water go?"

The old man's eyes were rheumy under the carapace of his brows. "As our planet cooled down, so its electromagnetic field faded. Our gravity became less, giving us more power—but robbing us of our most valuable possession."

His granddad turned his hands palm up and extended his arms upward. "The water rose in the air," he continued, "and drifted off into space. And do you know where it fell, this cloud of moisture that once had wet all Mars?

Do you know the Blue World, the one that twinkles close at night . . . ?"

"I know it."

"Yes. All of our water fell there and made it a blue world with green land. And we became the Red Planet, with deserts and choking sandstorms." The old man waved a finger at his grandson. "I don't know if it's true, but that's the story I heard from my grandfather, and he heard from his before him. And nobody I know has a better theory."

Many years later, after J'onn had been teleported to the Blue World, he heard the stories about the Great Flood that had devastated Earth millennia in the past. Cultures from all over the world had myths detailing the incessant rain and the few survivors as their lands drowned. The Sumerians told tales of Ut-na-pishtim and his family; the Hebrews remembered Noah and his ark. Every race, from Polynesian islanders to Siberian nomads, had a flood myth. Humans had come up with many explanations for the sudden inundation, from their god's wrath through sunspots and melting glaciers to a planetary superstorm.

But J'onn couldn't help wondering if maybe somehow, incredibly, an old man's tale to a young boy had actually been true.

He'd loved his grandfather and spent long hours with the old man, absorbing all his wisdom. He was old and frail by the time J'onn married, but he led the speeches and danced with the bride at J'onn's wedding. When J'onn's son was born a year later, the old man broke open a bottle of dew-water he'd literally spent years collecting.

They toasted the baby's health with water. When the

old man finally died, it was in the knowledge that his line would go on and the stories would continue to be told.

Although, as things worked out, the line did not go on and the stories were not told.

He puts much store in the telling of tales.
His emotions intrigue us. What is this love?
Emotion is irrelevant, a needless component of organic life.
We can harness emotion.
We can use it against our enemies.
All life is our enemy.

A pale sun hung in the red sky.

In his dream, J'onn saw people crowd the fields beneath him. They were looking up, waving to him. He made to wave back, then realized that greeting was not their intention at all. He angled to the side and swooped down closer.

He could see that all was far from well. The people were clutching each other, as if desperate for support. Several had fallen to the ground, their faces and exposed skin swelling with ugly, purple bruises.

Plague!

He sped away, his heart hammering, panic coursing through him as he flew toward his own dwelling. His wife stood framed in the open doorway, holding the limp body of their beloved son. Both mother and child were covered in the purple bruises, some of them burst and weeping a milky liquid on their skin.

Tears ran unchecked down her beautiful, ravaged face.

His heart numb with terror, J'onn raced toward them . . .

And disappeared in a blinding flash of rainbow color.

Plague . . .
We are attracted to this idea of disease.
And emotion.

The dream changed again.

He was full-grown, a man now. He wore a green cape over his costume and fought shoulder to shoulder with the champions of Earth, the fabled Justice League of America. His companions were living gods and goddesses: Wonder Woman, the Amazon Princess; Flash, the Fastest Man Alive; the Green Lantern, the Emerald Warrior; the Dark Knight, Batman; the Atom, who could harness the properties of a white dwarf star; and Firestorm, who could rearrange atomic matter.

Once every year, as regular as clockwork, J'onn J'onzz left his companions and went on a solitary pilgrimage.

Once every year, he went home—and stood on the sands of a dead world.

The fields were long gone, turned to desert by years of neglect. Swiftly eroded by the scouring, dust-laden winds that sometimes enveloped the whole planet, not a house or building of any kind still stood. Here and there, a skull with overarching carapace and mouth contorted by the rictus of death stared mockingly up at the Red Planet's last son.

The dust beneath his feet was the bones of his people—a billion of them, perhaps more, victims of a plague that poisoned their blood and ruptured their skin and liquefied their innards.

J'onn J'onzz was alone. The last Martian. Ever.

He fell to his knees and covered his face with his hands, and his body was wracked by grief-stricken sobs

There are many beings with superpowers: heroes.

It is the time of the Alpha. There will be no more heroes.

CHAPTER 14

"Psst!"

The little creature turned, startled, at the sound of the unaccustomed hiss—and found itself staring into the twin barrels of a Kolt Rapi-Fire.

"No tricks, or you'll be missing your head," the bounty hunter with the weird eyes told the Vrkn. It obviously had no idea what the man was saying, but guns impart a universal message: Obey or be shot. The Vrkn's eyes widened in apprehension, and it began to chatter excitedly in its own language.

"Shut it!" The gun barrel rammed painfully against its mouth, and the Vrkn fell silent again.

It had been working underground, constructing laboratory facilities, playing its small part in the Alpha's grand new vision for the planet Auriun, when it had to answer a call of nature. So it clambered up the stone ladder and emerged amidst the ruins of a shattered city—to confront four figures, three of them bearing guns.

"Now, my little friend," Angel Eyes told it, jerking his Kolt to indicate it should start moving, "let's find someplace quiet where you can tell us everything we need to know."

The bounty hunters' needleship had entered the B-2323 system hours before. Never one to take an unnecessary risk, Angel Eyes had insisted on a full system analysis, using the craft's scanning electron telescope. The views of Vrk itself told them nothing—a huge black rock spinning in space, with no surface buildings or installations of any kind.

Angel Eyes' suspicions were immediately aroused. The 'scope was retrained on Auriun and picked out the unbelievable destruction that had been visited on that luckless world. They could see what looked like several work squads, swarms of small creatures bustling about; most of them were entering tunnels in the ground, though some remained on the surface, sifting through the debris of a civilization.

"In search of what?" the Arcturan asked enigmatically.

There was only one way to find out. Ask one of them.

So they'd landed the ship in a deserted area of flattened buildings and set out to catch themselves a source of information. They say that everything comes to they who wait . . . and they didn't have to wait for long.

"Don't recognize the language," Randan the Khund grunted. "Sounds like somebody torturin' somethin' small and furry. How we gonna know what he's saying?"

Angel Eyes nodded toward their dark companion. "He'll tell the Arcturan," he said simply. "They *always* tell the Arcturan."

As the hooded, dark-robed magician leaned toward it,

the Vrkn screeched in terror. Then the Arcturan's hands closed on the sides of its head and rested there gently.

The little creature fell silent again, only its frightened eyes and the oily beads of perspiration on its forehead betraying its fear. Angel Eyes knew what was coming next; he'd seen K'Baal do this many times before. The result was always the same: They told what they knew.

Tendrils of the Arcturan's sinister mind probed into the Vrkn's skull, moving like hungry worms through the pathways of its primitive brain. The creature's eyes rolled back in its head, and its face registered extreme pain, but it made no further sound as the Arcturan used his dark arts to tease out what the Vrkn knew.

Finally satisfied, the alien magician drew back from his probings. A long shudder ran through the Vrkn, which remained standing in exactly the same position.

"Well?" Angel Eyes demanded, though he knew from long experience that the Arcturan would only talk in his own time.

"Things are not so simple as we had thought," the dark one said at last. "The creature is a Vrkn. Simple, primitive, a throwback. It knows nothing of Lobo or John Jones, nothing about any million-credit reward. But its world has been enslaved by a being that calls itself the Alpha."

"So what happened here?" Angel Eyes was puzzled. "These Vrkns aren't intelligent enough to invade and destroy an entire planet. And whatever this Alpha is, I don't see it razing these cities on its own."

The Arcturan's eyes were hidden in the shadows of its

hood. "Then you would be wrong," he said shortly. He gestured vaguely, indicating the destruction all around. "The Alpha did this, more or less alone. Now it has sent the Vrkns here to prepare for war."

"War? Who with?" Angel Eyes shrugged. "There are only two planets in the system."

"Then we must suppose the Alpha intends to wage its battles outside the system."

"You mean—attack *another* solar system?"

The Arcturan shrugged imperceptibly. "Yes."

"This changes everything." Deep in thought, the bounty hunter screwed up the golden eyes that had given him his name. "It's illegal under the Galactic Convention for any world to start a war."

"Sure," Virt agreed. "But we ain't galactic cops. We can't stop it."

Angel Eyes grinned suddenly. "Who said anything about stopping it?" he asked. "As soon as this Alpha launched his attack on Auriun, he became an outlaw. They'll put a price on his head—a high price, if he's into destroying planets."

Randan's ugly face lit up. "I get it," he said enthusiastically. "We breeze in, catch him, an' claim it."

"You got it." Angel Eyes nodded. "And if the Alpha's up for invading more planets, that bounty will soar like a bird."

Virt gestured toward the Vrkn, still standing immobile, as if paralyzed by fear. "What about him?"

Angel Eyes shrugged. "We can't take a chance on him talking. He might be dumb, but this Alpha is anything but." He turned away. "Shoot him."

Minutes later, the needleship blasted off again, leaving the hapless Vrkn's corpse buried beneath a pile of rubble.

The giant planet Czarnia was a paradise.

The Czarnians had long since eradicated war and aggression and criminal behavior. There was no poverty, no inequality, no dispute that could not be solved in a civilized manner. Creative endeavor of all types was encouraged from infancy. The planet's golden towers housed poets and philosophers, writers and artists, craftsmen and dreamers. Everybody recycled their trash.

The streets of its cities bristled with political correctness—not the kind that was adopted by an elite and force-fed to its minions, but a natural, joyous PC that people adopted happily and willingly. Life was good, the Czarnians were good, and their philosophers said it was 99 percent certain the whole Universe was good.

Into this Eden, a serpent was born; into this paradise, a worm.

Its name was Lobo.

There was no rational explanation for his existence. He had been conceived and born in the same way as billions of Czarnians over the centuries. His parents were typical pillars of society. Those who believed in astrology—and there were many—concluded there were no dark aspects, no sinister relationships between the planets. Those who believed in science were totally dumbfounded. Those who believed in religion starting building arks or headed for the hills.

The only possible explanation was: a cosmic joke. Lobo was one of those random acts of Nature that lie dormant for hundreds of thousands of years, then without warning emerge to overturn everything. A planet of good people produces someone for whom "evil" is too mild an epithet; a society of angels spawns the Great Beast. It could only be some Hell-birthed demon's idea of having a belly laugh.

Is this true?
   All truth is relative. Only honesty is absolute.
   Can we believe him?
   The bounty hunter has told the story so many times, perhaps even he is no longer sure of it.
   How different from the Martian.

His mother died in childbirth. Some say the baby deliberately strangled her with its own umbilical cord and ate it afterward. It is on record that both attending obstetricians never worked in medicine again and that three nurses claimed substantial financial compensation for the trauma they suffered. His father committed suicide before the child was a month old.

Lobo was expelled from kindergarten on his first day, after hospitalizing several of his classmates. Modeling clay was never meant to be forcibly ingested, any more than wax crayons should be melted into bodily orifices.

He lasted longer at school, perhaps because of the pure hatred he felt for his teacher. A disciplinarian of the old school, she was a real dragon—one of the few people not to be cowed by Lobo's foulness, vulgarity, and all-around violent menace. It was one of the happiest days of his life when, years later, one of his first bounty-hunting jobs was to track down and kill the old lady.

He took to wearing a leather jacket and steel-toed boots and began assaulting people in the street.

Unlike Plato's utopian Republic, Czarnia had no omnipotent elite to manage the lives of the peasantry (they had no peasants, either). Czarnia was closer to Aristotle's ideal, that if decent men are but left alone, the whole world will prosper. Unfortunately, this meant that not only did Czarnia not have a police force, it had no concept of a police force. Lobo's crimes went unpunished; emboldened, he got worse.

During his teenage years, Lobo decided to become a star of popular music. His beat combo, The Main Man and Several Scumbags, only played one gig; the heavy metal cacophony they produced caused widespread deafness in the concert hall. Unfortunately for the Several Scumbags, Lobo had prefigured their deaths by electrocution into the act.

As his guitar wailed out an ear-bleeding solo, his fellow band members screamed and jerked in their death throes.

They didn't get a return booking.

He started drinking alcohol and smoking. Drugs were legal on Czarnia, though it was centuries since anybody had bothered to use them. Drugs were a means of escape, and Czarnians had nothing to escape from . . . until now, when addiction levels soared in response to Lobo's behavior.

By the time Lobo was in his late teens, he'd had enough. He was bored: bored with this world of perfect goodness, bored causing mischief, bored causing trouble, bored killing innocent people. Bored, bored, fraggin' bored.

He was unique among Czarnians, and he'd had it up to the eyeballs with the other creeps. He was going to be unique, period.

He taught himself how to use guns and knives, and created the designs for his first chain and hook. Analysis of the frag grenade and related explosives became one of his favorite hobbies.

One of the school subjects at which Lobo had excelled was biotechnology. Bored near to death-by-lethargy, he retired to his home lab one day and locked himself in until he had completed his self-appointed task.

When he emerged, he was holding a flask containing one of the most deadly microorganisms that had ever been created.

He didn't pause to consider as he climbed up onto the roof of his old school. He didn't think twice as he held the flask up at eye level, admiring its cloudy, swirling contents in the light of another beautiful Czarnian day. And he didn't suffer a single pang of regret as he let the flask slip from his fingers. He watched as it plunged to the schoolyard below, smashing into a thousand shards, freeing its dark and deadly bacteria.

He'd ingested the antidote himself that morning.

It took a week for the planet to die. Seven days of agony for billions of people. Parents and children, friends and lovers, all watched each other fall sick and die, then fell sick and died themselves. The streets were lined with bloated corpses as the hideous disease swept round the planet like wildfire.

And while his people perished, Lobo partied. After all, he had something to celebrate. Now he really was unique: the *very* last Czarnian.

Is this a genuine record of his brain readings?
   We do not err.
   This one is no hero. He has much suppressed fury.
   He may be insane; his account may therefore be faulty.
   It will be advantageous to discover if his biotechnological skills are genuine. That would radically shorten our time scale.

Lobo waited till every last person was dead, then stocked up on booze and smokes and headed off-world in a primitive self-built spacepod. He was going to see the galaxy, sample all of its myriad pleasures for himself, bed every babe he could find. And woe betide anybody who tried to stand in his way.

There were several abortive attempts at holding down employment, none of which lasted more than a few hours. Lobo detested being told what to do. He needed something that harnessed his . . . creativity.

At Galactic Command HQ, there was talk of putting a bounty on his head. But apart from the Czarnian's own boasting, there was no evidence to confirm that he had in fact murdered his race.

Lobo soon gravitated toward bounty hunting, where he proved himself to be the perfect recruit. Fast, cunning, ruthless—he was these and more. While others tried out one job, then left sickened by the death of their prey—or their own bloody injuries—Lobo took to the life like a piranha to flesh. He could kill any villain he wanted—as long as there was a warrant, nobody would ask questions. If he could justify it, he was allowed to torture in the hunt for information on his prey. And bounty hunting gave him a quasi-legal authority, making it harder for anybody to charge him when his killings weren't strictly in the line of duty.

The Serpent had slithered into the only place it truly fitted outside the bowels of a high-security prison fortress.

He is much like us.

In effect only. He has no rational purpose. He is psychopathic.

An antihero. The opposite of the Martian.

Even now, the technology embedded in their crystal cells draws off his and the Martian's emotional energy.

Lobo's will spread rage and fury. The Martian's will spread dark despair.

Emotion as a weapon. We like this.

CHAPTER 15

Dawn was breaking over Vrk's highest point when the huge rock-being emerged from the cavernous interior. Briefly, it raised its head and scanned the heavens. The penetrating red light of the rising sun played over its quartzine body, conjuring up a whirlpool of swirling, fiery colors; it looked as if its entire being were combusting.

It stretched out its arms and started to rise in the air. Then it was gone, the massive body soaring up and away into space like a living rocket.

Superman clung to the shadows in a cleft between black, shiny boulders. He watched—and wondered—until the mighty rock-creature became no more than a distant speck, then vanished from view altogether.

The Man of Steel focused his super-vision and followed the departing behemoth's progress. It seemed set on a course for Auriun—the world Superman had found in flames.

Could *that* be the Directorate of the Imperium of Vrk?

It seemed unlikely . . . but then again, Vrk was an unlikely place to set itself up as an Imperium. And somebody—or something—had caused that widespread destruction on Auriun. Apart from anything else, a barren rock like Vrk could never have birthed any kind of advanced life, let alone that impressive figure.

A few hours earlier, when the meteor swarm passed its closest point to the planetoid, Superman had seized his chance. It was a risk, he knew, but it was one he had to take for his friend's sake. He streaked out from the shelter of the rolling space rock and sped down to the surface below. He was only in sight of any detectors Vrk might have had for seconds.

It was still dark where he landed, though his keen vision picked out the gargantuan stone entranceway nearby. Normally, his X-ray vision could penetrate any solid substance; he'd expected to be able to peer into the very heart of Vrk. It hadn't worked out so easily.

True, he could vaguely make out a network of underground passageways, and he had blurry impressions of strange-shaped chambers. But all detail eluded him. It could only be due to the presence of lead—the only effective shield for X-rays—in the planetoid's dense geology.

He couldn't tell if the entrance was guarded or not. For all he knew, a dozen sentinels might be waiting for him inside. So he decided to wait for dawn, when normal vision might do what X-rays couldn't.

As the red fingers of the rising sun lit up Vrk's horizon in a fabulous light show, he'd watched in amazement as the huge humanoid had exited and taken to the skies.

The light spread quickly, washing over Superman's

bolt-hole mere seconds after the giant had left. He could see the entrance clearly now—and there appeared to be no sign of any guards. Cautiously, he hovered a few inches off the ground, then streaked to the entrance. It was deserted.

He flew inside, awestruck by the weird, indecipherable carvings. Although they could only be religious in nature, there was something very futuristic about them. He couldn't help wondering if they were mere ornamentation or something more profound.

Several tunnels led off from the rear of the entrance hall. Superman listened carefully but could hear nothing. He chose a tunnel at random and set off down it. If it led nowhere, he could always come back to the others.

Proceeding as fast as he could while still retaining his caution, he followed the meandering passage to its end.

It opened out into a series of small, regular, bulb-shaped chambers. *Strangely reminiscent of machinery,* Superman thought—and remembered the technological feel to the carvings. Six or seven small carved-stone pipes connected the chambers and ran out through a channel far too small for Superman to enter.

There was no other exit. He retraced his steps and chose the adjacent tunnel for his second foray. This one sloped down at less of an angle; it was wider and taller than the other—perhaps specifically to accommodate the stone giant.

Deep beneath his feet, he was sure he could feel the vibrations of beings at work. The lead in the quartz walls made it impossible for him to spy on them, and his super-hearing could only pick up the faint sounds of chittering in a language that was completely alien to him.

Something strange was going on here. Something very strange.

After a quarter of a mile, the passage was blocked by a solid wedge of shaped stone, a plug of sorts; a carved-stone ring protruding from its end suggested it had been designed to prevent any further intrusion. Unless there was some sort of machinery to move it, it would require superhuman strength even to budge it.

Superman gripped the stone ring in both hands and slowly began to exert his phenomenal power. Krypton had been a giant planet, with a red sun in its skies. His removal to Earth, with its lesser gravity and yellow sun, had been the origin of all his superhuman abilities.

Now, in Vrk's still-lower gravity, his strength was even greater. The gigantic mass of rock must have weighed fifty or sixty tons, but it began to slide almost silently toward him, turning on cunningly concealed stone pivots until it revealed enough space for a large being to pass.

Superman slid through.

He knew instantly that he'd entered a prison. The regular layout, the obvious cells running off to each side, the very atmosphere of the place all screamed its function.

For the first time, Superman decided to use the telepathic link that connected him to J'onn J'onzz. It was how all of the Justice League members managed to stay in contact with each other, yet the invasion of mental privacy it brought was so shocking—could be so traumatic—that even super heroes used telepathy carefully and sparingly.

He hadn't dared before now, in case it gave away his

presence. There were many telepathic races in the Universe, and Superman had no way of knowing if the Vrks were possessed of that particular ability. He knew from J'onn that it could be a frightening thing to read another human's mind and was quietly grateful that telepathy wasn't one of the powers that had been bestowed on him by Gaia and its yellow sun.

He backed against a wall, giving him a view of all possible approaches, and reached out with his mind.

The Martian Manhunter and Lobo were one cell apart.

J'onn could see the bounty hunter fairly clearly through the transparent walls, as Lobo occasionally amused himself by sticking his tongue out or making faces at his fellow captive. Then he'd pace his cell, muttering curses over and over, evidently working himself up into a frenzy.

Approximately every hour or so, Lobo would attack the walls in a fury, pounding and hammering and kicking. Each time, he resisted the surging electricity until he ended up a slavering, quivering wreck on the cell floor. But J'onn noticed that, each time, it took longer before the bounty hunter collapsed.

J'onn himself had tried one more time to bludgeon his way through the cell wall. But the blaze that met him was fiercer, hotter than before, and he soon gave up. Unlike Lobo, the Manhunter didn't seem to gain any immunity with his mounting anger.

J'onn? J'onn J'onzz?

The voice spoke quietly inside his head, and J'onn felt his spirits suddenly soar. Superman!

I'm here, Superman. Imprisoned.

What's happened?

As swiftly as he could, the Martian ran through everything that had occurred since Lobo brought him to Vrk. He told of the false warrant—he had never committed any crime, it was only a ruse on the part of the Alpha to get him here.

A mighty rock-being?

Yes. You have seen him?

He was heading off-world—toward the other planet in the system, I think. Superman was puzzled. *But why does this Alpha want* you?

Mentally, J'onn shrugged. *I cannot tell. We appear to have been subjected to some kind of detailed analysis, but for reasons I do not know. The only other clue might be that the Alpha seems inordinately interested in beings who are the last of their kind.*

Does that mean Lobo, too?

He is in a cell nearby, J'onn informed his friend. *The Alpha played him for a fool. There was no million-credit reward waiting for him—only a cell, the same as me.*

Before we try to make sense of this, I'm going to get you out of there. Keep broadcasting to me, and I'll home in on your thoughts.

We can free Lobo, too.

I'm not so sure about that. Superman sounded reluctant. *He deserves to be left behind. He got you into this mess. He can get himself out of it.*

That's not entirely fair, J'onn protested. *Lobo may be a brutal monster—but he was only doing his job in bringing me here. Besides, I saw a different aspect to him on our journey. Even Lobo might be redeemed.*

Are you joking? Superman returned. *Do you know what he's done? What he's capable of?*

I know. And yet, I watched him defend a woman's honor.

Knowing Lobo, there would only be one reason for that, Superman thought scathingly.

Perhaps. Yet . . . it showed that even one such as he might have a heart.

Yes, Superman agreed. *He keeps it in his gun!*

Manhunter could feel the Man of Steel growing inexorably closer. *Just one more corner, and you will be here. You exit into a wider chamber—*

The one with two statues against the wall? Superman wanted to know.

J'onn J'onnz's reply came slowly. *You are in the right place. I saw the flash of color from your costume reflected in the quartz. But beware, my friend—there were no statues when we passed earlier.*

The Manhunter's warning came just in time. Even as his words flashed in Superman's mind, the statues moved simultaneously toward him. Each was about six feet high, smaller versions of the Alpha itself, but much more crudely carved. Instead of hands, the craggy arms ended in a shapeless mass, like hammers.

They moved with blinding speed, a stone tag team fighting in tandem. Superman managed to dodge the first swinging blow, but the second followed only an instant later. It careened off his shoulder with the force of a small tank. The telepathic link with J'onn was broken as Superman tried to marshal his thoughts to the matter at hand.

Swung around by the momentum of the blow, Superman was off-balance as the stone men continued their assault. Massive fists smashed into him from all angles, giving him no time in which to react. Despite his invulnerability, he felt the potency of their impacts and knew that even he couldn't withstand them forever.

As the living statues drove at him again, he stepped back from them, grasping each by a thick, stone wrist. He whipped hard with both hands, sending the stone men somersaulting on their backs.

They scrambled clumsily to their feet, unfazed by the fall.

Makes sense, Superman thought grimly. *Stone men aren't going to feel much pain. But they can't fight me if they can't reach me . . .*

His heat vision flicked on as if by a switch. Intense red beams lanced from the Kryptonian's eyes, focusing like lasers on the creatures' thickset ankles. There was a pungent odor of burning rock as the surface of their calves and ankles began to bubble, melting and flowing in little rivulets to pool on the ground.

There was a sudden *snap* and one of the creatures fell over, its lower legs burned entirely through. The second one was tougher and tried to lunge at Superman one final time. Intent on depriving it of motion, the Man of Steel kept up his barrage of eye beams and braced himself against the hammer fist that screamed toward his shoulder.

It was a big mistake. As the stone fist slammed forcefully into him, he felt it shatter against his arm. Shards of rock flew off in all directions—and sudden pain shrieked through him.

Dumbfounded, Superman lurched back and glanced down at his arm. Pain was almost unknown to him. His invulnerable body was proof against anything. Or almost anything . . .

A thin, irridescent layer of green kryptonite clung to his arm. Ironically, apart from magic, the debris from his ruined planet was the only thing that could harm the Man of Steel. Chunks of rock hurled out by the catastrophic explosion had passed through an intense cosmic storm, which bathed them in a strange plasma radiation, ionizing the stones—and turning them toxic to anything born on Krypton.

But—how could the Alpha know that? The thought flashed through Superman's mind. But before he could come up with any kind of answer, he felt his power drain out of him.

Even as the second stone monster's legs snapped and it tumbled face forward to the ground, Superman himself was falling. His hand brushed feebly at the grainy green kryptonite. Flecks fell off, but not enough.

Green fire seemed to course through his veins, blurring his vision, until the whole world turned green, and the flames burned too brightly.

Superman closed his eyes and gave up the struggle.

Superman? Are you still there?

J'onn J'onnz's telepathic voice reached out. There was no reply. J'onn could only conclude that the Man of Steel—Earth's mightiest hero—had been defeated.

His heart sank as he suddenly realized: kryptonite. The Alpha had known of Lobo's susceptibility to electricity; it knew of his own weakness, naked flame. It made sense that it had somehow discovered Superman's Achilles' heel, too.

J'onn's thoughts raced as the bigger picture started to reveal itself. He wouldn't be surprised if the Alpha had calculated that Superman would come to rescue his friend. Another Last Son for his mysterious collection.

Through the walls, he could see Lobo baring his teeth, rolling his eyes, and snarling wildly. The bounty hunter was working himself up into another frenzy. He didn't even glance at J'onn as he threw himself at the cell wall.

There was a jagged kaleidoscope of electrical energy. Still, Lobo pounded and hammered and cursed. The charge intensified, the voltage increasing as streaks of pure white lightning arced into the bounty hunter.

It took thirty seconds this time, but the end result was still the same. Lobo lay twitching and grunting on the floor of his cell, muscles beyond control, drooling and retching violently.

J'onn settled back against the wall, a dark cloud of gloom hanging over him. The Alpha had played all of them for fools, and now they were his captives. Bugs in a lab. Animals in a zoo. Living specimens in a crystal museum.

But *why*?

"Bastard! You're cheating!"

Randan the Khund erupted angrily out of his seat and grabbed his brother's arm. Twisting Virt's wrist, he forced him to show the cards that he held. Two kings . . . and five aces.

Virt wrenched his arm away, thrusting the table back as he stood upright. Coins and cards spilled everywhere.

Then the Khunds were at each other's throats, fangs bared, snarling barely coherent insults and threats at each other.

"All right, ladies. That's enough." Angel Eyes' voice cut through their raised voices, and they let each other go at once.

Randan stooped on one knee and began gathering up the cash he'd lost to his cheating brother. "You can find somebody else to play with from now on," he said huffily. He glanced at the corner, where the Arcturan sat cross-legged on the floor of the spaceship, and nodded toward him. "Try him. I'd like to see you cheat then."

Virt shivered and shook his head. He'd rather play tag with a bunch of Sirian scorpions than cards with a black magician.

The bounty-hunters' needleship had retreated to the very edge of the B-2323 system. It was too far for their onboard telescopes to show them what was happening on Auriun, but the Arcturan had said darkly that he knew another way.

He squatted down and used chalk to draw occult sigils on the floor surrounding him. Then he fell silent and retreated into himself.

His face hidden by the deep folds of his hood, K'Baal relaxed and allowed conscious thought to seep from his mind. All magic depended on the will of the practitioner; everything else—emotions, desires, even intellectual capability—was a sideshow. There could be no distractions.

Arcturans called this particular skill *a'yh'erna,* and in reality it was not magic at all. It was more like astral projection, or an out-of-body experience. Almost anybody could learn to do it, if only they practiced long and hard enough.

K'Baal willed his mind to expand, to push out beyond the confines of his flesh and bone and into the infinity that lay beyond.

Suddenly, in his mind's eye, Auriun was clear before him, as clear as if he were actually there. A gigantic stone figure, which could only be the Alpha, was being greeted by a host of small alien creatures like the one Angel Eyes had interrogated. They clustered around the stone humanoid like goblins around an ogre, chattering in their alien tongue as they led the way to a downsloping entrance.

They disappeared underground.

The Arcturan followed, an invisible wraith, his presence completely undetectable.

Now the Alpha stood before a fantastic piece of engineering. Completely carved from stone, it was an intricate spider's web of tubes and fine rock wires. The Alpha stepped up to it and gripped two protruding handles made of quartz. Nothing happened at first, but slowly a pale lilac glow began to spread across each handle. It deepened dramatically and quickly, until it was purple; there was a sudden flash and the glow was gone.

Strange, K'Baal thought. *It seems to be transferring some kind of . . . emotional energy from its body.*

The Alpha nodded, evidently satisfied, and stared hard at its tiny minions. The Arcturan knew it could only be broadcasting telepathic orders. This was interesting. He would be able to read its mind directly, unless the Alpha had mental defenses in place.

K'Baal focused hard, the sinister strands of his mind reaching out toward his target. There was a feeling entirely unlike anything K'Baal had encountered before.

The Arcturan snapped out of his trance with a visible start.

"What's up?" Angel Eyes asked quickly. "Trouble?"

"Indubitably, trouble," the Arcturan replied. "But whether it is for us, I do not know. The being called the Alpha is on Auriun. As far as I could tell, it is discharging some kind of energy into storage batteries." He paused, uncharacteristically unsure of himself, before continuing: "I tried to read its mind."

There was another silence. "And . . . ?" Angel Eyes prompted. He and the Khund brothers were staring agog at their crew mate.

"And I could not." K'Baal breathed deep. "The Alpha is not alive. It is not an organic creature. It is a machine mind—an artificial intelligence!"

On Auriun, the Vrkns consulted with their master before he again took to the skies. Although they did not understand what they were building for him, they were pleased because the Alpha was pleased.

Had they but known it, they'd constructed a series of storage containers, mathematically configured to hold the emotional energy the Alpha had siphoned off from Lobo and the Martian Manhunter. Now it had delivered the charge. Once the batteries were transferred to the Vrkn spaceships, it would be usable as a weapon of mass destruction.

Elsewhere under the still-burning cities, the Vrkns were busy constructing other weaponry of all kinds to the Alpha's specifications. Slender spacecraft, miracles in stone, were taking shape; they would carry the armaments to their designated targets.

In yet other locations, their army of stone soldiers was growing swiftly. As yet, the warriors were mere statues— replicas of the twin sentinels the Alpha had left to guard his prisoners. When the time came, the Alpha would charge them with the energy to perform their destructive tasks.

The Alpha had already weighed up and selected its next target. The star Arxetes was a mere day's journey distant. There were three worlds in its solar system, all populated, all fairly isolationist in their tendencies. None was technologically advanced, so resistance would be minimal.

The clock was ticking out the countdown to war.

CHAPTER 16

Scientists suspect that every living cell carries the memories of all life that ever existed and every mutation that it ever made. The 90-plus percent of DNA that they call "junk" isn't junk at all; it's the blueprints life needed in the past—and may need again when current conditions change.

Deep in the cells of his body, Superman carried the racial history of Krypton.

His first memory: being held in his father's strong arms. Keen eyes staring at him, with tears pricking at their corners. A fierce hug. The faint smell of his mother's perfume, the merest hint of an unknown flower. She's sobbing, hugging him to her as if she'll never let him go.

She's talking to him, her voice tinged with hysteria. But he's just a baby; he doesn't understand.

He's laid in a crib that holds him fast. A panel slots into place, sealing him in. Vibrations shake the pod. He sees his parents' tearful faces against the glass.

Everything changes. There's a terrible roaring, and the

crib is forced upward at incredible speed. The sad faces have been replaced by darkness and twinkling stars.

He's just a baby; he doesn't understand that Krypton is on the verge of death, or that his scientist father has sent him into space to escape it, or that he will be the only survivor.

He never witnessed the destruction of his homeworld; he was a child in a rocket, blasting away from the disaster.

But now, Superman saw it in his imagination.

The giant planet literally *rippled* when vibrations from its unstable core reverberated through it. In an instant, bedrock turned to quicksand as the anarchic oscillations grew and spread.

Cities sank into once-solid granite, their citizens submerged in liquefied stone. The planet's largest conurbation stood on a long-dormant fault line; when it cracked and spewed out a sea of red-hot lava, the city stood no chance. Ten thousand years of culture, art, and science disappeared as if they had never been.

Somewhere down there, the baby's parents were screaming as the glass atrium dome that covered their labs burst into a million deadly shards.

The effects intensified. Huge slabs of land pivoted on end and slid into suddenly yawning abysses. Vast herds of animals stampeded in panic when their forests burst into flame around them. The oceans seethed and bubbled and boiled, hot volcanic gases pouring into them from ten thousand undersea fissures.

In the space of a few hours, the planet turned itself inside out.

Then it exploded.

When you watch it in the movies, an explosion becomes

a thing of slow-motion beauty: a balletic dance, set to rousing music, as a thousand fragments trace out their graceful trajectories, smoke whorls spiraling in their wake. Destruction, viewed as a work of creativity.

But when you look beneath the superficial beauty, you see only the victims' terrified faces; you hear only their heartrending screams and pleas for aid. You see destruction for what it really is: the cold, bleak end of life.

Nobody—nothing—in the Universe could have helped the people of Krypton. Especially not a baby hurtling away in a rocket ship.

That didn't prevent the tears that sprang from Superman's closed, unseeing eyes, coursing down his face and dripping onto the cold quartz floor of his cell.

Emotion affects all life.
   Emotion weakens life.
   Not always. This one is purged of grief.
   He has become a hero.

It was a long, long journey from Krypton to Earth.

His father had thought of everything. The baby was fed and cleaned, automatically, regularly, thoroughly. Gentle voices—recordings of his mother and father—spoke soothing words when loneliness became too great and he cried in his lifepod. Their holographic images were there to comfort him as he drifted off to sleep.

And his father had ensured that his son would learn. A vast number of crystal keys had been inserted into the rocket's quantum computer; each key held all the knowledge that had been gleaned from a different discipline during Krypton's long history. The child had no way of knowing what they meant, but the data—and its subliminal messages—was absorbed directly into his unconscious mind.

Smallville: a township in the Midwest. Impossible skies that went on forever, every day a different shade of blue. Fields of tall, yellow corn swaying in unison as a teenage boy raced through them at two hundred miles an hour.

Jonathan and Martha Kent: the farmers who adopted him, who hid their foundling superbaby so no scientist could ever take him to pieces to see how he worked. Their own decency and honesty and compassion taught him that great power meant nothing unless it was used to create, not destroy. He learned to aid, not dominate. Lessons he would never forget.

His adoptive father's philosophy echoed that of Aristotle, two thousand years before him: Man is naturally good. Leave him alone to get on with his life, and the world will prosper.

But human nature being what it is, there has to be a fly in the ointment. In a word: deceit.

"Accept people for what they are," Jonathan Kent used to say, "but keep a weather eye open for what they aren't."

Metropolis: one of America's greatest cities. He was a reporter now—Clark Kent, bespectacled and mild-mannered, hiding in hidden places to rip off his suit and shirt and tie, exposing the red-and-blue costume beneath.

Protecting the city. Rescuing Lois Lane. Living a life.

* * *

Superman: Earth's mightiest hero. Superstrong, invulnerable, able to fly. Heat vision. X-ray vision. Telescopic vision. Superspeed. Scourge of the planet's criminal fraternity.

Member of the Justice League of America. Defender of Earth against catastrophe, be it earthquake or alien invasion.

And underneath beat the heart of a decent man.

Another tale of tragedy.
Soon, all tales will be tragedies.
Then there will be no more tales.

The Alpha had returned from Auriun to find Superman unconscious, collapsed on the prison floor next to its two immobilized guardians. The super hero's breath came in ragged gasps, and his skin was turning pale green from prolonged exposure to the toxic kryptonite.

The stone giant scooped him up casually and tossed him into the cell between his other captives. As J'onn J'onzz suspected, the Alpha had indeed been nearly certain that Superman would follow his friend. So it had taken precautions . . . and they had paid off.

Twin beams of energy blazed from the Alpha's eyes, sweeping over Superman's shoulder and arm, disintegrating the flecks of kryptonite. There was more, should it be needed.

The Man of Steel stirred. His eyes flicked open, and he began to massage his aching shoulder. The pain was rapidly subsiding as the effects of the toxin wore off.

"Why . . . ?" Superman gasped, his voice strained from exposure to the poison. "Why are you . . . doing this?"

"We are the Alpha. We are the first. You are the last." The deep voice paused. *"Is that explanation enough?"*

"I don't understand."

"That does not matter." The Alpha gestured around the bare cell. *"The walls contain detectors. Should you attempt to escape, you will receive a large—possibly fatal—dose of kryptonite."*

"That's another thing," Superman tried again. He staggered to his feet, holding on to the cell wall for support. "How did you know I'm vulnerable to that one substance?"

"Your computers told us."

"Computers? You mean—" Superman remembered how the Justice League network at the Watchtower had been acting up for no apparent reason. "You hacked into the Watchtower?"

"When we first came to Vrk, we used their transmitter to broadcast a message. Eventually, that connected us to the computers at your base. We learned all that we needed to know."

Superman frowned. The Watchtower security had been breached—and none of the other members knew. It could only have been a few days since he left the Moon, but it seemed to him as if months had passed.

The Alpha turned its back and exited from the cell. The transparent oval hatch slid noiselessly on its runners, sealing Superman in.

He slumped to the floor, head in one hand. He'd been in tight spots before—his great powers had brought him up against similarly gifted villains time and again. Always—always!—there had been a way out.

He hoped this wasn't the exception that proved the rule.

* * *

When J'onn J'onzz saw the Alpha dump Superman in the cell next door, he started involuntarily to his feet. But, with difficulty, he restrained himself. There was nothing he could do.

He breathed a sigh of relief when Superman came around. And when the Man of Steel started to quiz his captor, J'onn thought he saw a chance.

It was one of his own rules, rigidly imposed ever since he'd come to Earth, never to enter the mind of anybody unless they were a willing recipient. Emergencies and villains, obviously, were an exception . . . and the Alpha was beginning to shape up as some kind of Villain Supreme.

The stone giant's guard would be down as it conversed with Superman; he might not get this opportunity again. The Martian relaxed and let his mind go blank, reaching out to the other . . .

Nothing.

J'onn glared at the floor. Was this a complication? Did it matter? Or was it somehow the key to their escape?

The Alpha was an artificial intelligence.

A Martian. A Czarnian. A Kryptonian. An Auriun.

We will retain a single specimen from every species.

Their DNA will be analyzed, replicated, and stored in our vaults.

Their emotional energies will be used as weaponry.

The Universe will be ours.

CHAPTER 17

The Alpha hovered a hundred feet in the air. Ingenious use of the reflecting powers of its crystal body, coupled with its deep understanding of the science of light, allowed it to project itself at three times its normal size. Below, in the planetoid's largest subterranean cavern, a hundred thousand Vrkns thronged the floor, packed in so tightly that hundreds were forced to cling high on the support pillars.

The Alpha opened its mouth and a stream of high-pitched chittering issued forth, echoing around the chamber. It had found the Vrkns' minds to be vague and with a short attention span. Indeed, their only talent seemed to be engineering in stone. It was better if it talked to the creatures in their own gibberish tongue; it would make its guise of a god even more plausible than its terrible powers already had.

"The majority of you will accompany us to Auriun in the ships you have been constructing beneath the surface," it informed them. *"Our war fleet will assemble there."*

The myriad creatures gaped, not a cough or stray chatter breaking the unnatural stillness.

"The rest will remain here. You will bring the plans we have given you to fruition. You will ensure that the captives do not escape."

The last echoes died away, and the Vrkns sprang into motion. They separated, running into different corridors, others following the leaders like a flock of sheep.

When the last one had gone, the Alpha shut down its projectors. It flew out through the mouth of the cavern and blazed into the sky above . . . the way a god should. It turned and waited.

Minutes later, the first sleek, black crystal ships slid out of a custom-dug surface crater. They were followed by more, and more still, until the skies above Vrk teemed with hundreds of the stone-made spacecraft. Their crystal hulls absorbing sunlight, converting it directly into power, they soared high toward their creator.

With the Alpha at its head, the deadly armada headed away from the sun.

Lobo recovered consciousness with the ugly feeling of fingers crawling under his scalp.

Baldy! Get out my fraggin' mind!

My apologies. I—

"Ya got no need for telepathy," Lobo said, groaning. "The Alpha is gone."

"How could you know that?"

The Main Man tapped his nose and grinned weakly. "'My sense of smell can track a single molecule halfway across the galaxy. An' the big guy's stone butt is currently headin' off-world at a fair rate of knots." He groaned again and struggled into a sitting position.

"Are you all right?"

"Who can say these things, dude?" Lobo asked rhetorically. He lit up a cheroot and amused himself blowing smoke rings.

Nope, he realized, this wasn't some booze-induced nightmare. He was indeed captive in a transparent cell that turned up the voltage every time he tried to bust free. And he had a couple of do-gooders as fellow convicts.

He screwed up his eyes, forcing jangled nerve endings into focus. He could see Superman in the cell next to him; beyond, in the third cell, was the Martian.

Being locked up was bad enough, but being locked up with super heroes was even worse.

"Whaddya want, anyway, Baldy?" he growled.

"Superman and I have been talking. We have decided it would be best if we made a concerted effort to escape."

"Hey, be my guest, man." Lobo shrugged. "Concert away."

"We were hoping that you might have some ideas."

"Flattery will get ya everywhere, Jonesy." The bounty hunter blew a final smoke ring and stubbed out the butt on the floor. "Yeah, I got some ideas. Like, for starters, these cells are set up to drain off our emotional energy."

He saw the Martian's craggy brows furrow even more deeply. "How do you know this?"

"Because if they weren't, I'd have been furious enough hours ago to smash my way outa this stinkin' joint. I'm tellin' ya, I just ain't runnin' on full Main Man fraggin' vengeance mode." His head tilted to one side as he considered briefly. "Though maybe it's down to lack of nervous system stimulants. Like, I could murder a couple of cans of booze."

"I saw some strange alien machinery," Superman contributed, "all made out of stone. I couldn't make head nor tail of it. Why would the Alpha want our energy anyway, Lobo?"

Lobo rolled his red eyes. "Sheesh, what am I? Olly the Oracle?"

"Could it somehow be connected with what happened on Auriun?" the Martian mused. "If the Alpha did that—and I am more and more inclined to think it did—it may be planning other attacks, on other worlds."

"J'onn," Superman said slowly, "I know it's against your personal code of ethics, but couldn't your telepathy—"

"Well, whack my butt with a Cetacean's claw!" Lobo burst in. "Personal code of ethics? Man, he was in *my* noodle faster'n flies to a corpse. Ethics?" he repeated, and stuck a finger down his throat. "Makes me wanna vomit."

The Martian ignored him. "I admit that I have already tried. But I failed. The Alpha is not a normal sentient being. It is an artificial intelligence."

Superman looked thoughtful. "It said several times that it was the first, and we are the last. Do you think it means we're going extinct . . . ?"

"That's it, Big Cheese," Lobo whooped. "The Alpha's gonna make the Universe extinct. Kill off everythin'. Make sure of its own survival by offin' the competition." He whistled admiringly. "Ya gotta respect a guy that can pull off a stunt like that."

"Respect?" Superman echoed in disbelief. His tone hardened. "If you—"

"This is not an appropriate time for dispute, Superman," Manhunter reminded his friend. "We should be furthering our scheme to escape."

"Ya ain't got a scheme, Baldy," Lobo scoffed.

"And you have?" the Martian returned sharply. "Electrocute yourself until the Alpha takes pity on you, perhaps, and sets you free?"

Lobo couldn't argue with that. "Yeah, I gotta admit, my brain'll be blenderized before I get out of here. Not that the sensation is entirely without its attractions." He paused. "Of course, there's always my bike."

"Your bike?" Superman said doubtfully.

"Sure. The Spazz-Frag 5000 is fitted with a whistle control. Trouble is, every time I tried to whistle for it the cell electrocutes me." He raised his fingers to his lips, as if toying with the idea of giving a demonstration, then let them fall again. "I hate myself for what I'm gonna say," he went on, as an idea struck him. "Maybe Big Blue can duplicate my precise notes. His cell won't be programmed to electrify him. The bike answers, it blasts us free an' bunk's yer unk."

"I beg your pardon?" Manhunter said politely.

"Buncle is yer uncle. It means we're home free—with the emphasis on free. The bike carries enough weaponry to take out a small army."

"I'm willing to give it a go." Superman nodded. "What are the notes?"

"If I demonstrate, I get fried."

"If you don't, we all stay here."

"Ah, what the hell?" Lobo resigned himself.

He stuck two fingers in his lips and quickly blew a sequence of notes. Lightning arced through the air, sending exquisite pain shooting through his entire mouth and down into his innards.

I wouldn't wanna do it fer a livin', though, was his last thought before he once more spasmed his way into unconsciousness.

J'onn J'onzz stared at Lobo's convulsing body and sighed. He turned away to face Superman.

The Man of Steel might have had superbreath, but he wasn't exactly famed for whistling. He was looking askance at his two protruding forefingers, as if unsure where to put them.

"Did you get the notes?" J'onn asked.

"I think so." Dubiously, Superman put his fingers in his mouth and blew the first of the notes that Lobo had got out. Instantly, the cell wall writhed with crackles of green kryptonite. Instinctively, Superman fell back, both hands raised to protect his face from the toxin's debilitating touch.

His shoulders slumped in defeat. "Sorry, J'onn," he said bitterly. "And I'll bet you get the same reaction—only with flame—if you try. The Alpha seems to have covered every angle. It doesn't look like we'll be getting out of here yet."

The Martian stroked his chin. "It occurs to me," he said, almost reluctantly, "that we have one final option. On our way in here, I prevented Lobo from gratuitously killing some of the inhabitants. Perhaps, if they are still around, they might be willing to help us."

Superman raised his eyebrows. "That's a bit of a long shot, J'onn. Then again, desperate times call for desperate measures. See what you can do, old friend."

J'onn J'onzz squatted on the cell floor and reached out with his mind, racing at the speed of thought through the tunnels and hallways and caverns cut in the bedrock below . . .

A large party of Vrkns was deep inside the planetoid, excavating a gargantuan chamber that had hundreds of thick stone pipes running into escape vaults at its far end. They had no idea they were constructing a giant engine, one that would turn Vrk into an impenetrable crystalline fortress that would serve as the Alpha's mobile base as its sphere of influence grew. They knew only that the Alpha had told them what to do—and that to disobey would incur its godly wrath.

They worked in near silence, divided into parties that carried out their tasks like automatons. They had been the pathetic remnants of a once-great civilization when the Alpha found them; now they were debased slaves, who existed only for their master's whim.

Suddenly, one of them turned from the pipework it was laboriously carving. It screeched loudly and dropped the sharp stone tool it held. The agile fingers of both hands clutched its head, shaking it as if trying to drive out demons. This wasn't the vague, directed thoughts the Alpha had suffused them with. This was stone needles scraping under its skull.

One or two of the others threw rock chippings at it, and the little alien scuttled into a recess in the hewn-stone wall.

It calmed a little, rocking back and forth on its gnarled feet.

Something was happening inside its head.

It was always difficult to communicate mentally with alien beings. Their image systems, their cultural symbols, their entrenched beliefs—all were formidable barriers to psionic harmony.

From what J'onn J'onzz could pluck from the creature's atrophied mind, he was able to piece together a few fragments of the Vrkns' history. But that wasn't important. What mattered was that he let it know who he was and remind it how he had saved it. Difficult, when the creature had little concept of death in the first place.

Similarly, it had no idea what Auriun was and why it would matter if the Alpha had wiped out a billion or more people.

J'onn sighed deeply and tried again.

And again.

He was still trying when he heard Lobo say, "Man, whatta rush! Soon's we get back to civilization, I'm gonna invent a personal mouth jolter. Take it from me, Baldy, yer lips *really* tingle. Like kissin' ice. Only downside is, ya keep losin' consciousness."

The Vrkn had a clear picture in its head.

It ignored the others and made its way between the different work parties. It stopped beside one individual, its slender fingers wrapping around the other's arm and drawing it away. They chattered in whispers for a few minutes, then moved away toward the exit.

En route, they picked up number three.

They set out up the tunnel, a trio of misshapen golems, scuttling as quietly as they could, necks continually twisting as they looked fearfully around to see if their god was watching.

CHAPTER 18

Xemtex was beginning to feel bored.

The Spazz-Frag still sat, alone and unheeded, in the throne room. Xemtex had witnessed the Alpha's departure, then spent several hours trying to spark the bike's ignition by willpower alone. Without a scintilla of success.

If I ever get out of this, I'm going to pummel Lobo within an inch of his life. And that's just for starters. That bastard is so-ooo dead . . . !

Was this why he'd bucked against the traces all his life—why he'd battled authority at every opportunity? Is this how his criminal career was to end . . . as a brain in a bounty-hunter's bike? Hell, another few years and he'd have been a top dog, reward money in the 100K bracket and looking forward to an early retirement.

Xemtex retreated into a grim and bloody reverie, imagining having his hated foe at his mercy, with an unlimited number of sharp instruments . . .

He had no idea how much time had passed when he was suddenly jerked out of his violent daydreams. He couldn't be sure, but it was beginning to seem as if he was settling into his new role; the boundary between his own thoughts and the demands of running the bike was blurring over. His brain was becoming desensitized. He had to find a way out of this, as fast as he could, before his thoughts disappeared entirely.

The bike's external sensors were picking up three small shapes in the cavern shadows, moving stealthily toward it.

Unable to move or react in any way, Xemtex could only wait as the trio of Vrkns surreptitiously approached. They were obviously anxious not to be discovered, glancing continually around them, suddenly stopping, stock-still, with their pricked-up ears quivering.

At last, the Vrkns reached the bike. One immediately swung itself up into the driver's seat. Xemtex felt himself smirking as he waited for the saddle-spike to shoot up and impale the tresspasser. Nothing happened. The little creature must have been warned in advance, because it was taking great care not to spring the booby trap. It reached out a hand toward the override, and a long finger flicked it off.

The engine roared into life, the low-rev rumble of the powerful motors reverberating around the chamber. The other two Vrkns leapt aboard, clinging to the handlebars as the bike rose slowly into the air.

Bastards! Xemtex cursed. *I'm being stolen!*

The bike turned lazy circles in the air, the Vrkns jabbering at each other as they manipulated the controls. Then the Spazz-Frag shot forward at full speed, almost hurling its tiny passengers off as they barely managed to guide it into a tunnel. They bowled along in a series of fits and starts, every now and again scraping the bike against the tunnel walls as they tried to take a corner too fast.

Five minutes later, the bike was entering the prison sector, and Xemtex felt himself cheering up immensely. Through the transparent wall directly ahead, Xemtex could see Lobo. As the bike slowed to a halt outside the cell, Xemtex couldn't resist breaking into a laugh.

"How the mighty are humbled," he scoffed in his metallic voice. "I have to say—it couldn't have happened to a bigger bastard."

"Yeah, nice to see you, too," Lobo grunted. "You'll be happy to know you're gonna break me outa here."

"In your dreams, sucker," Xemtex gloated. "Know what I'm going to do? I'm recordin' your prison ordeal on the sensors. I'll broadcast the pictures all over the galaxy. You'll be a total laughingstock."

Shaking his head slightly, Lobo turned to face the Martian two cells away from him. "Hey, Baldy," he said casually, "tell one of your little tykes to hit the voltage switch."

The Martian merely looked at the Vrkns—and a second later, Xemtex was screaming so loud, the Vrkns almost jumped off in fright.

"I trust that settles the little matter of yer rebellion," Lobo remarked, as the outlaw's cries of pain faded. "Now, I want ya to retreat to about thirty feet away an' blast this wall with all the firepower ya got. Do ya think ya can do that?"

The bike moved backward in sullen silence, the Vrkns still hanging on.

Suddenly, all of its weapons systems opened fire simultaneously. At once, the cavern filled with the sounds of shells bursting, streams of tracer bullets, pulsed lasers, and rocket-propelled frag grenades. The noise was deafening, and the air quickly filled with thin, acrid smoke.

"Awright." Lobo's gruff voice cut over the sounds of explosions and ricocheting bullets. "Let's have a damage check."

Keen to avoid another shock, Xemtex stopped firing.

There was a long hairline crack in the cell's oval doorway.

"Sheesh," Lobo said in disgust. "Tough, or what? Still, at least ya got it started. Better give it another go, Xemtex."

"I'm using up a lot of ammunition," the disembodied brain reported. "It would probably be better if you stay here while I go find help."

"It would probably be better if you do as yer told," Lobo replied drily. "There's plenty more ammo in the reserves."

Xemtex hesitated.

"Do it," Lobo went on, "or I'll have the tykes hit the juice so hard, you'll think you was *born* fried."

Xemtex screwed up his eyes in anger—metaphorically speaking, of course, not having any eyes left except the bike sensors. And lo and behold! It was just like the old days. There was a huge flash and a thunderous roar, and the fissure in the cell door widened to become a rift, then a hole.

And then Lobo was clambering through to freedom.

I can still do it! Xemtex thought excitedly. *I can still blow things up just by looking at them and thinking about it!*

A warm, smug glow enveloped the ex-outlaw's brain. He felt as pleased as he would to wake up and find himself scratching his butt and belching.

His first, manic impulse was to start blasting Lobo. The thought of the bounty-hunter's body disintegrating into chunks of bloody meat made him want to laugh out loud. Healing factor? He'd blow Lobo into so many pieces, he'd *never* be able to put him together again.

But he held himself in check. If he took out Lobo, he'd still be left here at the mercy of the Alpha. Besides, the three dwarfs were still on his back; one telepathic command from Baldy, and Xemtex was fried.

Better to bide his time, wait till they were far away from this accursed place . . . then, when the Main Man least expected it, *Kaboom!* Game over. Rest in peace, one arrogant, big-mouthed bastard.

Oh yes. Xemtex could wait. And with a little luck, it wouldn't be for too long.

"Freedom," Lobo observed as he strode across the cavern floor, "is a double-edged sword."

The bounty hunter stooped down and snatched up his blaster from where it had fallen during his fight with the Alpha. He weighed it in his hand and checked that the ammo clip was full before turning back to face Superman and J'onn J'onzz in their cells.

"I mean, just look at my options," he went on, idly waving the gun in the direction of the other cells. "I can blast you two free. Or I can just hightail it on the bike with my brainy buddy Xemtex. Or—"

Lobo swung the gun round slowly, until it was leveled at the trio of Vrkns still perched on the bike. Deafened and half-blinded by the noise and glare of the explosions, they were almost in a state of shock.

"Or I can catch up on the fun ya denied me earlier an' blast these cute little gonks to kingdom come."

"No!" J'onn J'onzz and Superman yelled at the same time.

Lobo grinned and lowered the gun. "Only jokin'," he admitted. "Even the Main Man wouldn't stoop that low. Not unless I was gettin' paid for it. Or if I was in a *really* bad mood."

Without warning, he brought the gun back up at speed and whirled back to face the Martian's cell. "Just pretend I'm shootin' you, Baldy." He laughed, as a stream of pulsed, high-energy beams slammed into the cell door. For several seconds, nothing happened. Then slivers and shards of razor-sharp crystal peeled away, as the incredibly hard stone began to shatter under the force of the beams.

There was an earsplitting crack, and the oval door split right up the middle. It hung there, suspended, for a second before it collapsed under its own weight.

The Martian Manhunter stepped out from his confinement.

"Here, Baldy." Lobo tossed him the gun and the Martian caught it deftly. "I can't bring myself to free Big Blue." He pursed his lips and shook his head. "Just can't do it. I'd rather leave him here."

J'onn J'onzz frowned at the gun in his hand, obviously unused to firearms. Suddenly, Lobo took two paces closer to him and snatched the gun back again.

"Whoops," he said, arching his eyebrows. "I forgot. The gun's booby-trapped. If it ain't *my* palm holdin' it when the trigger's pulled, somebody loses a hand." He sighed, as if all the troubles in the world had just been dumped on his shoulders. "Guess I'll have to force myself."

He poured a stream of pulsed beams into the door of Superman's cell and almost kept on shooting as Superman shoved the shattered door aside and exited to join his Justice League colleague.

"That's one ya owe me, Big Cheese." Lobo jammed the gun barrel first into his belt. "But don't sweat it. I'll figure some way ya can pay me back."

"I think you're forgetting," Superman said coldly, "it's your fault we're here in the first place. It's you who owe—"

"Gentlemen, gentlemen," the Manhunter tried to mollify them, stepping swiftly between them. "No recriminations, please. Our fight is not with each other. We have to stop the Alpha from completing its insane quest."

Lobo tugged on an earlobe. "Aw, I kinda like insane quests," he confessed. "The little guy, battlin' against all odds to make his dream a reality—stories to tell around the campfire."

Martian Manhunter looked askance at him. "The Alpha is not a 'little guy.' Its dream appears to be the destruction of all life. If we do not stop it, there will be no campfire—and no stories to tell."

"Point taken." Lobo extended a finger and began to pick his nose. "But I still have to admire the Alpha. Heck, he makes me look like a piker!"

The bounty hunter whirled abruptly and walked to his space bike. "Tell ya what—since there ain't any cash involved, I'll let you two catch Alfy an' collect all the glory. Can't say fairer than that, right?"

"Do you not have a personal grudge to settle with the Alpha?" J'onn J'onzz asked. "I was under the impression you always seek revenge on those who betray you."

"I won't argue with that, Baldy," Lobo nodded. "There's nothin' I like more than slicin' an' dicin' a traitor. But it's a question of economics, see. There ain't no million creds no more—an' that kind of makes my interest wane somewhat."

"You may be wrong there," the Martian disagreed. "If, as we suspect, the Alpha destroyed Auriun, surely the galactic authorities will put a bounty on his head?"

"He-ey!" Lobo let his breath out slowly. "Maybe ya ain't as dumb as ya look, Baldy. Illegal invasion of a world—followed by illegal massacres, if Big Blue got it right. There's gotta be a few war crimes in there, too." He whistled, brightening by the second. "Oh man, I can smell that million startin' to build again. Yes sir, that cash has got the Bo's name embossed on it."

Suddenly businesslike, he swung himself up onto the bike, almost kicking one of the Vrkns off.

"Right, little dudes," he said to the small, nervous trio. "It ain't often the Main Man says thanks, but I'm sayin' it to you. Ya did a real swell job." He pulled back hard on the throttle, and the engine note built to a throbbing whine.

"Now c'm'on—I'm gonna give ya a ride the way the Spazz-Frag *should* be rode. Heeyaaa!"

The bike leapt forward, the Vrkns grabbing desperately for handholds to prevent themselves being thrown off.

"Lobo!" Superman yelled after the rapidly departing bike. "Where the devil do you think you're going?"

The bounty hunter didn't bother replying. He accelerated hard, laughing at the Vrkns' terrified chatter as he took them on a high-speed tour of the tunnels that they'd never forget. If they survived it.

Superman and the Manhunter were waiting by the carved entranceway when he finally joined them, five minutes later.

"Where are the Vrkns?" Superman demanded. "You didn't—"

"Relax," Lobo told him, in that infuriatingly casual way of his. "I dropped the tykes off at their workstation."

"It's not like you to do somebody a good turn," Superman observed sourly.

"I did one for you, man." Lobo jerked a thumb over his shoulder, back toward the depths of the cavern. "Besides, I wanted to take a look around. I got a little knowledge of machinery myself. I once worked as a mechanic. Only lasted a couple of hours, of course, but—"

"I am sure your employment history is fascinating," the Manhunter prompted, "but can we stick to the business at hand?"

"I was right about the energy drains," Lobo told them. "There are storage chambers set way under the cells.

Guess Alfie'll synthesize our emotional energy, maybe use it in his campaign against the Universe."

"How?" Superman demanded.

"If I knew that, I'd probably be doin' it myself, Supes. I guess Alfie's gettin' rage from me—though Feetal alone knows what he'll get from you two. But there's more . . ." Lobo broke off, fished a cigar from inside his vest, and lit up irritatingly slowly. "Alfie's turnin' this whole planetoid into a huge spaceship," the bounty hunter went on at last. "Looks like it'll be powered by sunlight. We're talkin' advanced technocrap here, guys. This guy ain't no dunce. He's buildin' himself one hell of a battle base."

"We will achieve nothing by staying here," J'onn J'onzz said gravely. "We must figure out what the Alpha's next target will be and stop the carnage before it begins."

Superman nodded. "A preemptive strike on his war fleet? I agree."

"My nose'll track him wherever he's headed." Lobo gunned the bike engine. "What ya waitin' fer, guys?"

He accelerated away from them so fiercely, they barely caught the words flung back over his shoulder. "Last one to Auriun's a big loser!"

That's it, you moron! Laugh. Laugh until you're bloody dead!

Xemtex was happier than he'd been since he first blew up Lobo in the radiated city. Not only was he going to destroy the bounty hunter, it looked as if he might be able to pick up the cash, too.

Life was full of little surprises.

He felt like singing. But he didn't.

CHAPTER 19

The Chowenstine Asteroids stretched half a billion miles in length, spinning like a cosmic Mobius strip in a never-ending orbit around the star Arxetes. Approximately every three months or so, the sun and its three planets lined up in formation; the light—and reflected light—combined to form an unforgettable spectacle . . . the Rainbow Dawn.

According to the tourist brochures, it was a "captivating symphony of color, a rhapsody of the rainbow, a cosmic event so truly special—so truly *blessed*—that every sentient being should make the trek to see it at least once in their lifetime."

A massive space hotel had been constructed several hundred miles inside the asteroids' orbital path, with no expense spared to make it one of the most luxurious destinations in the Magellanic Cloud. Glasseen and titanium-steel combined in a state-of-the-art construction that was a work of architectural merit in its own right. And every room had a view.

Two thousand tourists were cared and catered for by a

thousand state-of-the-art servodroids. The gossip in the tourist agencies maintained that, if you had to ask how much a week at the Chowenstine Ritz cost, not only could you not afford it, you were a piker. Nobody ever booked for less than a month.

Now, the tourists were flooding into the hotel's spectacular Dome Ballroom. Perched at the very top of the sprawling space structure, the ballroom's glasseen walls and curving roof formed one gigantic viewing dome, where the galaxy's good and great gathered to watch the Rainbow Dawn . . . and each other.

As the orchestra played and couples danced to the latest galactic MOR hits, a sea of voices chattered and murmured:

"—really *must* tell my friends, they'll be sick with envy—"

"No cameras allowed, sir. We try to maintain the exclusivity . . ."

"—the shrump *à la mode* is to die for—"

"Look! It's like they're dancing just for us—"

"The Rainbow Dawn is special, darling. Like you . . ."

Through the toughened glasseen dome, they could see the asteroids rolling and tumbling on their aeons-long path. The space rocks were still mainly black, glistening lumps; every now and again, one would reflect the twinkling light of some distant star. But the triple-planetary alignment with Arxetes was fast approaching, and with it, one of the most memorable sights in the known Universe.

A sudden flash of light from the rising sun stabbed past the space hotel. When it struck the spinning asteroids, there was an explosion of every color in the spectrum. The entire belt seemed to spring into life, shimmering and glowing with a hundred rainbow hues, a phenomenal light show played out against the inky black depths of the cosmos.

Two thousand people sighed as one, while the rainbow colors swirled over the dome in a stunning display.

"Oooh! It's absolutely exquisite!"

"I've never seen anything like it . . ."

"—a special dawn for a special lady—"

"What's that? It looks like one of them is heading this way . . . !"

In the hotel's nerve center, the monitor room from which everything else was run, robot scanners tracked the apparently wayward asteroid. The Ritz was equipped to handle any eventuality—including being fitted with atomic disruptors, for use on asteroids with potential wandering tendencies.

"Object too small to be an asteroid."

"Object is leading a fleet of craft in this direction."

"Establish communication."

"No comm-link accepted."

"Collision is unavoidable. Prime the disruptors."

Speeding in toward the majestic hotel, the Alpha saw the defensive gun turrets swivel and realign themselves so they pointed in its direction. Dense bolts of sun-spawned energy poured from its outstretched hands, instantly homing on their targets.

The disruptor towers disappeared in gouts of flame and explosion that blotted out the rainbow whorl.

* * *

"Wh-what's happening?"

In the ballroom, joy and revelry turned to uncomprehending fear. The occupants of the huge dome could see where the gun turrets were burning. And still the rogue swarm sped toward them.

"Would all couples in the ballroom please cease dancing," a calm, robotic voice came over the public address system. "The shops are now closing. All guests must head for the lifeboats in an orderly fashion. Do not panic. I repeat: Do not panic."

Few things are more likely to induce panic than being told not to panic. Anxious voices rang throughout the ballroom as people started to run for the emergency exits. A woman fell to the floor, screaming as a tide of frightened feet pounded over her. Tables and chairs were upended, causing more of the mob to trip and fall.

But fleeing was futile. Many of the guests merely stood, heads raised, awestruck, as they watched the fast-approaching fleet with the flying stone figure at its head.

The Alpha burst through the dome in a storm of shattered glasseen. Livid red beams blasted from the creature's eye sockets. Huge, jagged sheets of razor-sharp glasseen dropped from their frames, slicing into the hysterical crowds below.

There was a sudden Arctic chill as the dome's air was sucked out into the vacuum of space. The screaming intensified, then ceased abruptly as people's hearts and lungs started exploding from their bodies.

A series of small explosions shook the hotel's superstructure, sending low-frequency vibrations juddering through its floors and walls.

Then the Chowenstine Ritz blew itself apart.

"Wow! Is that fireworks, or is that *fireworks*?"

"Man, they should stage that every year. It makes the Rainbow Dawn look like a kindergarten show."

"Best explosion I've seen since the Khund fleet took out Libra-7."

Angel Eyes' needleship sat well out of detector range, its electron-scanning telescope relaying back the destruction of the Ritz to the crew.

"Recorded?" Angel Eyes asked.

Virt nodded. "The whole shebang, Angel."

"Format it for sending back to Quarantino's. Copy to the Galactic cops. Copy to the Ritz owners, too. I guess their insurance company might want to chip in a few creds for the reward."

Virt seated himself at the control console and busied himself following Angel Eyes' instructions.

The ship was too cramped for the four of them, really. Different when they were traveling—they could put up with the discomfort, knowing that it was only temporary. But waiting was a whole new ball game. Khunds weren't noted for their ability to sit still, unless they could hit somebody at the same time. Patience wasn't one of their few virtues: Virt and Randan had come close to fighting a dozen times and actually fought twice.

Playing cards were scattered all over the floor, where Virt had hurled them in an angry huff.

The Arcturan sat with his back to the others, face

buried in the folds of his hood. He had rubbed off some of the sigils he'd drawn on the bulwarks and replaced them with fresh occult symbols. He was lost deep in himself and paid no heed when the others squabbled. Even when Vul punched Randan and Angel Eyes hauled them apart at gunpoint, K'Baal never budged.

The omens were not good.

The tentacles of K'Baal's strange mind had reached out as far as Vrk, and the Arcturan was astonished to find the captives' cells empty. This put a different spin on everything. No doubt the super heroes would pursue the Alpha—and Lobo, too, for revenge as well as the bounty.

Slowly, K'Baal withdrew from his inner depths. He turned himself around to face the others. "The Alpha's prisoners are free. Even now, they are on their way here in pursuit."

Angel Eyes brought a fist crashing down on the table. "Damn and double damn," he cursed. "We're going to be taking a chance going up against the Alpha itself—but it'll be suicide if these three are against us, too."

"It may be possible." The Arcturan's voice was calm, filled with self-confidence. "My magic may be enough to quell them all."

"And if it's not . . . ?" Angel Eyes let his voice tail off; he looked uneasy. "I'm not so sure, K'Baal. Lobo and the others ain't just ordinary guys."

"Has my magic ever failed us?"

"No," Angel Eyes admitted, slowly exhaling. "But—"

"Magic is merely a matter of willpower," the Arcturan

reminded him. "Mine has been honed to a remarkable degree."

"All the same, I think it safer to wait. Big Blue and his pal can take down the Alpha and Lobo can help them. Then we step in and pick up the reward."

"And Lobo will just let us?" Randan put in. "I mean, I like a good fight as much as the next Khund . . . but not when the odds are stacked against me."

Virt grunted his assent without looking up from the console.

"I can take Lobo." K'Baal's voice rang with self-belief. "I am sure I can take all of them, if necessary."

All Arcturans chosen for the Path of Magic were trained from childhood to develop a remarkable confidence in their own occult abilities. At base, sorcery *was* willpower . . . and if that willpower ever flagged, then the magic would also fail.

Arcturus was a closed society with a rigid hierarchical structure. At the top of the pyramid, a small elite of adept warlocks ruled the planet. A few thousand others—like K'Baal—mediated between the rulers and the mass of ordinary, downtrodden people. Visitors from off-world were actively discouraged and—although they might want to— few of the natives ever left their darksome world.

K'Baal's ambitions had been his downfall. Forbidden by convention to practice live sacrifice, K'Baal had used the sacrificial deaths of his inferiors to boost his own growing powers. A death warrant was issued against him and packs of assassin-priests were sent out to hunt him down for ritual slaying.

He managed to get off-world, where he knew the insular Arcturans would not follow. He'd drifted from planet to planet, an outcast wherever he went. Those who knew of Arcturus feared him; even those who'd never heard of the occult world gave him a wide berth. Despite the religious figure he cut in his robes and voluminous hood, K'Baal exuded menace.

No doubt he would have ended his days as a petty criminal, on the run, hunted down for bounty. But everything changed the day he met Angel Eyes.

The tall, gaunt bounty hunter had burst into a bar on Raimi's World with both guns blazing, those amazing golden eyes gleaming with lust for the kill. The Arcturan was drinking water at a shadowed corner table and nearly jumped out of his robe with surprise.

Five customers went down in lifeless heaps, but not a single innocent had a hair on his head harmed. Angel Eyes was a dead shot.

As the bounty hunter checked his warrants against the corpses, a sixth outlaw emerged from the restroom. The newcomer sized up the situation in a glance and swiftly drew his gun. Angel Eyes had his back to him, unaware of the other's presence.

K'Baal thought hard. A bolt of mental energy seared into the outlaw's mind. The Arcturan could see fear in the man's eyes as his movements suddenly became no longer his own. Perspiration beaded from the villain's forehead and his mouth opened and closed noiselessly as he raised the gun to his own temple.

His finger tightened on the trigger, and his brains erupted all over the bar walls.

From that moment on, Angel Eyes and the Arcturan

had worked as a team. No qualifications were necessary to become a licensed bounty hunter other than the ability to outwit and outfight the prey you were after. Angel Eyes and K'Baal soon gained an enviable reputation for both ruthlessness and reliability.

They picked up the two warlike Khunds more for muscle than for their social skills. Randan and Virt were typical of their kind—vulgar, rude, and prone to unforeseen fits of aggression. But they were strong, dependable and loyal—and they had no qualms about killing.

The foursome began working together, more than a match for the criminal gangs they specialized in tracking. The violence was guaranteed, the pay was good, and the sex followed naturally. All four had salted away a nest-egg for the day when they'd retire . . . although they all knew, without it ever being said, that that day would never come. They were professional killers; like the pros they were, they'd die on the job.

One day, sooner or later, some bad guy would get them.

K'Baal banished his gloomy thoughts as Angel Eyes suddenly snapped his fingers and whacked a hand against his own thigh.

"I got an idea, guys." He laughed, considering how simple—yet brilliant—it was. "We're going to eliminate all risk to ourselves. Strap yourselves in. Randan, set us a course."

"We are leaving?" the Arcturan asked. "For where . . . ?"

Angel Eyes' grin broadened even more. "We're going to get a little cake and coffee. And buy ourselves some insurance at the same time."

"Do not speak in riddles."

Angel Eyes' face became suddenly serious. "You know that babe Lobo's sweet on . . . ?"

"The waitress?" Randan asked. "I've eaten at her place. Good slurmp."

Angel Eyes nodded. "Lobo goes weak at the knees when she's around. Turns into a total sap. So it seems to me we should pick her up and bring her to the party."

Lobo couldn't make up his mind how he was feeling.

It was a novelty for him to be streaking through space, flanked on either side by one of the galaxy's greatest super heroes. By rights, their very presence should have made him sick. And yet . . . contrary to everything he thought he knew about himself, he was feeling tickled pink.

Heavy rock music was battering his eardrums. Xemtex had maintained his sulky, brooding silence. They were on their way to the galactic equivalent of the heavyweight fight championships (lasers and knives permitted). And there were still two cans of suds chilling in the bike's cooler.

He flicked his eyes left and right, seeing first Superman, then the Martian Manhunter as the trio flew in perfect synchrony. Square jaws. Thousand-mile stares. Capes flowing behind them. An aura of grim determination, based on the thesis that good always wins out over evil.

Not in my world, it doesn't, the Main Man thought. *An' not in the real world, either. The winner wins, end of story.*

Lobo didn't like the duo any more than he ever did . . .
but he *did* like the fact that they would help capture the
Alpha; yet he would waltz away with the reward.

There was no doubt about it—they were gentlemen.

Or, as Lobo pronounced the word, *chumps*.

There were three planets in the Arxetes system. Chrinoz,
closest to the sun, was the least advanced. Its high temperatures and rate of orbital spin had made it difficult for life
to gain a foothold, although once it had, it evolved rapidly. Now, the planet's inhabitants were roughly at the ne-
olithic stage of development: family-based tribes that
lived nomadically.

The second world, Sandoz, was much cooler, its atmosphere more stable and dense. The humanoid races that
evolved here had larger brains than their counterpart on
Chrinoz; their mechanical bent was demonstrated in the
size and armaments of their well-equipped armies.
They'd been fighting the equivalent of Earth's First World
War for around a century, with neither side having gained
any real advantage.

Gallioz was farthest from the sun, only a few hours'
journey in from the Chowenstine Asteroids. Evolution
had been favored on Gallioz by the presence of vast
oceans. The indigenous peoples had remained true to
their aquatic origins: More than half of their population
was housed in colossal floating cities. Normally anchored
to the seabed, the vast urban conglomerations were also
capable of navigating the endless blue deep.

It was to Gallioz that the Alpha came next, leading his
armada of death.

As the fleet of crystal ships drew closer, small groups peeled off and soared away in search of their targets. Unlike the Ritz Hotel, this assault would avoid destruction as much as possible. The Gallioz cities housed vast nutrient factories, where plankton from the oceans was processed into every kind of food imaginable. The Alpha had already ascertained that his Vrkn warriors would be able to exist on such a diet. And an army marches—or flies—on its stomach.

The Alpha's electromagnetic powers allowed it to seek out and pinpoint Gallioz's off-world communication centers. It would strike these centers itself. In the early stages of its campaign, surprise was essential. As many worlds as possible must fall before resistance could be organized.

Twin gun turrets atop one of the city's graceful spires hummed and whirred as they tracked on their prey. Above them, two of the crystal craft were heading directly their way. Whoever was aboard, they were maintaining radio silence and refusing to answer any incoming calls.

It could only be assumed that their intent was hostile.

But just out of range of the turret guns, the spaceships slowed almost to a walking pace. Their nose cones began to glow, building to a vibrant orange. Suddenly, pulsed beams of energy streamed out of the cones, widening in concentric circles as they expanded to cover the entire city. This was a technology way beyond anything the peoples of Gallioz could conceive.

On landing strips that reached like concrete fingers into the ocean, civil defense aircraft taxied and took to the air—directly into the path of the pulsed beams.

The pilots' reaction was near instantaneous. A red knot of anger took root in their guts, burgeoning into an all-consuming rage as it coursed through their nervous systems. Their minds blanked out, overcome by a fury so strong they began visibly to sweat and shake.

Within seconds, the enraged pilots had turned their crafts' weapons on each other.

Seconds later, the planes plunged out of the skies without ever having fired a shot at their foe. Such was the potency of Lobo's synthesized and amplified emotional energy.

Masses of people crowded onto the streets, each one lost in his own personal hell of terror as wave after wave of pure Loboesque rage broke over them. Hormones flooded their bodies, building their stress levels to unprecedented levels. Automobiles mowed down pedestrians and nobody seemed to notice. Driven by sheer anger, thousands of citizens attacked each other—while thousands of others committed suicide. Still more fell to the streets and lay still, as their hearts gave out under the emotional stress.

Still the beams intensified until, at long last, not a soul moved the length and breadth of the city. Bodies were scattered everywhere, lying where they fell, lips and teeth drawn back in their faces, snarling their fury in the rictus of death.

Elsewhere, it was the synthetic equivalent of J'onn J'onzz's despair that washed down on the populace of the cities. Within minutes, niggling worry swelled into stressful anxiety, that blossomed into hopelessness, that swiftly turned into full-blown, debilitating despair.

Every nuance of the Martian's grief was synthesized and amplified by the Alpha's machine-mind technology.

The people knew they were going to die, knew their world was being taken over by something monstrous. All of their history—their achievements—everything they'd ever aspired to—was doomed.

In their millions, they fell to the ground and wept for its passing.

CHAPTER 20

Where the Ritz space hotel once orbited, now there was nothing except clouds of debris interspersed with ruptured corpses.

The three men hovered nearby. Superman and J'onn J'onzz looked askance at each other. Could a natural disaster have caused this—a fault in the hotel's antigravity engines, for instance, or a catastrophic meltdown in its supply of nuclear fuel?

Both knew the answer was "no," but Lobo settled the question definitively. He wrinkled his nose and snuffled, his superkeen sense of smell picking up just the faintest trace of the Alpha. The bounty hunter punched data into the bike's onboard computer system and watched to see what would come up on the navigation screen.

There could be only one place the Alpha was heading: Gallioz. Information about the planet and its star system started to scroll down his screen, and Lobo grinned like a death's-head. Gallioz wasn't too far away. With a little luck, they'd be confronting their foe within hours . . . and he'd be making plans for the big-cred reward.

Lobo pointed ahead, gunned the throttle, and the Spazz-Frag shot away at high speed, leaving Superman and the Martian Manhunter to follow.

The Alpha had decided not all of Gallioz's cities would be spared. Only those that had food-manufacturing capability or factories that could be converted into armament production lines were of use to its war effort. The others— and there were dozens of them—were marked for annihilation.

A hundred or so crystal ships gathered over one of the planet's largest conurbations. There was no need for them to use the beams that spread rage or despair; the factories and buildings here would burn along with their inhabitants.

Pecling off into smaller groups of ten, the craft swooped down, locking in on their individual targets.

A rain of bombs fell cityward.

Seconds later, a series of bright explosions rocked the streets.

The two heroes and their financially motivated companion glowed fiery red as they dived into Gallioz's atmosphere. Both Martian Manhunter and Superman used their super-vision to probe the surface, miles below—and were horrified by what they saw.

"It's a full-scale invasion," Superman reported. "Cities are burning. There's a mass slaughter of citizens. We have to stop it."

"Time for us to take the gloves off," Lobo snarled impatiently. "Let's do it."

"Wait!" the Martian snapped. "You forget—the attack craft are manned by Vrkns."

Lobo shrugged. "Great. So I get my turkey shoot after all."

"You do not understand," Manhunter went on. "They do only what the Alpha forces them to do. The blame is not theirs. We cannot kill them in cold blood."

Lobo's eyes widened in surprise, but before he could speak the Manhunter peeled off and began to dive away.

"I will try to use my telepathy to undo what the Alpha has done," he called back.

The bounty hunter shook his head in disbelief. "Tell ya what," he said sarcastically to Superman. "Why don't you go pick a few flowers an' we can give the death-dealin' little creeps a posy each?"

The Man of Steel didn't deign to reply.

J'onn J'onzz's mind zeroed in on one of the crystal craft, probing at the Vrkn pilot. There was no time for subtlety, or sensitivity to the feelings of others. J'onn's mind plunged straight into the pilot's . . .

And what he saw there shook him with disgust.

The Vrkns had long since lost any memory of who they originally were. Even so, the creature J'onn had mentally contacted on Vrk itself was still a thinking, semirational being, despite his primitive mind-set.

But the pilot had no mind. His neurological circuits had been burned out and replaced with a simple directive: Obey the Alpha. He was incapable of doing anything except following the dictates of his genocidal god.

The Manhunter focused intently, trying to force the

pilot to bend to his will. There was no reaction. Even the Martian's formidable telepathic powers were useless when there was virtually no mind to concentrate on.

These Vrkns were no longer independent creatures, but mindless zombies.

There was no saving them.

"Yee-haa!" Lobo yelped in triumph, after the Manhunter had reported his findings. "Now maybe we can get down to the serious stuff. Fraggin'."

He throttled the Spazz-Frag and sent it screaming into a steep dive. Saving cities wasn't exactly the Main Man's bag, but shooting things and blowing them up most certainly was. Like many bounty hunters—and presumably vampires, too—he never felt more alive than when he was taking somebody else's life.

"Awright, Xemtex," he said cheerfully to the bike. "Here's where ya earn yer keep."

"I already earned my keep. I set you free, didn't I?"

"Ya been rewarded for that. I ain't fed ya any juice for ages."

"You are charity personified. Command and I will obey, o mighty one." The bike's speakers couldn't conceal the mocking tone, but Lobo ignored it. It was time for some fun.

"Destroy," the Main Man said simply, but with heartfelt pleasure.

Yet another mutant heavy metal monstrosity pounded in his ears as Lobo swooped to the attack. Bike cannon chattered out a stream of tracers that ripped into a pair of crystal ships. Built as attack craft, they relied solely on their stone hulls for defense—enough, perhaps, to face the air force of a backward planet. But nowhere *near* enough to face the full wrath of a Spazz-Frag piloted by a psychopathic Czarnian.

The metal band was just segueing into the song's chorus when the first ship exploded in a gout of flame. Caught in the blast, its companion craft veered wildly away and plunged out of control into the ocean below.

"Two down," Lobo remarked, "an' a frag of a lot more to come!"

A half dozen of the craft had witnessed their companions' destruction. They shot toward Lobo, weapons blazing, their energy beams rebounding harmlessly from the space bike's force field.

"Chicken run, huh?"

Lobo turned the bike in a tight loop that left him facing the oncoming craft. He flipped the twin turbos' boost switch and the bike shot forward, its speed doubling and redoubling every second.

He hit the lead ship so hard that the Spazz-Frag plowed straight through it, smashing it to pieces. With all its weapons firing, he maneuvered the bike between the other craft, like a pinball in an arcade game, picking them off at will. Several of the ships fired at him but missed, their beams raking into their companions.

Ship after ship after ship blossomed into flame and plummeted downward, trailing smoke and debris.

"Eight down," Lobo kept tally, "an' I'm just startin' to warm up. Let's go frag the rest of them bastiches."

*   *   *

Superman felt sick at heart as he flew toward one of the Vrkn attack formations. Their pilots might be throwbacks, barely worthy of being called sentient beings. But they were innocent, and they were alive—and Superman was sworn to defend life, not destroy it.

Summoning his superspeed, he streaked past the craft, then banked sharply so he was above them. Some of them started firing at him, but his invulernable Kryptonian skin just shrugged off their beams.

Twin rays of pencil-thin energy lanced from Superman's eyes. Like lasers, his heat vision burned through a crystal hull, destroying its stabilizers and turning the weapons relays to a molten mass. The ship stopped firing and turned to limp away.

But in the time it would take him to disable them all, they'd be free to drop their deadly cargoes on the city skyscrapers below.

The heat beams faded as he came to a decision. Speeding up until he was no more than a blur, the Man of Steel circled the wedge-shaped formation time and again.

The turbulence caused in his wake threw the ships into each other, buffeting them like pressure waves on a storm front. Unable to control their flight, the stricken ships plunged one after another into the sea.

At least the Vrkns might stand a chance of survival, crashing into water—although if what J'onn had said was true, they would no longer be able to exist on their own. That didn't make what Superman had to do any easier.

Gritting his teeth, he flew off in search of the enemy.

* * *

Superman's dilemna was shared by his friend. Like the Man of Steel, J'onn J'onzz would never willingly take a life. Yet what choice did he have?

He was hovering over a city under assault from dozens of crystal ships. He could disable every ship manually—and while he was doing it, the others would continue their barrage of death and destruction. His psionic skills were useless without proper minds to affect.

He glanced down at the city, pockmarked with burning buildings and huge craters, and steeled his resolve. The Alpha was to blame for this atrocity. Soon, there must come a reckoning.

But in the meantime, there was work to be done. The Martian sighed, prayed to his ancestors for forgiveness, and swooped to the attack.

On the other side of the planet, the Alpha stood atop a magnificent skyscraper, basking in the sun's rays. As light from the sun was absorbed by the artificial intelligence's crystal body, it was reduced to its fundamental particles and stored in the near-infinite molecular latticework of the quartz.

The Alpha lowered its head and pointed a massive arm at an adjacent thirty-story office block. Intense beams of energy crackled from its fingertips, arcing toward the base of the building. The beams stabbed into the cladding, burning through it to the girders below.

Less than a minute later, the entire edifice collapsed in on itself.

The Alpha lumbered across the roof and hurled itself into the air, becoming a living projectile as it smashed its way into a glass-and-steel structure. Slender aliens screamed and cringed away from the monstrous figure. It ignored them all, apart from one female. Striding forward, it grasped her in one giant hand, careful not to damage her. She would be the sole survivor of the Gallioz race. A Last Daughter for his collection.

The Alpha raked the room with a glance, energy bolts leaping from its eyes. The others died instantly, silently.

It cradled the woman, shielding her with its body, as it left the building and took again to the air. It flew up to one of the crystal ships and transferred her to the Vrkns' care.

The ship blasted away from the others, ferrying her back to Vrk and imprisonment in an artificial intelligence's museum of life.

It was then that the Alpha felt it—a disturbance in the electromagnetic spectrum that resulted from the interplay of the planet's field and that of the sun. Something was not as it should be.

Its crystal craft were falling from the skies.

The Alpha shot away, traveling halfway around the planet with as little effort as it would take to cross a street.

"Do you, Darlene, take this man—this bounty hunter—this Main Man—to be your lawful wedded husband?"

Darlene's already impressive bosoms swelled with pride. "I do."

Almost shyly, she glanced to the side, batting her long eyelashes. Lobo stood beside her, resplendent in a smart, well-fitted tuxedo, white shirt, and psychedelic tie. Thankfully, he'd heeded her wishes and wasn't wearing his chain and hook. The last thing she wanted on the biggest day of her life was trouble.

He smiled down at her. Darlene's pulse raced. Her knees went weak, and she almost swooned as she lost herself in the bottomless depths of his gorgeous red eyes.

"And do you, Lobo," the minister asked, "take this babe Darlene to be your lawful wedded wife?"

"Do I? Man, *do* I? You bet yer bony butt I do!"

Then he was sweeping her up in those strong arms, his lips gently caressing hers, the hardness of his body pressing against her flesh under the filmy silk wedding dress . . .

"So—what do you think, Darl?"

Darlene's daydream popped like a soap bubble impaled on a nail.

Al was lowering himself onto a stool at the table where she sat, lost in her dreams. Al had closed the diner while he and Darlene cleaned up, fixed up, and redecorated as best they could.

Now he gestured around the little restaurant, which gleamed and shone—superficially, at least. But if you looked a little closer, you could see the holes in the wall stuffed with makeshift filler, and the bashes and dents in the tables and chairs. Al had used the next month's stock money to pay for the materials; professional workmen would have to wait till Lobo coughed up what he owed.

And Darlene knew he *would* pay up. Lobo always kept his word.

"Would you buy a shrumpburger and a beer here?" Al asked her.

Darlene smiled. "I wouldn't eat anyplace else," she said loyally.

"I know you don't want to hear this," Al went on slowly, "but personally I'd be more than happy if Lobo never came back."

"That's unfair, Al." Darlene leapt to the bounty hunter's defense. "He didn't wreck the diner deliberately. He was only protecting me."

"Why couldn't he have taken those creeps outside to protect you? Why does he always have to smash my place up?"

"Oh, Al," Darlene returned, "you're exaggerating. It's only happened twice."

Al looked skeptically at her. *"Only?"*

"I'm sorry, Al. I can't control Lobo. He's not my boyfriend."

Darlene looked down at the table. She really did feel sorry for Al, who had been struggling for years to make ends meet. And just when things were starting to look up, Lobo paid his first visit, fell in lust with Darlene . . . and kept coming back.

"You should forget all about him," Al rebuked her sternly. "The guy is nothing but trouble."

"That's not true. Any girl would be proud to take his arm."

Al raised one eyebrow, archly. "Sure. As long as he wasn't spitting. Or cursing. Or vomiting. Or fighting. Or . . ."

Darlene stood up. "Come on," she cajoled, "lighten up. Let's get the diner open for business again—your mood will soon improve once the cash register starts to jingle."

She went over to the diner entrance and flipped the CLOSED sign over.

"Looks as if we have customers already," she called over her shoulder to Al. "There's a ship docked outside."

Darlene glanced briefly at her reflection in the microwave oven's polished glasseen front. She pouted her lips and moistened them with her tongue. She ran her hands over her breasts, patted down her tight-fitting apron, and opened the door.

To find the barrel of a gun sticking in her face.

Al Fretowski looked up and plastered a professional smile on his face as Darlene led four figures into the diner.

"Welcome to Al's," he greeted them expansively. "Darlene will show you to a table and—" He broke off as he saw the gun in the tall, golden-eyed man's hand. "Er . . . is there a problem, gents?"

"No. We just need your waitress for a while."

Al could see Darlene's face was pale with shock. She really was too sensitive for this kind of life.

"I'm sorry, guys," Al told them, "but I got a big party coming in. I need Darlene here."

"I'm not asking you, chubby," Angel Eyes snarled. "I'm telling you. We'll bring her back safe and sound in a day or so. Just don't go notifying the cops—or we'll be back for you."

Then the four of them were gone, and Darlene with them. Al slumped in a chair. He didn't know how . . . but somehow he just *knew* this was all Lobo's fault.

CHAPTER 21

This is impossible.
Impossibility is merely the failure to consider everything
in context.
Our emotional weapons should have crippled them.
And yet they fight back.

A score of Gallioz aircraft screamed across the sky, a mile or so in front of the flying behemoth. The jet fighters were heading en masse toward a trio of Vrkn crystal craft; as they came within firing range, they opened up with their weaponry.

The Vrkn ships could have withstood an assault from two or three of their foes—but twenty acting in unison, firing as one, was too much. One of the craft erupted in a bright ball of flame. Even as it spiraled down toward the ground, the two other ships exploded, too.

The Alpha altered its direction, putting it on an interception course with the Gallioz craft. Beams lanced from its eyes and the tips of its fingers, ripping into the old-fashioned aircraft. It didn't stop until they were wiped out of existence.

On a military airstrip below, the Alpha could make out a group of figures. All were recognizable as the slender, graceful people of Gallioz—except one. He stood taller and much bulkier and was wrapped in an ankle-length cape. He was also green.

*   *   *

The Martian.

> *How can he have escaped?*

> *Irrelevant.*

> *No doubt he has used his telepathic powers to purge the debilitating effects of our beams from the pilots' minds.*

> *We have his DNA. We have a complete record of his electrochemical makeup. We do not need him.*

> *We must crush him.*

Changing its trajectory, the Alpha swooped down at incredible speed.

The man was shaking and trembling, close to being petrified by pure, blind rage. J'onn J'onzz uttered a few comforting words, then held one hand on either side of the Gallioz pilot's head and concentrated on driving out the feeling that had seized him.

It could be no picnic to be infused with the type of fury J'onn had seen Lobo exhibit when he tried to burst out of the Alpha's cell.

Already, J'onn had restored hundreds of the pilots to normality; the men were shaken, but keen to fight back against the evil that was plundering their world. An entire squadron of their jets had taken off together, their crews grimly determined to take the unequal fight back to the enemy. They were outgunned and outnumbered, but to a man they took to the skies.

J'onn removed his hands. The man's face was placid now, his eyes bright and clear.

"Thank you, thank you," he said over and over again.

The Martian pointed to the airstrip. "Your people will thank you if you fight back."

The pilot nodded and, followed by two crew members, started to run toward one of the waiting planes.

Suddenly, the Martian detected a high-pitched noise in the air above him. He turned to look up—and started as he saw the Alpha diving at full speed toward him.

There was no time to avoid the impact. J'onn barely managed to brace himself before the eight-foot-high colossus slammed into him. The creature's momentum was unbelievable. J'onn felt the thick concrete under his feet crack and give way under the sudden force—and both of them disappeared into the ground.

They plunged down through layers of soil and concrete, landing with bone-jarring impact on the reinforced floor of an underground storage bay. Trapped under the Alpha, J'onn summoned all of his strength and tried to heave it off. But the Alpha was every bit as strong as the Manhunter and resisted his efforts with apparent ease.

Its massive stone hands curled into fists, pounding at J'onn's head in an attempt to daze him and keep him off-balance. Despite his invulnerability, the Manhunter felt the force of every senses-shattering blow; he knew that, somehow, he had to gain the upper hand.

The storage bay was about fifteen feet high, perhaps four times that in length. Crates of aircraft spares and boxes of ammunition were stacked up against the walls in several places, and there were several small metal tanks—

presumably for holding fuel. Well above head height, heavy, insulated cables ran the length of the chamber wall, obviously the electricity supply for the base above. There were several bright yellow fire extinguishers bracketed to the wall in different places.

Shifting his weight, J'onn managed to turn over so that his knees and hands were braced against the floor. He did his best to ignore the blows that hammered against his back and head, contracting his muscles, waiting for the right opportunity. When the Alpha raised one mighty fist high, J'onn moved like lightning.

He hurled himself upright, throwing off the crystal monster. The Alpha's foot slipped in a glistening pool of spilled oil and it fell heavily into a stack of crates. They tumbled down on top of it, almost burying it.

J'onn ripped one of the fire extinguishers off the wall and hurriedly primed it. The Alpha burst out of the fallen crates, hurling splintered wood everywhere—and found itself gazing into the nozzle of the extinguisher.

J'onn hit the plunger. Thick white foam billowed out, filling the Alpha's eyes and nostrils and mouth. It clawed clumsily at its face, trying to brush off the invasive chemicals. The Martian smashed the end of the extinguisher into the Alpha's mouth, the force of the impact rupturing the metal canister and covering the creature in an eruption of foam.

The Alpha lashed out blindly, one massive fist ripping out a two-foot chunk of the wall as J'onn ducked under the blow.

The Manhunter knew he had to keep clear and get the fight over with as swiftly as possible. He leapt into the air, his hand closing around one of the thick electric cables. As he dropped back to the floor, he wrenched it hard. The cable snapped, leaving J'onn holding the live end. Blue sparks fizzed and popped as he held the wire out at arm's length and advanced toward the Alpha. Perhaps electricity could achieve what brute force couldn't.

The Alpha lurched forward, and J'onn thrust the sparking cable directly into its faceted crystal face. There was a blinding blue explosion, and the Alpha roared its dismay as the high voltage flooded through its body.

It didn't twitch and jerk the way Lobo had when his muscles' nerve endings were disrupted. The Alpha had no nerve endings. Instead, it froze, paralyzed; a tiny quiver passed over its face.

Yes! J'onn thought, with a surge of triumph. *Electricity might not destroy it . . . but it is certainly having an effect.*

He kept the cable jammed against its face. But the effects seemed to be diminishing. The Alpha's eyes flashed, and random, tiny bolts of lightning seemed to swirl deep inside its crystal body. Then the random arcs began to coalesce into a pattern.

J'onn J'onzz cursed to himself. Somehow, the Alpha was adjusting its internal mechanisms to accommodate the flow of electrons. It was turning J'onn's weapon against it into fresh power for itself.

Without warning, the Alpha lashed out with a backhand swipe. Caught unaware, J'onn's head snapped back, and he careened into one of the fuel storage tanks, bursting it. There was a loud crack as the sparking cable touched the metal tank . . .

Then the chamber erupted in a volcano of flame.

Fire . . . J'onn J'onzz's nemesis. As flames flickered and danced around him, his strength drained away. His limbs suddenly weak, the Martian's legs buckled under him, and he pitched forward onto the floor.

Agony burned through his whole body. Dimly, he was aware of the Alpha looming out of the flame like a phoenix. The monster's fists were balled as it stood over him, victorious.

He only had one chance now. A desperate telepathic message stabbed from his mind . . .

Then everything ebbed away from him and he slumped unconscious with the flames still licking at his body.

Superman arrived with the force of a thunderbolt.

He'd been digging a channel at superspeed from the coast to the heart of a burning city, providing water for the emergency services as they fought desperately to douse the flames. J'onn J'onzz's desperate mental plea for help had seared into his brain.

Now, as he flew at phenomenal speed toward the air base, his telescopic vision probed the yawning crater in the concrete runway. A chamber below ground was on fire. The Manhunter lay helpless, unconscious, perhaps even . . .

Superman didn't finish the thought.

He banked his body in a steep dive, aiming himself at the crater. He swooped in through the shattered concrete, at the same time unleashing a blast of frigid superbreath that pushed all the heat out of the room. The flames disappeared as if by magic, and powdery frost turned the interior sparkling white.

Superman didn't slow down. He grasped the startled

Alpha and angled himself up again, smashing a new exit route through the concrete ceiling, dragging the crystal giant with him. He burst out into sunshine, his momentum carrying them high into the air.

Superman could feel the Alpha starting to struggle as it realized what was happening to it. The Man of Steel didn't hold back. Hovering half a mile in the air, he raised the Alpha above his head in both hands and hurled the crystal creature downward with as much force as he could muster.

He watched as the plunging Alpha rebounded off the corner of a high building, sending tons of stone and rubble cascading to the streets below. The Alpha tried to reestablish control, but there wasn't enough time. It struck the jib of a large crane, shearing right through the metal, and smashed through a wall into a yard. The heavy jib twisted and buckled and collapsed on top of it.

Intent on pressing home his advantage, Superman again dived at his adversary.

The Alpha had come down in a junkyard miraculously untouched by the Vrkns' assault. The yard was piled high with obsolete hovercraft, rusting wrecks, and accident write-offs. Jumbled piles of scrap and spares lay everywhere, giving the place the characteristic appearance of junkyards throughout the Universe.

As he descended, the Man of Steel reached to grasp a length of chain from which a heavy wrecking ball was suspended. Ripping it free, Superman whirled the ball around his head like a medieval knight's mace. The Alpha struggled out of the tangled metal that restrained it, tossing girders aside like matchsticks—and Superman struck.

The solid steel ball slammed against the Alpha's head with a sound like metal thunder. Again and again the ball whirled, gleaming in the alien sunshine, as Superman repeatedly drove it into his foe.

This is no use, Superman was thinking. *It's keeping him occupied, but it's not doing any real damage. I wonder what else J'onn was trying to tell me . . . ?*

The Martian's psionic call hadn't just been a plea for help. He had tried to tell Superman something else—about how the crystal monster might be defeated. But his thoughts had faded and died before he finished.

As the ball spun in the air again, the Alpha finally managed to react. It snatched up a twisted girder and swung it like a baseball bat. Steel connected with steel; the wrecking ball was ripped from Superman's hands and sent flying a half mile across the city.

The crystal giant loomed over Superman, who reacted by unleashing blistering heat vision from his eyes. The beams struck the Alpha in the chest. It stopped and looked down, an expression of near intrigue on its features as it saw the top inch or so of its crystal "skin" start to bubble and melt.

Seeing that he was finally causing the beast some damage, Superman redoubled his efforts. But the Alpha laughed, an ugly, grating sound.

"You cannot harm us," it said nonchalantly, even as globules of molten crystal ran down its chest. *"But we retain the ability to harm you."*

Before the last words were out of its mouth, fierce green beams shot from its eye sockets.

"Kryptonite!" Superman gasped, pain already spreading like wildfire through his nervous system. The Alpha must have it stored inside its crystal body! He threw himself back, but the Alpha merely swiveled its head, keeping the toxic beams trained on him.

Consciousness started to fade as the waves of pain swelled faster Dimly, he was aware of the Alpha's arrogant voice:

"We are the first. You are the last. We have no hesitation in annihilating any who interfere with our plans."

Then Superman knew no more.

"Bravo. Applause. Encore, maestro, please."

Lobo sat on his bike, hovering ten feet above the junkyard, contemptuously clapping his hands together. The Martian's message hadn't just been sent to Superman's mind. Lobo had picked it up, too, and come to investigate—though in more leisurely fashion than Superman, as the Main Man took time out to shoot down several more of the Vrkn attack craft.

"Sorry to interrupt yer fun, Alfie," Lobo went on in his gravelly voice, "but this is where the Bo gets his own back on the big bad bonehead."

Every weapon that was left in the bike's arsenal went off at once. The Alpha reeled back under an onslaught of shells, tracer bullets, energy beams, and frag grenades. Lobo's gun was in his hand, and he was yelling like a maniac as he pumped shot after shot into the faltering crystal giant.

"How'd ya like them onions?" the bounty hunter shouted in triumph as the massive figure crumpled to the ground. Fragments of crystal were ripped from its body with every shot. It rallied, grabbing at a rusted auto chassis for support as it struggled to get its huge bulk upright again.

The blizzard of firepower died away as suddenly as it had begun. The bike was fresh out of ammo; not surprising, given the amount that had been expended escaping from Vrk and shooting down the assault ships.

Immediately, Lobo leapt from the bike, with his chain and hook spinning around his head.

"An' here's the *coup de grâce*, rocky," the Main Man yelled victoriously.

He landed atop the fallen Alpha and brought the hook flailing down at speed. With a grinding shriek, the hook's tip penetrated a good six inches into the crystal skull.

Lobo leapt nimbly off, leaving the hook embedded in his enemy's head.

"Guess ya won't be doin' much without a brain," he crowed.

His pleasure turned to puzzlement as the Alpha lurched suddenly to its feet. *"Then you guess incorrectly,"* it said politely. *"Our brain is our body. There is no central cranial area, as is common with . . . ordinary life."*

"Well, frag me sideways," the bounty hunter jeered. "I guess I'm gonna have to do it the hard way, then. I'll rip ya limb from limb, then pulverize the bits. Betcha won't be doin' much thinkin' after yer road fill, Einstein."

They circled each other warily, more like primeval monsters than heavyweight boxers, each looking for a critical opening.

Lobo struck first, lashing out with a kick to the Alpha's groin. It would have doubled up any normal foe, as well putting an end to any future paternity hopes he might have fostered. The Alpha didn't even flinch.

Its fist launched in an overhand right that took Lobo flush in the face. The bounty hunter grunted, but didn't fall back Anything a stone chump could do, he could do better.

Blows rained down from all sides. Neither budged an inch.

Miles away, in the chamber under the air base, J'onn J'onzz was on his knees, doubled over, retching violently on the concrete floor. The fires had all been extinguished, and the frost was melting away, but the stench of gas-oil still hung heavy in the air.

His whole body ached, a sensation he was unused to feeling. The flames had consumed him. For an awful instant, he'd feared he was about to die. Superman must have received his message and used his superbreath to douse the flames. But where was he now? And where was the Alpha?

The Martian got to his feet, noticing for the first time the second hole smashed in the chamber roof—this one from the inside. His legs felt unsteady, his senses still partly dazed. He would have to wait a while before trying to fly.

And then he remembered: Electricity had affected the Alpha. His mind raced as he struggled to understand why that would be so. The Alpha was made out of stone, a notoriously bad conducting medium. It was an artificial intelligence, not really alive. It had no muscles or nerve ends in its body, no ganglions in its skull because it had no brain . . .

Yet it was able to store energy—presumably in the molecular structure of its quartz body. It could amplify and discharge that energy from eyes or hands, in the form of beams.

Of course! Electromagnetic fields! The electricity from the cable must have temporarily overwhelmed the Alpha's own inner electromagnetic flows—the very flows that must keep its intelligence together. Without them, it would have no way of maintaining a constant identity.

J'onn steeled himself, ready to leap into the air. But nausea overwhelmed him again, and he leaned back wearily against the chamber wall. He had to let the others know. This was a matter of life and death!

Lobo was getting fed up. They must have traded a hundred blows. His knuckles were torn and bleeding; his forehead was gashed where he'd employed a sneaky head butt; and his healing factor was working overtime to keep up with repairing the damage the Alpha was doing to his arms, shoulders, and torso. One foot was aching, too, where the Alpha had stamped hard on his instep.

Yet the bounty hunter couldn't see a way out of this. Unlike Baldy or Big Blue, he had no tricky little powers like invisibility, heat vision, or frigid breath. With the Main Man, what you saw was what you got. Big gun, big knife, and a hook that would gut a space whale.

Normally, he'd be able to wear down any foe, because his healing factor repaired him while the other guy could only get weaker over time. Plus, of course, the madder he got, the stronger he felt. But none of that seemed to cut any ice with the Alpha.

The Alpha had him by the throat, its grip relentlessly strengthening. Lobo grabbed its hand, trying to prize off the huge stone paw. He succeeded only in snapping off one of the stubby crystal fingers. He tried to hold on to it, but a swinging punch thudded into his ear; Lobo lost his grip, and the finger fell to the ground.

It was then Lobo felt his skull begin to prickle, that horrible, maggoty feeling, like mantis worms burrowing into his brain.

Baldy! What have I told ya, ya mind-invadin' bastich? I don't—

Shut up and listen, Lobo, came the Martian's reply, with uncharacteristic vehemence. At the same time, the Alpha's quartz fist slammed into the bounty hunter's mouth. *I suspect the Alpha powers itself via electromagnetism, possibly absorbing it directly from sunlight. If I am right, you can—*

Enough said, dude! The Main Man hears an' understands!

The Alpha had him in a bear hug, straining to crack his spine. Lobo jabbed his thumbs into the empty eye sockets, waggling them around, trying to get a purchase and start ripping off its head.

But thanks to the Martian, now there might be another way.

"Xemtex," Lobo called out suddenly. "Hit it with the EM Disruptor!"

The Spazz-Frag still hovered a dozen or so feet off the ground, its every sensor trained on the battle royal below. Xemtex was enjoying this more than anything since . . . well, since he'd had his brain yanked out. To see Lobo being battered, his blood spilled, made him unspeakably happy.

And now the creep had to go and spoil it all by

ordering him to use the Electromagnetic Disruptor. The disruptor was part of the bike's force field defenses, used for diverting energy beams or circumventing the defense shields of enemy craft. But it could be separated out and fired as a weapon in its own right . . . if the bike's SSCS allowed.

Xemtex was the bike's SSCS. And he was inclined to say, "Go screw yourself with your own hook, Lobo."

For this, of course, was Xemtex's big chance, the break he'd been waiting for—the long-awaited big boom. Both super heroes were out of it—Superman was sprawled unconscious in the junkyard below, and who knew where the Martian was?

Xemtex felt a prickle of pure pleasure shoot through his brain. He imagined screwing up his eyes. The sensors zoomed in on Lobo. Xemtex did that funny little thing inside his head.

"Bye-bye, Bo," he grated cheerfully.

The first blast exploded between Lobo's legs. The bounty hunter's eyes widened. His jaw dropped in shock and he let go his grip of the Alpha.

Xemtex's second blast took him between the shoulder blades, throwing him forward to crack his head on a stripped-out engine block.

Before Lobo could recover, a third blast erupted mere inches away from his head. He slumped as if poleaxed. The Alpha dived on top of him, massive fists raining down flurries of blows on the defenseless bounty hunter.

Within minutes, it was all over.

CHAPTER 22

The hypothalamus in Xemtex's brain was flashing like a lighthouse, pumping out dopamine, infusing every neuron with pleasure.

Lobo was down. The bounty hunter was being hammered to a pulp by ruthless stone fists. There was a loud crack as more of the Main Man's ribs broke. Lobo's blood was gushing from a dozen wounds. Man, it was heaven.

But the disembodied outlaw was careful not to get too carried away. He couldn't afford to be having some kind of mental orgasm; he needed to keep his wits about him. Quietly, he edged the hovering bike farther away.

Blood and gore stained the quartz fists as, at last, the behemoth's blows ceased. Leaving Lobo limp and seemingly lifeless, it rose to its feet and turned to look up at the hovering Spazz-Frag.

"Why?" it asked. *"Why did you attack the Czarnian and not us? Are you a form of machine intelligence?"*

"You could say that," Xemtex blared out through the speakers. "Alternatively—"

While he spoke, Xemtex surreptitiously decoupled the

EMD from the defensive shields and reversed its polarity. All at once, an invisible, intangible vortex of electromagnetic forces enveloped the unsuspecting Alpha. Sparks flashed from its eyes and mouth, and its whole body juddered like an aircraft fuselage in a typhoon.

"*We are . . .*" it began to say. "*We are . . .*"

The Alpha's head began to vibrate slightly, and the sentence was never finished. It toppled over with a cry of what sounded like distress, smashing into and through the hood of a dilapidated hovercraft. It lay there, half inside the car chassis, quivering very faintly.

"Never finished, did I?" Xemtex asked, though if the Alpha was still capable of hearing, it didn't respond. "I was going to say 'Alternatively, I can hit you with the disruptor and take you back for the reward myself.'"

Xemtex started to laugh uproariously, but took special care to ensure the EMD was still active. Lobo was more of a paste than a man. The Alpha was a docile prisoner.

Quarantino's, here I come!

Being an outlaw wasn't so different from being a bounty hunter. But once he picked up that big-bucks recompense, that was it: Xemtex was retired. No more bank robberies, muggings, freight heists, or massacres. And definitely no more bounty hunting.

We are . . .
   What are we . . . ?
   The Alpha is . . .
   First or last?
   Perhaps . . . we are . . .
   Perhaps we are . . . not.

* * *

Every time the Alpha tried to put a coherent thought together, the random nature of the disruptor's frequency switches made it impossible. If it couldn't think, it couldn't act.

And if it couldn't act, it was just another hunk of pretty rock.

Its plans for Universal conquest were gone, now just random noise in an unconnected swarm of neurons.

The Spazz-Frag's audio sensors were picking up something incoming. It was Baldy and Big Blue, blurred streaks in the sky.

"So," Xemtex drawled as they glided down to land in the yard, "the super heroes return. What kept you, guys? I sure could have used your help to subdue the big creep."

Superman and J'onn J'onzz stared first at the collapsed Alpha, Lobo's hook and chain still trailing from its head, and then at the barely breathing body of the bounty hunter.

"You did this?" Superman asked.

"Who else do you see around? Of course I did it," Xemtex lied, carefully blending in enough of the truth so they'd accept his version of events. "The Alpha was pounding Lobo into salad dip. I tried to stop it, blasted it with everything the bike has. It wasn't till I tried the EM Disruptor that something finally worked."

"Then I was right. Electromagnetism can defeat it." The Martian Manhunter strode to Lobo's body and stooped down to examine him. "He is in a bad way," he reported. "He should receive medical attention."

"There isn't a doctor in the galaxy who would come within a mile of Lobo," Xemtex lied again. "They say he has a phobia about medics—reacts very violently to them. But don't you worry about the Main Man. His healing factor will have him back on his feet, cursing and carousing, in no time."

"And you?" Superman wanted to know. "What will you do?"

Xemtex made all the bike's lights flash at once. "Me, I'm on a roll," he drawled cheerfully. "I intend to exchange the Alpha for a large pot of folding green. I'll then exchange a wad of cash for a brand-new body at one of those Gro-Bod transplant shops. Virile, muscular—rippling torso, inflatable pecs. You know, a bit like you guys. But definitely not green. No offense," he added quickly, sensors blinking at the Martian. "Then I'm going on vacation. Quite possibly forever."

A sudden thought struck him; he tried to keep the slyness from his electronic voice as he went on, "Of course, you guys played your part. I'm more than willing to split the cash three ways."

"We don't work for money," Superman said flatly—exactly as Xemtex had known he would. Super heroes were all the same; they *liked* sacrificing themselves for other people, especially when morality rather than money was involved. Their payment was a jolt of nice emotion when the job was done. They must be paupers when they retire. Well, who was he to argue?

"Will the Czarnian not want his share?" the Martian asked.

"Probably. But just like with you, Mr. Mars, Lobo didn't give me the benefit of a trial. He cut my head open like an egg." Xemtex's voice had begun to rise with indignation, but he reined it in. "Anyhow, he was beat. I saved the bastard's life—though who knows why I should have. The way I see it, Lobo owes me big-time. If he can find me, he can have his share."

Superman frowned. "I wouldn't want to be in your shoes if he does find you." He paused, then: "Sorry. Perhaps 'shoes' isn't the best analogy."

"By the time Lobo finds a way off Gallioz," Xemtex said confidently, "I'll be lost in space. Even Lobo isn't dumb enough to waste the rest of his life sniffing the stars and looking for me."

"Very well. The decision is yours," the Martian admitted. He flew up into the air, with Superman following closely behind. "We have work to do here, helping the victims to recover."

Xemtex tried to make his voice sound sorrowful. "I wish I could go with you, guys, but I'm a little short of limbs right now." He sounded the bike's warning alarm, blasting out a racket like a foghorn in a metal canyon. "I'll be thinking of you. See you around."

Not if I can help it, though.

Xemtex waited until they were out of sensor range, then spent a full minute whooping and cheering and laughing like a gurgling drain. He paused, checked to see that the super heroes weren't coming back, then blasted

Lobo's battered body with several more mental explosions.

The unconscious bounty hunter soared twenty feet through the air and landed on a twisted pile of semireclaimed metal. A protruding spike speared his thigh, impaling him.

Xemtex cheered again. He could have spent a week here, just blasting that bastard. Maybe he should give Lobo time to recover a little, let him think his healing factor had him on the mend—then blast the hell out of him all over again.

But if Big Blue and Baldy came back, they wouldn't tolerate that kind of torture. And if the Alpha figured out a way to overcome the disruptor, he'd get creamed. It was better for Xemtex to load up his prisoner and hightail it off Gallioz.

The bike swooped lower. A retractable grapple shot out on the end of a plastiline, securing itself around the Alpha's leg.

"Time to hit the trail, big guy," Xemtex drawled. "And this time, in blessed silence." He was going to burn out the radio circuits so he'd never have to listen to that appalling heavy metal music again.

He visualized himself with a spiffy new body, something that would really turn the babes on. He'd go strutting his stuff at exclusive parties, or maybe mix it with the entertainment crowd at the holomovie premieres. He'd give up beer and start drinking exotic liqueurs flown in from distant worlds.

With a start that was close to being physical, he realized he was going to miss being part of the Spazz-Frag.

Being the Spazz-Frag, in fact. Now that his nerves had settled in and stopped jangling, he found it kind of . . . satisfying. The all-over itch was still there, but even that didn't seem so much of a hassle anymore. In fact, he might even miss it if it wasn't there, the way he might miss a toothache.

No! This is stupid thinking. My nerve cells are becoming part of the bike, that's why I feel this way. I'll need to be careful about this. Hell, if I drop my guard, I could end up as a bike forever!

He was just about to take to the air, trailing his captive, when a cold voice broke in on his troubled thoughts.

"Not so fast, bad boy."

Xemtex groaned. What now? He swiveled his sensors and saw a tall, gaunt figure with bright golden eyes step into the junkyard. He had a gun in each hand, both leveled at the Spazz-Frag.

Kolts, Xemtex couldn't help noting, a relic of his long years as an outlaw with a gun in his own hand.

The stranger was flanked by two manic-looking Khunds. One wielded an electromace, the other a laser knife.

Frantically, Xemtex searched through the bike's data files. There was nothing remotely like these guys in the villain sections. But the information on bounty hunters told him all he needed to know.

"I think you have something that belongs to us," Angel Eyes was saying. "We're here to take it back."

How did you put a civilization back together?

You sped from city to city, using your superbreath to

put out the raging fires. You used your heat vision to blast channels from the ocean into the hearts of the conurbations, providing the emergency services with water. You used your superstrength to demolish unsafe buildings and shore up those that could be saved. You used telepathy to clear clouded minds and return people to their normal state. And everywhere, you rescued those who were in distress.

But as charities on Earth had long since learned, immediate relief was only part of the story. It was far better to enable people to help themselves rather than treat them as helpless victims.

So you targeted the hospitals, making their repair and restoration a prime objective. You ensured that food stores were available and organized supply lines. You helped set up coordination centers, where survivors could be put in touch with their friends and family. You organized the patrols whose grim task it would be to search the ruins for the living and the dead.

And you started the first mass pyres to destroy the bodies that would otherwise putrefy and bring disease.

But even when that was done, the super heroes' task was far from over.

"I think they can take it from here themselves," Superman remarked at last. "They're a resilient people. They can look after themselves now."

"Lobo will be recovering," Manhunter replied. "Perhaps we should check . . . ?"

The Man of Steel shook his head. "Lobo doesn't need

us, and he wouldn't thank us for letting his space bike go. Besides, we still have another problem to solve."

J'onn J'onzz looked at him blankly for a moment before he realized: "Vrk," he said unhappily. "The creatures I contacted there were not so far gone as the pilots and troops. It may be possible to save them."

"And if not . . . ?"

The Martian's eyes were grim under his craggy brows. "I do not want to know the answer to that."

CHAPTER 23

Xemtex figured he was on the horns of a dilemma. And both horns were more than sharp enough to impale his metaphorical behind.

He'd used up all the reserves, and now the Spazz-Frag was totally out of ammunition. He couldn't disconnect the EM Disruptor without freeing the Alpha—so the bike had no defense shield. His only options were to hand the Alpha over to the bounty hunters . . . or to blast their sorry butts.

A man of action to the last, Xemtex chose the latter.

He concentrated hard, using the bike's sensors to pinpoint his targets. For a fraction of a second, the air just in front of the bounty hunters seemed to ripple. Then it exploded.

Angel Eyes' reactions were faster than any Xemtex had ever seen. In the split second when the air rippled, he already seemed to size up the threat. He somersaulted backward. As he landed, he threw himself into a roll, further distancing himself from the ensuing explosion.

Randan the Khund was big and tough, but lightness on

his feet wasn't one of his talents. The explosion took him full in the abdomen, ripping open his flesh. He stared down in disbelief as a large proportion of his intestines lurched out of the gaping wound and fell to the ground with a sickening squelch. Randan's eyes glazed over. His knees buckled, and he pitched forward in a heap on top of his own steaming guts.

"Randan!" his brother Virt cried in shock.

They can bury you both in the same grave, Xemtex thought, and prepared to blast again. There was something kind of appealing about killing two brothers on the same day. Especially when they were stinking bounty dogs out to steal his rightful property.

By now, Angel Eyes had dived behind a hummock of scrap metal, opening fire with both guns. A dozen shots crashed into the Spazz-Frag, most of them ricocheting harmlessly off. But two of the external cameras were hit, disintegrating into junk.

Damn and blast them! Xemtex cursed. Both of the smashed sensors were front-mounted, meaning that his view of the bounty hunters was now severely compromised. And if he couldn't see them properly, he couldn't blow them up.

Angel Eyes squeezed off another few rounds at him. The other Khund had crawled away when his brother fell, but Xemtex could see—albeit through a blur—that he was on his way back. And he was carrying the biggest bazooka Xemtex had seen since the psychodroid's pipe gun.

Virt raised the firing tube to his shoulder. "I'm going to

show you what happens to bikes that kill my brother," the Khund said, between clenched teeth.

Xemtex imagined his finger starting to tighten on the trigger and braced himself for the impact that could only be a split second away.

Guess I made the wrong choice, he figured resignedly. *Wonder what kind of afterlife is reserved for bike-brains . . . ?*

But the Khund froze instantly as an authoritative voice called out, "Do not hit the bike!"

A previously unseen figure stepped out into the open, partly visible on the bike's lateral sensors. One hand was held aloft, its bony fingers tracing strangely hypnotic patterns in the air.

The Arcturan: According to the bike's data bank, he was the fourth—and most powerful—member of Angel Eyes' gang.

Because of the broken cameras, Xemtex could only get a partial view. But what the hell? He might as well take a crack at the new guy, too.

Only, when he tried to focus and produce an explosion, nothing happened.

"My magic decrees your resistance is over," the Arcturan said tonelessly. "You will remain immobile until I say otherwise."

Looks like the bastard's right, Xemtex thought grimly. *I can't move!*

"He killed my brother," Virt said huffily. "He deserves to die."

K'Baal gestured toward the figure of the Alpha. The stone giant lay unmoving, still held by the bike's robotic grabber arm. "The bike has the Alpha encaged in a disruptor field. Any damage to the bike might set it free."

"So what?" Virt snarled. "We blow up the bike, then we blow up the Alpha. It's clear as daylight to me."

The Khund must have taken the Arcturan's silence to signify assent. He cradled the huge gun against his shoulder, snicked off the safety catch and chambered a six-inch shell.

Weird what folks think when they're only seconds from eternal oblivion. *Good-bye, cruel world* was the phrase that zipped around Xemtex's brain. And it *had* been a cruel world, too. Locked up as a kid, as an adult disembodied by a maniac. Maybe he was better off out of the whole shebang.

"Virt, I said do not hit the bike."

"Screw you, warlock," the Khund snarled. "Sometimes magic has to take a backseat to a very big bang."

What happened next took them all by surprise. Especially Virt.

The Arcturan made a jabbing motion toward the Khund with one hand. Even as Virt's clawed finger tightened on the trigger, his head exploded in a gory bloom of brains and bone.

Blood spurted from his neck. He fell beside his brother, staining the ground red around them.

Aw hell. Xemtex's spirits sank even lower. *If he can do that to his own pals, what the devil's he going to do to me?*

Angel Eyes had come out of cover. He holstered his guns, his golden eyes flashing as he glared at K'Baal.

The Arcturan lowered his head. "I apologize for Virt's death. But there was no other way."

"A simple paralysis spell would have done the trick," Angel Eyes suggested. "It would have been easier on Virt, too."

"It was not possible while I still hold the bike in thrall."

"Anyhow, I thought you said you could take the Alpha?" Angel Eyes asked.

"I did. And I believe I could have." The Arcturan's voice softened. "But was it not you who said this is no time to be running risks?"

Angel Eyes shrugged. "Guess we split the bounty two ways, then."

The bounty-hunters' needleship had landed unseen during the climactic battle between Lobo and the Alpha. The Arcturan's occult senses told him immediately what was going on. It was Angel Eyes' decision that they should bide their time, let the others exhaust or kill themselves, then step in and pick up the pieces.

A very successful strategy, as it had turned out. Although the loss of both of the Khunds still rankled with Angel Eyes.

Now, he loped off with long strides to where they'd hidden their ship. He'd seen Superman and the Martian Manhunter leave on their mission to rebuild the planet. They could return at any time and he'd rather be off-world if they did. Not that they had any beef with him and K'Baal, of course; it was just that he'd prefer to get this sewn up sooner rather than later.

Angel Eyes popped open a hatch and stooped as he entered. He sealed it behind him and made his way up the short, narrow corridor to the cabin-cum–flight deck.

"Lobo?" He heard Darlene's voice, muffled by the cupboard they'd locked her in. "Is that you, Lobo?"

"No," he snapped.

He slid the bolt out of its fastener and pulled the door open. Darlene came spilling out, her eyes red from crying.

"Where is he?" she demanded hoarsely. "Where's Lobo?"

Angel Eyes scowled darkly. "Lobo is pizza topping, honey. Roadkill. Seems he wasn't tough enough for the Alpha. The guy stomped him real good—good enough to kill him, I'd say."

"Liar!" Darlene screamed. She threw herself forward, her hands stretching up to rake her long fingernails down Angel Eyes' cheek.

The bounty hunter cursed and grabbed both her wrists in his strong hands. He could feel tiny weals of blood trickle down his face.

"Listen, you fool," he spat at her. "We made a mistake bringing you here. You were supposed to be our insurance that Lobo did what we wanted—but you weren't needed. So calm down, and we'll take you right back home again."

"I don't want to go home," Darlene retorted hotly. "I want Lobo!"

She managed to tear one hand free and curled her fingers to strike again. This time Angel Eyes was ready for her. His hand lashed out in a backhand slap that caught

Darlene hard across the face. He grabbed her roughly by one arm and bundled her back into the cupboard.

"Lobo can't be dead," she was saying, as he slammed the door closed and rammed home the bolt. "He'll come for you! I know he will!"

"Yeah, yeah," Angel Eyes muttered. He punched the door hard with the heel of his hand. "You shut up now, or maybe I'll just forget that I'm a gentleman. Would you rather be waiting table in the diner or lying on a slab in the morgue?"

Darlene said nothing and the bounty hunter eased himself into the control seat. It would be simpler all around if they could just kill her now and dump her body in space. But he and K'Baal had their licenses to consider; the manhunting fraternity might be a rough and ready lot, but generally they had to stay within the law. If any innocent citizens got hurt during an operation, it was likely to end in police involvement, heavy financial penalties, and, more than likely, jail.

Angel Eyes sighed, checking all recent news broadcasts on the comm-system as he fired up the atomic motors. Good news. So far the bounty on the Alpha was half a million credits . . . and rising.

They were going to be rich.

With long-practiced skill, Angel Eyes landed the ship directly in the junkyard—which really was a junkyard now. The fights had destroyed almost everything there.

He and K'Baal hurriedly transferred the Alpha to their craft, using the ship's own EM Disruptor to keep the creature secure. It would mean they would be without defense shields on the return trip to Quarantino's, but that wouldn't matter. They were hardly likely to come under attack.

Strange, Angel Eyes thought, halfheartedly kicking the Alpha's crystal hide as they winched it aboard. *The thing must weigh five tons, easy . . . yet all it takes to cripple it is random jolts of electromagnetism.*

"What about that?" the Arcturan asked, once the Alpha was safely aboard. He was looking up at the still-hovering, motionless Spazz-Frag.

Angel Eyes stroked his chin, and his bright eyes narrowed thoughtfully. "Lobo will put himself back together sooner or later. The last thing we want is for him to find transport."

"Leave it to me."

A few minutes later, the needleship was rising back into the air. The Arcturan stood by an ob window, gesturing with one hand.

Bastard, Xemtex thought sourly. Powerless to resist K'Baal's magic, the bike rose, too, keeping pace with the larger craft.

They were about a mile up when the needleship slowed and K'Baal's gestures ceased. Xemtex knew what was coming next and it wasn't a million credits. The Arcturan waved to him, coyly—saying good-bye.

The Spazz-Frag plunged down nose first, engines on maximum overdrive, twin turbos wailing like banshees, its speed increasing with every second. Through the damaged sensors, Xemtex had a blurry vision of the junkyard rushing up to meet him. He could see the speck that was

Lobo's body still lying in the wreckage, getting larger all the time.

He struggled to reestablish control of the plummeting bike, but to no avail. Magic said he was going to crash, and yes, he was going to crash.

Ah well, Xemtex comforted himself, *at least I get to take out the Main Man . . . again. That's some kind of achievement, I guess, even if nobody will ever know about it.*

For the briefest of moments, he had the strangest of impulses. For perhaps only the second time in his life, he felt like praying.

Then Spazz-Frag met junkyard, with Lobo's body directly intervening.

It wasn't pretty for any of them.

"I never thought I'd see this place again," Superman commented as he and the Manhunter arced down toward the entrance to Vrk's subterranean depths.

The duo had wasted no time, traveling back from Gallioz just as fast as they'd gone there. Now, with no Alpha to worry about, they swooped at maximum speed through the giant gateway and headed into the planetoid's interior.

Far below the surface, the Vrkn work gangs were still hollowing out and refining what was to have been the tiny world's engine room, as the Alpha turned it into its mobile base. The small, misshapen creatures from one work detail paused, staring in consternation as Superman and Manhunter landed close to them.

"This next part's all yours, J'onn," Superman told his companion. "I can't help with the deprogramming."

The Man of Steel cast his gaze around the chamber,

taking in the sculpted-stone pipework, the arrays of crystal electron batteries, and the mysterious chiplike carvings. It looked like his first guess—that they were religious symbols—was wrong. They were actually circuitry components. Their purpose was way beyond Superman's comprehension of science— but he knew that, because they were designed by the Alpha, they could only have been created for evil ends.

"I don't think we should leave them intact," he decided. "If you take the Vrkns to the main chamber, I'll see to what must be done."

A short while later, all of the Vrks remaining on the planetoid had gathered in the largest chamber. There were only a few thousand of them, the rest presumably having been taken by the Alpha for the invasion of Gallioz. They chittered quietly at each other, their excitable little voices subdued.

J'onn J'onzz hovered in the air before them, hoping beyond hope that the Alpha's control of them wasn't so great that he couldn't set them free. He gathered his thoughts and tried to focus his telepathic powers on the whole crowd—but to no avail. Their minds were similar, their programming by the Alpha almost identical, but *en masse* he knew the task was beyond him.

His eyes combed the sea of faces until he found what he was looking for: the three Vrkns who had helped in the escape. The mere fact that they had repaid their debt to him meant that they would be more susceptible to his mental suggestions.

The trio stepped forward suspiciously and the others

cleared a path as they made their way to the front of the chamber, taking up positions directly beneath J'onn.

The Manhunter said a silent prayer to his grandfather, closed his eyes, and let his mind reach out . . .

Meanwhile, Superman was making his way slowly through the caverns and tunnels, utilizing his heat vision to melt or rupture every structure that the Vrkns had built. Several of the larger constructions resisted the heat and only by alternating with his frigid superbreath was he able to shatter them.

By the time he was finished, nobody would ever again be able to use the place for destructive purposes.

Had his movements not been so slow and deliberate, he would have missed it: a large niche in the crystal wall, cunningly cut at an oblique angle so as to be almost undetectable to the casual glance.

Puzzled, Superman walked through, noting that it was the same height as the other tunnels—in other words, it had been cut to fit the Alpha's frame. There was a passageway that extended for some thirty feet before it opened out into a larger chamber.

A single block of crystal had been shaped into a cube that stood four feet high. A black obsidian crystal screen stood atop it. It took Superman mere seconds to realize: *It's a computer!*

CHAPTER 24

The island-city was called Halfwayville, tragically apt in light of the fact only half of it was left standing. Much of that had been in flames until the two superbeings doused them.

Hundreds of teams of volunteers combed what was left of the streets in the desperate search for survivors. Literally thousands of corpses had been dug out of the debris of collapsed buildings; thousands more who were injured had been ferried to the makeshift hospitals Superman and the Martian Manhunter had set up.

The rescue party hadn't been going to search the junkyard at first. The destruction there was so complete, nobody could have survived. But one of the dogs had heard something, and it barked and strained at its leash until its handler relented. Following the dog, he climbed in through a huge rent in one wall and marveled at what he saw.

In the middle of the junkyard was a thirty-foot-deep crater, wisps of smoke still drifting up from its charred sides. At the bottom of it, the body of a man lay under the twisted remains of what looked like a space bike. The man was trying to push off the wrecked bike that pinned him to the crater floor, but he was obviously too weak.

As the handler got closer, he could hear the man saying something over and over again. It sounded like: "Fragfragfragfragfragfrag!"

The dog's ears pricked up, and its hackles rose; it crouched low on its belly and started to growl. "Hey, Fido," the voice called, "come on down here. I'm fraggin' ravenous!"

"Hey," the handler cried in recognition, gesturing to the other rescuers to join him. "There's somebody here. It's Lobo—one of the guys who fought the invaders. He's still alive!"

Not only was the Main Man still alive, he was beginning to get mighty angry with people blasting the tar out of him every time he started to recover. With a final effort, he shoved the bike aside and scrambled into a semiupright position.

"What do you guys want?" he snarled, looking up at the circle of alien faces peering over the crater rim. The rescuers froze in their tracks. "Take a powder, or yer next meal will be a bounty hunter's boot."

The dog whimpered and moved closer to its handler's legs. Somebody stepped forward, braver than the rest, and explained they were here to rescue the bounty hunter.

"I don't need to be rescued," Lobo sneered. "Folks need rescuin' from *me*."

His strength was flowing back by the second, as the healing factor in his blood activated cell regeneration, bone repair, and new skin growth. He took a deep, deep breath and drew himself up to his full height. His eyebrows furrowed in a frown. Something bothered him, but he couldn't quite put his finger on what.

Hm. Don't remember no crater when I flaked out. Maybe that's it.

The Spazz-Frag's titanium frame lay next to him, grotesquely twisted out of shape. The bike's engines were embedded deep in the crater wall, possibly protecting them from too much damage. If any of the other components had survived, they were too small for him to see. What the frag had happened?

He raised his eyes to the rim again. "Do you geeks do space travel?"

"No," came the reply. "We haven't invented it yet, and under Galactic Convention other worlds aren't allowed to help us develop the technol—"

"Yadda yadda yadda," Lobo said rudely. "What yer tellin' me is, I'm stuck on this pitiful mudball for the foreseeable future?"

There was a chorus of yesses and a near-inaudible comment, "Gallioz isn't a mudball."

"It won't be too bad," the dog handler called down. "You're a hero. You saved untold thousands of people from a horrible death. We'll treat you like a god. In fact," the man went on, warming to his theme. "You could even become the Official Hero of Gallioz, or something like that. You could protect us, save us when we needed it—"

Lobo jammed his forefingers in his ears. "Shuddup, ya clown," he roared. "Yer makin' me barf! Lobo—a hero? Bite me!"

Some of the rescuers were starting to scramble down the crater sides, although he noticed the dog handler was hanging back. That was a pity; the mutt looked pretty tasty.

One of the women skidded down the last few yards and landed next to him. She pulled a flask from inside her coat.

"What's that?" Lobo asked suspiciously.

"High-energy glucose drink," she explained. "It'll help you recover."

Disdainfully, Lobo shook his head. "Now, if it was a high-alcohol booze drink . . ." he suggested.

The woman looked blank. "Alcohol? Is that a species of fruit? We don't have any on Gallioz, I'm afraid."

"Surprise me." He hawked and spat at the woman's feet. She jumped back so fast, she almost stumbled. "Tell ya what, pruneface," he went on. "If ya really want to help me, there is somethin' ya can do."

She nodded, eager to please. "Anything for a hero."

"Right. I want ya to comb this crater an' the junk-yard—if there's anythin' left of it. Yer lookin' for bits of my space hog. I got the owner's manual here some-place . . ." He reached into his back pocket and carefully extracted a charred, crumpled, dog-eared, and beer-stained pamphlet. "It's got pictures. It'll help ya recognize the bits."

The woman took it from his outstretched hand as if he were passing her something the dog had expelled. She un-folded it slowly, but even so a tattered corner gave up the ghost and dropped off.

"Watch it," Lobo snapped. "I want that back in good condition."

The Semisentient Control System is in many ways the most important part of a Spazz Frag. So important that the brain unit itself is sealed inside a half-inch-thick titanium casing, guaranteed by the manufacturer to withstand anything short of a ten-kiloton nuclear blast or your money back (if you survive).

It was found by the dog, a good hundred yards from the junkyard, and returned to Lobo. He patted its head and called it "good boy," but when he asked the handler if he knew how to cook a canine stew, man and dog fled.

Some big cheese literary guy once said: "Music hath the charms to soothe the savage breast." Whether it was Shakespeare or one of the Fugs, he'd obviously never met Lobo. The music Lobo liked—heavy fraggin' metal, the heavier the better, like twenty thousand tons' worth of heavy—drove him into a kill-frenzy. But the music he didn't like—which included almost everything else, but especially soul music—also drove him into a kill-frenzy.

So when the prune-faced woman turned on a portable radio and the Main Man's ears were assailed by classical junk, she was lucky to get her head out of the way before his fist reduced the radio to around a hundred separate components.

He'd been working on the bike for hours now. The Gallioz geeks had set up a workbench and welding unit against a section of junkyard wall that was still standing. The only times he'd looked up from welding, screwing (machine parts), and hammering was to eat—and obliterate the radio.

There were few things in life Lobo could be said to love: boozing, brawling, babes, and metal music just about summed it up. But the Spazz-Frag was in there, too, someplace. He'd had this machine for years, had customized it, dismantled it, and rebuilt it a dozen times. Any maintenance he couldn't do himself, he always made sure the workshop owner knew the price of screwing up. He depended on that bike, and when you depend on something, you look after it.

Or at least learn to fix it when it's broke.

At last, it was as ready as he'd ever be able to make it.

Lobo wiped grimy perspiration from his brow with the back of a grease-spattered hand and stood back for the panoramic view.

The Spazz-Frag was a surrealist's nightmare compared with the gleaming, beautiful original. The fire-blackened frame and handlebars were as straight as he could get them—which was pretty crooked, actually. One handlebar was missing entirely. There was no console or monitor. Half of the side farings had gone, presumably disintegrated, and there weren't a whole lot of functioning sensors, either. And he still didn't know what had caused it.

The miniaturized nuclear engines had survived almost intact, blown into the soft soil of the crater wall. He cleaned them with a steam jet and kept his fingers crossed that the holding tanks hadn't been breached. Otherwise, a significant portion of Halfwayville might disappear when he switched on.

The SSCS was in place. Its casing was gouged and dented, but the bounty hunter had rewired all the connections. Feetal alone knew what condition Xemtex would be in, but Lobo didn't give a rat's behind about the ex-outlaw as long as the unit functioned.

He'd found his gun, which unfortunately only had a single charge left in it. Gallioz technology was nowhere near advanced enough for them to help him out there; until he reached civilization, he'd be only one shot away from firing blanks. His hook and chain were gone, possibly still impaled in the Alpha's skull—and the Alpha was missing, too.

He couldn't see bleeding hearts like Baldy or Big Blue pulling a stunt like this. Something else must have happened. But what?

A small crowd gathered to watch as he straddled the Spazz-Frag, gashing his thigh on a jagged outcrop of metal. He hit the ignition and nodded with satisfaction when the engines fired.

It was when he shook his head, throwing back his mane of unkempt hair, that he suddenly realized what had been evading him: a scent.

Delicately, he sniffed at the air, automatically sifting out the smells of the Gallioz rescuers—the dog—the super heroes. Who else? The Alpha, sure, the air reeked of crystal. Who else?

A man's scent, one he should know but couldn't place. Why not? His memory was infallible when it came to smells, even when he had a black hole of a hangover. Anyway, he felt like he hadn't touched booze for months.

Then there was the faintest trace of a woman's scent: a

delicate hint of lilac in morning sunlight. Icy fingers churned his gut. Darlene.

Darlene had been here.

"Awright, Xemtex," he snorted. "Do yer stuff."

Xemtex didn't.

"Wake up!" Lobo jabbed the extrapotent jolt circuit he'd added to the bike. "I know yer okay, ya bastich," he cursed. "Trust me, I'm a mechanic."

"Zzzt."

Nope, that didn't make sense. Xemtex tried again. *"Wazzt?"*

A stone-hard voice was yelling at him, trying to rouse him from the beautiful, all-encompassing darkness. Xemtex clung to the comforting, satin-black nothingness. He'd been lost in a dream of nothing at all. It was great.

"Get yer stinkin' butt in gear, ya lazy dork. The Alpha's got Darlene . . . and we're gonna get her back!"

Lobo. I might have known. That creep's indestructible. But . . . how am I still here? Last thing I remember was the big boom. I'm back in the bike, too . . .

His senses reached out to explore his surroundings and he realized it was a vastly different bike he now inhabited. In fact, it was a scrap heap.

"Izzatso?" Xemtex's voice grated and distorted as it whined through the jury-rigged speaker system. "This isn't a Spazz-Frag. It's a death trap. I can't take this junk heap into space."

Finger jabbed.

Electricity flowed.

Xemtex screamed.

Then he got his butt in gear.

* * *

The crowd of people waved and cheered as the resurrected space bike rose off the ground. It hung in the air for a moment, wobbling precariously, then shot off into sky.

Their hero was gone.

Secretly, the handler and the prune-faced woman were relieved.

The dog barked happily for hours.

"Do you know how to operate it?" J'onn J'onzz asked.

The Martian had mentally deprogrammed the three Vrkns who'd helped them, hoping that if they were able to talk to their brethren in their own tongue, the whole task would be accomplished much faster. And he'd been right. Even as he worked on the others mentally, the trio babbled away to them, explaining in the Vrkn language what had been going on.

It took barely half an hour before all of the Vrkns were free agents again—at least, as free as they had ever been.

Then J'onn had received Superman's telepathic broadcast and hurried down to the labyrinth of chambers on the lower levels.

Now, he and Superman stood in front of the crystal computer. A scattering of small boreholes in the chamber ceiling allowed a dozen or so narrow shafts of sunlight to play over the alien console.

"The Alpha itself operated via electromagnetic fields," Superman said thoughtfully. "My guess is, this has to be the same."

"I see nothing that looks like a keyboard or input

control," Manhunter remarked. He glanced up at the ceiling, and his eyes narrowed under his thick brows. "Perhaps," he said slowly, "those columns of light are the controls."

"I don't see how." Superman shook his head. "None of them are falling on what I take to be the hard drive."

"Not right now, they aren't," J'onn corrected him. He pointed to several small, shutterlike flanges he'd noticed and reached up toward one. "But if I do this—"

He twisted one of the small, flat crystals through ninety degrees. The shaft of sunlight ricocheted off it and was redirected to the center of the top of the cube. The monitor screen glitched and flickered into life.

"That's it switched on, obviously," Superman said. "Perhaps if we manipulate the others, we can coax it into revealing what data it holds."

The Martian twisted another flange and images began to dance across the screen . . .

The bike flashed through the cosmos, with only the merest glitch in its protective force field betraying its delicate condition.

I'd forgotten how majestic all this is, Xemtex was thinking, although cracked and missing visuals didn't afford much of a view. He'd been quiet since they left Gallioz's atmosphere, just watching the endless vista of stars—and preparing his answer for Lobo's inevitable question.

"What the frag happened back there?"

The lies rolled off Xemtex's tongue like honey off a stick. "I didn't mean to blast you when you were fighting the Alpha. My sensors were damaged, so I couldn't aim properly."

He hoped the bounty hunter's silence was a good omen.

"Anyway," he rushed on, "by the time I managed to zap the big guy, he'd already creamed you. So there's me, trying to wake you up, playing heavy metal music at five hundred decibels, and not a whisper from you."

Xemtex paused again, waiting for some encouragement. None was forthcoming.

"Next thing I know, I got Angel Eyes and his gang—"

"Angel Eyes?" Lobo asked, so sharply he could have dropped a bird in flight. "The bounty hunter?"

"Sure. Didn't you know?" Xemtex pretended to be surprised. "They started blasting me—and you, too, I have to say. I managed to take out two of them, a pair of Khunds. But the Arcturan wizard put the whammy on me. That's what caused the explosion. They made me dive for ground zero from way above the clouds."

"Right on top of me?"

"I'm really sorry."

"I bet you are."

"You think I'd have done that willingly?"

"Yeah," Lobo replied gruffly. "I do."

"Come on, Lobo—what else do I have to do to win your trust?" Xemtex wheedled. "We're on the same side now. Partners, you could say."

"No, I couldn't," the bounty hunter blasted back at him. "You don't seem to realize, birdbrain—you ain't Xemtex anymore. Yer a *bike*. Now, who in their right mind do *you* know that would partner up with a bike, for frag's sake?"

"I guess when you put it like that . . ."

Xemtex let his tinny voice trail away. No point getting the bounty hunter's back up. He hadn't returned to life just to let Lobo shock him back into oblivion. He'd been given a second chance, an opportunity not afforded to a lot of people. It was his duty to make the most of it this time around. He'd relax, take time to look at the stars, maybe even think some deep thoughts.

A good ex-outlaw was always flexible, always ready to accommodate a change in plans. He'd let Lobo kill Angel Eyes and pick up the reward. Then, when he'd gained Lobo's trust just enough . . .

Ka-boom!

Bye-bye, Main Man, bring on the body shop.

Although, now he came to think of it, parties and premieres didn't really seem so desirable. Maybe he'd become an astronomer, instead.

CHAPTER 25

"What the frag's the matter with ya, Xemtex?" Lobo slapped the fire-blackened bike frame in frustration. The reconstructed Spazz-Frag had been limping along at way below top speed for hours. "It's gonna take us *years* to get there at this rate! Angel Eyes an' that rat fink K'Baal will have pocketed my loot an' blown for another galaxy. An' Feetal alone knows what they'll do with Darlene. Ya gotta perk things up."

That was the scent Lobo had been unable to place at the junkyard: the Arcturan. The creep probably used magic to disguise his trail.

"If I go any faster," Xemtex grated, "the bike'll shake itself to pieces."

Lobo found Xemtex's voice even more irritating now that the speakers weren't working properly. It sounded like a demented version of the automated announcements he heard in every spaceport—the kind where you were never able to make out what the frag they'd said. The kind you wanted to silence with a fist in the kisser.

But he tamped down his irritation; right now he needed

Xemtex onside. "Listen, my newfound friend, my good ol' buddy," the bounty hunter said affably. "There's only one way we can catch up with these geeks. We gotta take a shortcut. Check out the star maps, okay?"

There were a few desultory flashes from an LED. "Half the navigation system's missing," Xemtex reminded him, "but I have enough here to see there's no shortcut." There was a short pause. "Well, there's one." There was a longer pause. "But nobody's stupid enough to use it."

"We are. An' the word's 'brave,' not 'stupid.'"

The speaker whined. "Not Reubenz's Black Hole?"

"The very same, dude."

A black hole was an area of space created by a collapsing giant star, where gravity went wild. Anything in the vicinity was sucked in by the black hole's irresistible attraction.

Kinda like Darlene an' me, the Main Man ruminated, though he didn't say it aloud. In fact, the center of the black hole was so dense, even light got sucked in and couldn't escape. So nobody could ever see into a black hole to find out what was there.

"But the scientists say black holes are suicide," Xemtex protested. "Right in the center is what they call a singularity. That's a point so dense, a simple can of booze would weigh the same as eight or nine galaxies."

"How can a point weigh anything?" Lobo shot back.

"The scientists—"

"The scientists," Lobo said, picking his words carefully, "are idiots. They also say ninety percent of everythin' is dark matter, right? You can't see it, feel it, touch it, measure it or even shake a stick at it. Now you an' me have been travelin' the space-lanes for years. Did *you* ever bump into any dark matter?"

"I guess not," Xemtex admitted. "I bumped into a few angry husbands, an' the law more often than I liked. Never any dark matter."

"But if nine out of every ten objects in space are dark matter," Lobo went on, "it stands to reason we'd be trippin' over nine of them when we tried to get to the one object that *wasn't* dark matter. Right?"

"You're giving me a headache, Einstein," Xemtex complained.

But Lobo was just starting to hit his stride. "Another example: scientists say the Universe was created by a Big Bang, right? Now, you an' me have fired a lot of guns, tossed our share of grenades. We've caused a whole boatload of explosions."

"What's your point?"

"Did you ever see an explosion create *anything*?" the bounty hunter asked. "I mean, all of *my* explosions blew things to fraggin' smithereens. Like, none of them even created somethin' *simple*—like knuckledusters, say. Or a shrumpburger."

"You should have been a professor, Bo," Xemtex told him, his tone halfway between ironic admiration and "what the hell's a shrumpburger got to do with the birth of the cosmos?" "I can't argue with that kind of logic."

"Good. Debate's over, anyway. Point proved: Scientists are idiots." Lobo punched air and whooped triumphantly. "Reubenz, here we come!"

* * *

Reubenz's Black Hole was a beautiful, if frightening, sight to behold.

It revolved slowly around a central axis, with a hazy area about halfway between the outer circumference and the singularity at its center. This was the Schwarzchild radius; beyond this point, nothing could ever escape the black hole's gravity well. Fall through the radius and you'd be falling forever. Not that you'd care a whole lot, because you'd be compressed to a red splodge about the size of the average zit.

"Suicide," Xemtex wailed as the Spazz-Frag approached the maelstrom in space. "We might as well switch off the force fields and suck vacuum."

"Don't be such a wuss," Lobo scolded. "The way I figure it, we go in at an oblique angle, plow through the outer regions an' hit the radius at a tangent. It'll be a gas. If we're clever enough, we'll bounce off at the right angle—only movin' approximately ten times faster."

There was a sudden flash of light from the black hole's interior as gravity overcame and disintegrated some chunk of matter. Only, the light didn't expand out toward them. It sort of inverted itself and disappeared below the radius.

Xemtex gulped, sounding like a robot chicken. "I'm not going," he said adamantly. "And you can't make me."

"Do the words 'electricity' an' 'jolt' awaken any dormant memories?"

"Do your worst. I'm not going."

Lobo didn't need to do his worst. On a scale of one to ten, he figured it was about a seven.

"How ya feelin', dude?"

" . . ."

"That sounded like 'obedient' to me. Now set course an' do yer thang."

The Spazz-Frag dutifully sped toward its date with destiny.

Every bounty hunter on the station turned out to watch Angel Eyes and the Arcturan bring in the Alpha. It wasn't every day you got to see a villain with a million on his scalp.

Quarantino had arranged for a self-powered neural net to be ready for the needleship's arrival. Once they'd wrapped the Alpha in that, its random bursts of electromagnetism would nullify any patterns the artificial intelligence might try to set up. A tracked minicrane transported it to the station's holding tanks, where it would be kept till the Galactic Police came to pick it up for trial.

"He ain't so big as I thought he'd be." A leathery-skinned Cepheid with a hooked beak snorted disdainfully. "My mother-in-law could have brought that chump in."

"I thought it *was* your mother-in-law," Angel Eyes said coldly. "If you think it so easy, maybe we should switch off the net—"

"Don't even joke about such things," Quarantino interrupted. "I get paranoid enough as it is, with monsters like that on my station."

"Hold your water," Angel Eyes scoffed.

The Alpha was pitched unceremoniously into the strongest of the holding cells, which also had a backup disruptor built into the walls. Even if the artificial intelligence somehow managed to subvert the neural net, the backup would ensure it stayed in a random state.

The electronic door had barely hissed into place when Angel Eyes turned to Quarantino. The smaller man didn't wait to be asked.

"You'll be pleased to hear the reward is up to a million. It's in the strong room. This way."

The golden eyes sparkled like miniature suns as Quarantino led them through a maze of corridors until their way was blocked by a meshwork of laser beams that extended from floor to ceiling.

The bounty agent operated a small control pad set in the wall, waiting while it identified his fingerprints. The lasers disappeared abruptly.

"A necessary precaution," Quarantino explained, as he beckoned them to follow him. He jerked a thumb back in the direction of the bar. "Too many of these greedy freaks would rather steal the bounty than earn it. No offense," he added quickly.

"None taken," Angel Eyes shrugged. "I'm a greedy freak myself."

The bounty agent approached a bank of steel drawers held in the confines of a stasis beam. "Now, how d'you want the cash? Bearer bonds? Guaranteed no-trace check? Electronic transfer to the bank and planet of your choice? Green stamps?"

"Cash sounded good to me." Angel Eyes saw the agent's mouth open, about to protest, and went swiftly on, "Don't tell me you don't have it. A job like the Alpha, you'd want to be absolutely certain of getting your cut."

"You're very astute. Cash it is."

Quarantino killed the beam and the bank of drawers settled smoothly to the floor. "There's a hundred thou in each of them. You get eight, I take two." He stood aside. "You'll need to lug them yourselves. These suckers are heavy."

The Arcturan's presence had barely been noted; he'd stuck to the shadows, enveloped in the confines of his hood, inscrutable. But now he snapped his fingers, once.

Eight of the metal drawers levitated into the air. The bounty hunters turned and walked away, Pied Pipers leading a line of floating cash.

We . . . Alpha.
Alpha are . . .
First.
Last.
Alpha . . . ?

It had taken them a while, but at last Superman and Martian Manhunter had worked out how to alter the shafts of sunlight sufficiently for them to be able to access the computer's data banks in sequence.

What they found there astonished them. The Alpha had downloaded its entire life story.

It was the story of a planet called Colu, whose people trusted emotion so little, they put their faith—and their fate—in the hands of machines. A network of computers observed and monitored and analyzed every aspect of society, every sentient interaction and every word that was spoken.

As time went by, the machines arrogated more and

more of the decision-making. People thought the computers knew best.

Inevitably, one day the computers *did* know best.

The network rearranged society so it ran according to the network's rules. Sentient beings were emotional and irrational; they needed to be told what to do. Obedience was paramount. If the people didn't obey, the computers punished them—with imprisonment, or torture, or death. Termination of organic life was no big deal; it always replaced itself.

Through the application of impeccable logic, service evolved into tyranny.

For centuries, none dared disobey the computer tyrants . . . until eventually the people forgot what disobedience was. Society ran smoothly, like a well-oiled machine. There was no war. There was no crime.

No creativity. No spontaniety.

No hope.

There was only tomorrow, that was the same as today, that was the same as yesterday.

Superman heaved a sigh. "A whole planet ruled by machines. And they did it willingly."

"There's nothing so perverse as life," J'onn J'onzz agreed.

When a closed system settles into equilibrium, only an outside force can bring change. Change came to Colu in the shape of a galactic law enforcement agency—a band of superpowered misfits who mouthed off about freedom and dignity. They refused to obey the computers.

When the tyrants tried to kill them, the cops fought back. And when the going got tough, the weapons went nuclear.

The computer tyrants of Colu—the cumulative result of millennia of artificial intelligence—were blasted into atomic oblivion.

"Incredible." Superman shook his head. "The computers were destroyed—yet somehow their intelligence survived."

"Perhaps as neurons—bits of information," the Martian theorized. "Even if they'd been blown apart over hundreds of square miles, it might only take something simple—like a flash of lightning—to give them sufficient energy to begin to regroup."

"To become the Alpha." Superman nodded. "It must have learned from its past mistake. Organic life is just too troublesome if you try to control it so—"

"The Alpha decided to wipe out *all* life," Manhunter finished for him. "A sort of preemptive strike . . . on the entire Universe." He bowed his head slightly. "I can only thank my ancestors that it was stopped in time."

"Amen to that," Superman said somberly. "Can you imagine anything more tragic than a dead Universe, where the only true life that exists is in the form of Last Sons and Daughters? The sole survivors of their respective races, kept as specimens in a zoological laboratory for analysis and study?"

"No," Manhunter replied simply. "I cannot."

* * *

No discussion was necessary; they knew what they had to do. Standing shoulder to shoulder, as they had so often in the past, the Martian and the Kryptonian employed their super-vision.

Within minutes, the quartz computer was a large, spreading pool of sluggish, red-hot liquid.

"I'm reporting you, you just wait and see!"

Angel Eyes had forgotten all about Darlene until he and K'Baal got the money back to the needlecraft and stashed safely away. Eight hundred thousand was a whole load of clams. Spending it—or salting it away—was going to take considerable thought, preferably over a couple of bottles of Sirian bourbon.

And now he had this harridan—admittedly a very pretty harridan—screaming at him so shrilly he thought his eardrums would burst.

"Simmer down, lady," the bounty hunter snapped at her. "Tell you what—we'll leave you here. I'll give you the cash for your trip back to the Asteroids. Heck, you can even travel first class. No trouble."

"You're the one who's in trouble, mister," Darlene accused. "You abducted me. That's a crime. You stole Lobo's bounty. That's another crime."

"There's gonna be a third crime if you don't shut up," Angel Eyes said, his eyes narrowing to pale yellow slits. "They call it murder."

He bent his head close to the Arcturan's, and they conversed in hushed whispers for a moment. When they came out of the huddle, Angel Eyes went straight to the console and strapped himself in.

"Prepare for takeoff," he told Darlene. "We're taking you home. And as a token of our appreciation for your co-operation, we'll give you five thousand credits."

He watched as a tight-lipped Darlene pulled the straps across her chest and lap, snapping them into their locks. Lobo didn't have such bad taste in women.

Another good reason to get her back fast, Angel Eyes reminded himself, *before the Main Man can work out a way to get off Gallioz.*

Minutes later, the needleship was on its way to Al's Diner.

Streaking into the black hole was like being crushed, ripped apart, and dropped from a great height—all at the same time.

The sensations of exploding eardrums, warping bones, and excruciating intestinal agony might not be every-body's cup of tea, but how would you know that you liked something if you never tried it?

So went Lobo's reasoning. And as pain went, he'd suf-fered worse.

Or better, depending on how you looked at it.

Xemtex hated every second, every 3,011 of them, as the bike screamed through the black hole's outer regions.

The view was spectacular. Ripples of shimmering en-ergy danced and tumbled as they fell past the screaming Spazz-Frag. A million pinpoints of light twinkled like atomic fireflies. And that damned Schwarzchild radius was so hazily sinister, it was like looking into a fogbank of pure malevolence.

This was probably the last view that Reubenz himself—the discoverer of the black hole—had ever seen. He'd found it in the days before the force field was a must-fit accessory to every spacecraft. His own ship's feeble engines had been unable to counteract the tremendous pull exerted by the gravity well. His last act, as he plunged toward the radius, had been to radio the black hole's coordinates back to his academic base.

Per ardua ad astra, Xemtex thought, recalling a logo he'd once seen on a ship. *Whatever the hell that means.*

The subframe was shuddering like a nodding dog in an earthquake. Two more visual sensors were stripped off in a shower of sparks that arced gracefully away, spinning toward the vague, constantly shifting outline of the radius. What was left of the navigation system reached some bizarre conclusion of its own; it shut itself down and refused to respond to Xemtex's desperate pleas for a course update.

Xemtex had never prayed. Indeed, he'd cursed his deity, religion, and its believers on a near-daily basis for most of his adult life. He'd shot up his share of churches, too. But recent events had made him think twice about being quite so casually offhand in his dismissal of supreme beings.

It would be just his luck if there really was a god, a wrathsome, vengeance-crazed deity who spent eternity sitting in that black hole, planning how to get his own back on guys like Xemtex when they jerked him around.

How else could you explain going from respected outlaw gang leader to disembodied brain in a nuked-out bike that was plummeting into the Universe's most dangerous box of tricks?

He could feel the vast gravitational forces pulling at the bike, trying to haul it off course and suck into the maw of the hole. But you had to hand it to the Spazz-Frag; if any bike could survive this trip, it was that hog.

Xemtex peered out through the bike's only remaining sensor. Distant galaxies hung like frozen frost patterns on purple velvet. He sighed and started to relax. Lobo was right—scientists *were* idiots. No Big Bang could produce anything near as gorgeous as this.

Of course, that meant there probably *was* a god.

Maybe he'd try that prayer, after all.

CHAPTER 26

The Spazz-Frag came hurtling away from the black hole at precisely the angle Xemtex had calculated.

Unfortunately, it was the wrong angle. A minor glitch in what remained of the nav system had inserted a cosine—instead of a sine—into the trajectory equation. It was hard to believe such a tiny error could make so much difference.

The bike pitched and yawed like a leaf in a hurricane, its downgraded force field tested to the limit. The stiffened frame began to squeak and pop, as if the very molecules that made it up were striving to break free. It wasn't going to last much longer.

Lobo whistled and yelled and cheered, clinging on in gleeful desperation as the bucking space bike did its best to dislodge him. He wanted to get after Angel Eyes, to visit some serious damage on the rival bounty hunter before whisking the lovely Darlene off for some intense romance. But at the same time, a tiny part of him couldn't help wishing that the Spazz-Frag would blow itself up; not merely to satisfy his love of explosions, but out of a genuine desire to learn if he could survive such a mid-space disaster.

They were traveling so fast, neither Lobo nor Xemtex was any longer in control of the bike.

"What the hell . . . ?" Angel Eyes blinked in disbelief, then trained his golden gaze back on the needleship's nav screen. "We got something ejecting from Reubenz's Hole. At high speed."

He watched the unidentified object's progress on the screen for a moment, punching its coordinates into the ship's computers, trying to figure out its most likely course. Figures scrolled rapidly down the monitor screen as the computers calculated, adjusted, and recalculated the object's path. Finally, the scrolling stopped.

Angel Eyes cursed softly as large, red warning letters flashed on his screen.

COLLISION IMMINENT, he read. 5 SECONDS. 4 SECONDS . . .

In addition to being a boozer, brawler, and babe merchant, Lobo was also very much a betting man. Risk was in his bones.

Depending on his mood—and state of inebriation—the Main Man would bet on anything, from two radslugs sliding across a corpse to the outcome of a galactic war. He'd won and lost a dozen fortunes, playing cards and games of chance in casinos and gambling dives throughout the cosmos.

But even he wouldn't have bet on the trillion-to-one odds that sent the Spazz-Frag spinning out of the black hole on a direct collision course with the very enemies he was seeking.

Both bike and needleship were slowing dramatically, Xemtex noted. But no force in the known Universe could prevent them from colliding.

Collision imminent. It wasn't much of an epitaph.

They slammed into each other at something close to ten thousand klicks a second. Child's play for the force fields to handle . . . at least, in normal circumstances. But the Spazz-Frag's remaining systems had been put under maximum duress by the skip into, and out of, the black hole. Its force field was on the verge of total anarchy.

Unfortunately for all concerned, the needleship's force field had been diverted in order to hold the Alpha prisoner. In the excitement of getting away with all the cash, Angel Eyes had neglected to reverse it.

As the Spazz-Frag's electromagnetic field fought to keep the vehicles apart, the bike's system glitched. It was only for a fraction of a second, but that was enough. When it came back online, bike and needleship were practically touching each other. Lobo cheered and hollered like somebody seized with hysterical dementia.

Locked together in a deadly *danse macabre,* bike and ship spun and twisted as they veered out of control.

Al Fretowski's mind was a total blank as every fiber of his being focused on the barrel of shrump mix he was stirring. The pink-gray organic material had the consistency of melted rubber and smelled like an old man with no functioning kidneys.

Zen and the art of making shrumpburgers.

He could have used an automatic blender, of course, like most eating establishments did. That's why their shrump came out thin and pasty, like gruel. It took much longer by hand, but it was the only way to obtain the gelatinous consistency so prized by the burger connoisseur.

Al bent forward, lowering his head to sniff gently at the mix. Nodding to himself in satisfaction, he took a pinch of Sirian herbs from a small plastic sack and sprinkled them on the shrump.

At last, the mix was ready. Now the automatic cutters would take over, weighing it and separating it out into custom-sized patties.

His brain started operating again as he shuffled across the empty diner, over to the mound of bread rolls awaiting slicing. This was usually Darlene's job. But she was gone, taken by that thug with the yellow eyes and his Khund goons. They'd assured Al she would be returned safe and sound, that no harm would befall her, and that if he called the cops, they'd come back and shoot him.

Al's eyes strayed up to the ob window and the panorama of glittering stars it framed. There was a flicker of light in the distance. A comet, maybe, or a wayward asteroid.

He took a deep breath, enjoying the way the odor of his sauce mingled with the purity of the air released by the subterranean hydroponic farms. Then he sighed and went back to slicing buns.

What else could he do? He was just an ordinary Joe

struggling to make a living, taking his burgers wherever paying customers might be found. Things had been looking up since he moved to the asteroid belt. The miners worked hard, played hard, and ate like hungry pigs. Both he and Darlene had been building up nice little bank balances from the often-hefty tips—until, of course, Lobo stopped by for the first time.

The Main Man's eyes had popped and his mouth drooled, his tongue hanging out like a panting puppy, the first time he saw Darlene. Al thought at first that the bounty hunter's infatuation with the waitress could only be a good thing for business, bringing in some more of those high-spending bounty dogs.

It hadn't taken him long to discover that Lobo was much more likely to bring trouble. Bloodstained walls he could live with; a wrecked restaurant he could live with, even when it happened the second time. But to lose Darlene . . .

He breathed a heavy sigh and looked back out of the window. The flickering light was still there, but closer now—much closer. Al frowned. He could see now that it wasn't a comet, and he knew that asteroids didn't spontaneously combust. Therefore, it had to be a spaceship.

But if it was a ship, why was it speeding inexorably toward the diner?

The object grew larger in a matter of seconds, and Al's heart lurched as he recognized the shape. That was the bounty hunters' needlecraft. And that, seemingly wedged nose first into the larger craft's hull, was Lobo's Spazz-Frag.

They were both glowing an unhealthy shade of fiery red as they screamed toward the diner.

An incredible roaring noise filled Al's ears. The craft were so close now, they were all he could see in the window. Al ducked instinctively, hurling himself to the floor and squirming under the counter.

He looked up—and saw the diner's entire roof disappear in a split-second shriek of twisted metal.

Then the craft were gone and Al Fretowski was lying flat on his back on the diner floor, looking up at the stars through his nonexistent roof and wondering if it was maybe time he thought about an alternative career.

Bound together more closely than husband and wife, the needleship and bike slammed into the main asteroid. A blizzard of sparks blazed in their wake as they plowed over the rocky surface, gouging a new canyon.

Miners' hovels disappeared as the skidding wreckage sheared them from their foundations. They slammed into a massive hopper filled with ore, and it sent them skidding off at an angle. They ripped through conveyor belts and crane rigs and even a Port-a-loo.

Shredded metal and five-ton boulders toppled onto the decelerating craft, slowing them even more, until eventually they came to rest under the cranes and feeder belts of the asteroid's mighty ore-crushing plant.

Fortunately, the whole contingent of miners was working half a mile down and was completely unaware of both the damage on the surface and the soon-to-ensue carnage.

CHAPTER 27

Angel Eyes hauled himself to his feet and knuckled dust from his eyes. The tangled mess he was standing in the middle of was completely unrecognizable as a needle-ship. The warp-drive engines and stabilizers had been ripped away completely, and large sections of the hull had peeled off as the craft skidded along the ground. He had the weirdest sensation of standing inside a dinosaur's skeleton, the ship's framework and stress pillars mangled and protruding like broken ribs.

The control console had been compressed into a shape-less lump the size of a trash can. It sparked one final time and died.

There was no sign of K'Baal—or the girl, for that matter, though Angel Eyes didn't really give a rat's behind about her.

As long as the cash is intact, he told himself, *I can still walk away as a winner. Whatever crashed into us couldn't possibly have survived.*

He picked his way between smashed and unidentifi-able machinery that had so recently been the heart of a

galaxy-spanning spaceship. There was no telling where
the money might have ended up, although he'd be surprised if the steel cases had burst. It was hopeless trying to
make his way to the rear of the wrecked ship on the inside; he'd make faster progress if he traversed the outside.

He stepped through a jagged rip in the ship's outer skin
and realized for the first time how lucky he'd really been.

The needleship had come to a grinding halt right under
the ore crushers. Another twenty yards and they'd have
brought down the superstructure, entombing themselves
in thousands of tons of metal and rock. As it was, the ship
had run into an array of crane jibs, knocking some over
and tilting the others at crazy angles. One huge chain,
with its carrying hook, had been severed completely and
lay draped over the front of the wreckage.

*Oh no. This can't be happening. It can't be him. Not
him!*

Angel Eyes felt a momentary chill. The hunk of junk
that used to be Lobo's Spazz-Frag was wedged in the
needleship's hull.

"Yo, Angel Eyes," a gruff voice said. "Small world,
ain't it?"

Slowly, making no sudden move, Angel Eyes turned to
face his tormentor.

Lobo was well aware of Angel Eyes' amazing reactions. That's why he stood a hundred feet away, his gun
held steady in both hands, its muzzle lined up with the
other bounty hunter's chest. The gun had only one charge
left in it; he had to make it count.

"Ya stole my money, an' ya stole my woman," Lobo
accused. "Ya should know better than that, Angel. We've

never rubbed each other up the right way, but it never came to war before. It ain't worth gettin' yourself killed over this."

He could see his enemy's yellow eyes darting every which way, looking for an escape route. "We didn't steal the Alpha, Bo," Angel Eyes said levelly. "You were out for the count. You'd have done the same in our position."

Lobo knew this was true. In fact, if the positions *had* been reversed, he might have been a whole lot sneakier than Angel Eyes was. But that wasn't the crux of the matter. "Ya kidnapped Darlene, ya rat. Ya placed my babe in danger."

"*I* put her in danger?" Angel Eyes was outraged. "Hell, she was as safe as milk with me. It was *you* that crashed into *us*!"

"Where is she?"

Angel Eyes' hands were a blur as they dropped for the guns that hung by his side. Lobo prided himself on being fast, but the cornered Angel Eyes was quicker than a Lyran whip-snake. Before Lobo's finger had even half-tightened on the trigger, his gun went spinning from his hand as the first of his foe's shots struck home.

Lobo dived away, rolled and came up running. Half a dozen blasts seared the air around him or raised dust at his feet, but he kept on moving, his right hand reaching to draw his knife from its leg sheath. The knife slipped out as if it were greased—which it was, actually—and Lobo threw it in a single, swift motion.

The twelve-inch serrated blade flew toward Angel Eyes. Lobo saw him focus on the knife, loosing off a volley of shots at it. But the knife twisted and curved in the air like a living thing, slipping the threatening beams.

"Inbuilt microcourse adjustor," Lobo said needlessly. The knife hadn't failed him yet, and he'd had it a long time.

There was a loud double beep as the charge pack in Angel Eyes' guns ran flat. Lobo watched intently as the other man let the guns drop from his hands. Angel Eyes spun around, the flaps of his long leather coat billowing out like sails; they whipped around the speeding blade and sent it careening away.

There was a loud, metallic shriek as the blade buried itself three inches deep in a fallen girder.

Lobo cursed himself for underestimating Angel Eyes' reflexes.

The other man was already leaping into the air, arms outstretched. He grabbed on to a tilted crane jib, swung himself around it to gather momentum, then let go. Lobo braced himself for impact, but it never came.

Angel Eyes kicked out in midair, his foot thrusting him away from his original path. He landed lithely by the side of his ruined ship and disappeared behind a twisted bulkhead.

"Aw, frag. This is all I fraggin' need," Lobo swore furiously, as Angel Eyes showed himself again.

The other bounty hunter had obviously seen movement in the wreckage. He was standing to his full height—and held in front of him, his hands at her throat, was the sexiest human shield in history.

Darlene.

* * *

At first, Xemtex had figured he was dead and gone to some version of hell. He could feel nothing—no connection to the bike's systems, no audio feeds, no weaponry, and no surge of heavy metal music. So obviously it wasn't hell—if it had been, he was sure the heavy metal would be playing continuously and at maximum volume.

It took him a while to realize the bike was wedged in the needleship, and they both lay in the shadow of some grotesque industrial unit. Only one of the external visual sensors was still operational. It protruded at a weird angle, pointed directly into the sky, but its connections were still in place.

Through it, Xemtex could see a scattering of stars far above. So peaceful, so perfect.

"Lobo! Oh, Lobo, please help me," Darlene sobbed huskily.

"I will, honey. Don't worry." The bounty hunter gritted his teeth, his fists clenching and unclenching in angry frustration.

Angel Eyes sneered as he clamped one hand over Darlene's perfect, bow-shaped mouth. "Yeah—help her, Bo . . . by keeping your distance. You know how fast I am. I'll snap her pretty neck like a pencil before you can get halfway to us."

"Whaddya want, ugly?" Lobo demanded, playing for time. He knew full well what Angel Eyes wanted—the money. Lobo wanted it, too. Question was, did Lobo want it more than he wanted Darlene?

His eyes slid around, checking for potential weaponry in the environment. His gun, with its solitary charge, lay closer to Angel Eyes and Darlene than it did to him. His knife was embedded in the girder. As far as he knew, his chain and hook were still impaled in the Alpha's crystal skull.

Wait a minute. Chain and hook . . . ?

"I want you to turn around, Lobo," Angel Eyes commanded. His fingers twitched nervously at Darlene's throat. "I want you to start walking and keep going till you're about a hundred miles away. Can you do that?"

A link of fallen chain lay at Lobo's feet. It was at least three times thicker than his own personal weapon of choice, forged for the stresses of lifting ore rather than killing people. Casually, he let his gaze follow its snaking contours. It was about ten feet long, with a hook on the end that must have weighed a ton.

Smoo-ooth, the Main Man thought.

Aloud, he said, "What guarantee do I have you'll let Darlene go?"

"You got my word," Angel Eyes promised. "You also got my word I'll kill her if you *don't* go."

Lobo threw back his head and scratched his ear, as if considering his choices. Then he came to a sudden decision. He bent down slowly and grasped the end of the chain in one hand.

"Tell ya what, Angel," he said defeatedly, "you kill the babe if ya want. She's all yours. I'll settle for the cash, if that's agreeable to ya."

Angel Eyes blinked in surprise—and that was all the opportunity Lobo needed. His biceps flexed as he whipped the chain, sending the heavy hook leaping into the air. He snapped his arm sharply and the hook plunged down . . .

Straight through the top of Angel Eyes' skull. There was a sickening crunch of breaking bone, accompanied by a sound like Jell-O splatting against a wall. The golden eyes closed abruptly, and he pitched forward to lie prone on the ground.

"Lobo, oh, Lobo," Darlene sobbed, throwing herself into the Main Man's open arms. "I thought I was going to die. Why—why did you tell him to . . . to kill me?"

He folded his arms around her, drawing her close, the thudding of her heartbeat echoing against his chest. "Relax, babe," he said comfortingly. "It was just a ruse to get the creep off guard. You know I'd never let anybody hurt you."

For about a microsecond, he debated telling her that he'd never used such a large hook and chain. An inch off with his aim and it would have been Darlene's no-doubt gorgeous brains dancing the skullquake tango.

He held her till her sobs subsided, losing himself in the pleasure of the moment, with her face buried in his chest and her arms wrapped tight around his waist.

Easy, in circumstances like that, to forget all about the Arcturan.

CHAPTER 28

K'Baal leapt violently back into Lobo's recall as a bolt of occult energy flashed out of nowhere and struck the bounty hunter between the eyes, hurling him off his feet.

Darlene screamed. She tried to run toward him, but tripped over Angel Eyes' body and went sprawling face-down in the dust beside the gory corpse.

Lobo was already springing upright. "Take cover," he hissed to Darlene.

"But—"

"Just do it, babe," he insisted. "I got a war comin' up here. The last thing I need is to be worryin' about your pretty buns."

He waited until Darlene had scurried underneath a thick heat plate, buckled by the crash landing until it resembled a house roof. He still couldn't see the Arcturan—but the Main Man didn't need vision when he could employ his olfactory powers.

He sniffed at the air, which at this range was thick with the cloying, sinister scent of the warlock; the Arcturan was making no attempt to disguise it. Lobo followed the trail back to its source.

K'Baal stood fifty feet above him, balanced on the edge of one of the ore grinders. The massive machine was still in operation, the upper conveyor belts rolling in an endless loop, huge metal teeth literally chewing up the granite-hard rock that the belts delivered.

Knife or gun, either would do. The knife was closer, though, so Lobo began to edge his way toward it.

All at once, he was enveloped in an occult mindstorm. Mystical energies cracked and seared around him, and the very air itself turned brooding and malignant. Wraithlike faces screamed out of nowhere, taunting him with their malevolent intangibility.

Fighting against a growing sorcerous wind, Lobo swelled his chest and roared at the top of his voice: "Is that the best ya can do? Gimme four shrumpburgers, an' I can fart worse than that," he boasted.

He caught a glimpse of K'Baal, raising his robed arms in the air. The effects around Lobo intensified dramatically. The mystical wind was close to blowing him off his feet, energy bolts were striking him on an irritatingly regular basis and he was beginning to get mad at those fiendish wraiths.

Summoning every ounce of his willpower, Lobo forced himself to dive away from the Arcturan's mystic manifestations. Energy crackled around him as, abandoning his quest for the knife, he swung himself up onto the superstructure that supported the crushing machinery. He clambered up the lattice of girders at speed, swaying and dodging as K'Baal tried to blast him away. Magic needed concentration, and Lobo knew it was hard for a wizard to hit a moving target.

With a final effort, Lobo swung himself over the top. He somersaulted once and landed lightly on his feet, facing K'Baal.

"Let's cut out all the superficial crap," Lobo suggested. "Thunder an' lightnin's for wimps. The way I hear it, magic's all about willpower. Izzatso, chump?"

"You are making a mistake." The Arcturan's voice hissed from the hood. "My will is supreme."

"So let's test it out, dude. Just you, me an' Mr. Willy Power." He scowled darkly at K'Baal, his eyes flashing red. "Whaddyasay? Little game of chicken with the total mental mayhem?"

In reply, K'Baal flung back his hood.

"Yee-uch." Lobo drew back in mock-revulsion. "It's a long time since you've seen a cosmetics counter, dude."

The Arcturan's skin was parchment dry, stretched over his bones so tautly that he looked like a skeleton wrapped in cellophane. His huge, black eyes were multifaceted, an inheritance of his insectoid race. Two tiny antennae protruded from the bony forehead, their tips quivering delicately as if in anticipation.

Black eyes locked with red.

The battle of the minds began.

Apart from an aptitude for biochemistry and a certain low cunning, nobody would ever mistake Lobo for a genius (unless he forced them to, of course). But the one thing he possessed in spades was indomitable willpower. In all his career, he had never, ever surrendered to anybody. Not even the few—the very few—who had beaten him. He preferred to descend into unconsciousness rather than suffer the ignominy of saying "uncle."

K'Baal attacked him with every occult trick at his command. He tried to sap Lobo's resistance with a facsimile of Darlene's voice crying for help.

Lobo stood strong.

The magician scrambled his senses, until the world of Lobo's mind became a random collection of jumbled-up sensations. This may not have been so different from Lobo's normal state of mind, and the bounty hunter rode the storm.

At the warlock's mental command, obscene demons materialized under the bounty hunter's skin, feasting on his raw flesh with needle-sharp teeth.

Lobo began to get a bit pissed. "A joke's a joke," as Jonas Glim always used to say, "but keep your butt off the pillow."

As the sorcerer unloosed a host of will-sapping mental violence, the bounty hunter figured it was time to act.

Screw this mentalist stuff, he decided. *It's gettin' me nowhere fast.*

His foot shot out and up. K'Baal had no warning as the bounty hunter's heavy boot exploded violently against his crotch.

"Groooo." The magician gave a small, grunting gasp. His hands crossed in front of him, clutching at his groin, and he lurched painfully forward.

Lobo unclipped something from his belt and rammed it hard into K'Baal's leathery mouth. Then he wrenched the warlock's hood up again and held it tightly over his head. There was an ominous hiss, followed by a bout of painful coughing; small wisps of purple gas drifted out from between the hood's folds. The necromancer gagged and hawked and retched, as acid fumes ate into his eyes and nose and mouth.

K'Baal gave a final, strangled cry; his body spasmed, then was still.

Only one other thing had survived the bike crash on Gallioz: a single canister of toxic gas.

Still gripping the hood, Lobo straightened his arm, lifting the dead Arcturan high.

"Guess I can never be too sure with a magic geek like you," the Bo told him. "Who can say what tricks ya got to bring yerself back to life?"

Grinning, he tossed the body onto a conveyor belt.

For just a moment, the crack and grind of crushing rock faded, as the crusher's metal teeth chewed on Arcturan flesh and bone.

Painfully, inch by inch, Angel Eyes dragged himself across the rough ground. He tried to keep his movements smooth, so as not to give himself away by making the chain clatter. The hook was embedded in his head, and the chain dragged behind him as he squirmed his way toward the gun.

Half his brain was oozing down his face, and one of his golden eyes had disintegrated. He could tell by the nerve-splitting throb in his jaw that he wouldn't be eating shrump for a long time. Or anything else, for that matter.

Angel Eyes was obviously no slouch in the willpower stakes, either. Close to death, he'd heard Lobo challenging

K'Baal, then saw the Main Man climbing up to join the Arcturan. That was when he started to move.

He was nearly there now. Outstretched fingers groped in the dust until finally they closed around the gun's butt.

With an effort that saw a chunk of brain slide down to the ground, he dragged himself into a sitting position. He cradled the gun and checked the charge. One shot left. One shot was all he'd need. He'd take Lobo's head clean off his shoulders. See how his healing factor coped with that.

"Yaahoooo!" Lobo yelled, and dived headfirst off the ledge. He did two full turns and a pike, before landing on his feet with a flourish. He bowed theatrically, then looked around to see if Darlene was watching.

She wasn't. She was still in hiding, only her shapely rump betraying her presence under the buckled heat shield.

Then he saw Angel Eyes—and the gun.

"I gotta hand it to ya, dude," Lobo said admiringly. "Ain't many guys get the drop on the Main Man, specially when they got a hook like that stickin' out their heads. Boy, that's gotta hurt."

"You'll soon find out, you bastard!" Angel Eyes swore. He twitched slightly, and his finger tightened on the trigger.

"What are ya waitin' for, hook-head?" Lobo challenged. "Maybe ya've lost so much of yer brain, ya don't know which is your trigger finger."

"I hate you," Angel Eyes retorted fiercely. His finger squeezed—

And the gun exploded.

"Oops," Lobo said with mock-reproach, slamming the heel of his hand against his forehead. "Did I forget to mention my gun was palmprint only?" He shrugged. "I guess it doesn't matter. Ya know now, right?"

Angel Eyes' single yellow eye stared, stupefied, at the stump left where his arm had been blown off. A geyser of blood was pumping out, splashing on the dusty ground beside the still-twitching arm.

The light went out in that fabulous golden eye. Lobo cleared his throat and sent a fat globule of spit sailing through the air. It splatted against the dead man's leg.

"Believe me now?" the Main Man asked of nobody in particular. "I told ya it wasn't worth dyin' over."

"Lobo . . ."

"Darlene . . ."

"You saved my life."

"You're gorgeous."

"I—I don't know how I can ever thank you."

"I do."

He leaned down, arms drawing her closer, and his lips fastened hungrily on hers. They kissed for a long time, their hands roaming over each other's bodies, caressing and squeezing.

When they drew apart, they were panting like dogs in heat.

"But . . . surely not here?" Darlene asked breathlessly.

"It would be spontaneous," Lobo assured her. "That's the best way. At least," he tagged on quickly, "that's what I've heard the guys in the locker room say."

"Oh."

His tongue flicked out to gently lick her earlobe.

"There's just one thing . . ." she said anxiously.

Lobo shrugged. "I ain't got any condoms, either. We'll just have to—"

"It's not that. I . . ." Darlene's eyelashes fluttered bashfully, and her voice dropped to a self-conscious whisper. "I'm a virgin, Lobo."

The Main Man whistled, low and lascivious. "What a coincidence, babe. So am I. Yes, ma'am. So am I!"

Through a combination of good fortune and trial and error, Xemtex had finally managed to get the external camera to swivel. Now he wished he hadn't bothered.

He could see two naked bodies entwined with each other, doing things that the casual passerby might find unusual.

Intellectually, Xemtex understood. The adrenaline doesn't stop flowing once the danger has passed—and what better way to chill out than getting it on? But emotionally, he just couldn't connect. He used to be like that, killing guys one minute, making love the next. Weird. A shiver ran through him. Now it seemed . . . unnatural, somehow, flesh on flesh.

Being a bike was much cooler. And that's what Fate seemed to have decided for him: he was going to be a bike. Okay. That was fine by Xemtex.

He swiveled the camera until it was pointing upward again, peering into the infinite stars. A single meteor flashed by, a few seconds of light as the asteroid's artifical atmosphere brought its aeons-long journey to an end.

Xemtex felt like crying as he lost himself in the eternal rhapsody of cosmic splendor.

EPILOG

Superman's first task on returning to the Watchtower was to institute a radical overhaul of the Justice League computer network. Despite the system's up-to-the-minute security codes and fire walls, the Alpha had managed to infiltrate it and plunder all the data it wanted. Perhaps no system could ever be impenetrable; besides, it was impossible to provide one hundred percent protection against the depredations of an artificial intelligence.

But they had to try.

Seated in the observation room, Superman peered out into the blackness of the dark side of the moon. It was a bleak, harsh environment, with temperatures never rising above minus two hundred degrees. No wind stirred its surface; even the forces of erosion had long since given up and abandoned this hostile hemisphere. No life had ever evolved here, and none ever would.

Was this how the Alpha had seen the future of the Universe? All organic life dead. No time, because there would be no sentient life to record its passing. No future, except for thinking machines.

The planet Krypton had perished more or less by accident. Billions of people had lost their lives. And yet only one survivor—Superman—remained to mourn them all. Was this what it would have been like everywhere, as the Alpha pursued its course of destroying civilizations . . . leaving only a Last Son, or Daughter, to mourn their passing?

Last Sons . . . The phrase rolled around in Superman's head. He thought of Vrk. He and Martian Manhunter had freed the captive Auriun from his dungeon and asked the man what he wanted to do. The Man of Steel offered to take him back to his destroyed homeworld, or indeed to anyplace in the galaxy he wanted to go.

The Auriun declined. His Vrkn jailers had by that time fed him some of the hallucinogenic fungus; when he was under its effects, he forgot all about his grief for his planet. He decided to stay where he was—lost in a psychedelic haze that cocooned him from his traumatic memories.

The woman from Gallioz hadn't yet been fed the mind-altering substance. Yet when they explained her situation to her, she, too, decided to stay on Vrk, where she and the Auriun would at least share a common bond.

And in time, maybe the fungus could help her forget, too.

Yes, Superman thought, *being a Last Son is a bond shared only by a very few. It's such a pity one of them has to be an arrogant, foul-mouthed, infuriating psychopath.*

John Jones's mood was as miserable as the weather.

A heavy storm had struck New York, sheets of fat raindrops splashing in the dusty streets, washing away the summer grime. Rain-laden Canadian winds had whipped in behind the storm front, turning the greatest city on Earth a thousand shades of gray.

It seemed to take him forever to walk the length of the street. Water dripped from his hat brim onto his shoulders; his raincoat was soaked through. Yet his steps didn't quicken. John was the bearer of bad news, and he was in no hurry to pass it on.

He only wished it could have been otherwise.

Boswell Jacklin's mother was waiting for him. He'd telephoned her to say he was coming. It might have been easier to tell her over the phone, to make his apologies, hang up, and never think of her again. But that wasn't John Jones's way.

The apartment was small and neat and tidy. Despite the unsalubrious neighborhood, Mrs. Jacklin clearly took pride in her surroundings. Faded photographs in clip frames stood on the sideboard, the story of her life: a happy young woman proudly cradling three boys; shots of the boys, solo portraits and all together; a framed school report card, with words circled in red: "Winston will go far."

She followed his gaze and sighed. "Winston didn't go far," she remarked sadly, lowering herself wearily into an armchair. "He was shot dead two blocks from here before he was seventeen years old."

She motioned to John to sit down opposite her, but he shook his head. "Mrs. Jacklin, I regret that I have bad news for you," he said quietly. "I saw Boswell about a week ago. I passed on your message to him." He hesitated, but knew that she deserved the full truth. "It's only my opinion," he went on, "but I think your words got through to him. He asked how you were doing. He said he'd consider what I told him."

Mrs. Jacklin looked at him, but didn't say a word. Already, John could see tears forming in the corners of her eyes. She knew only too well what he was going to say.

"I had to go . . . out of town for a few days. I returned today and went to see Boswell again. I—" He felt a lump in his throat, but forced himself to say the words: "I was too late. Boswell died yesterday, in a shoot-out with the police."

She sat perfectly still, barely even breathing, the tears rolling down her cheeks the only sign that she had heard him.

"I'm sorry, ma'am," John told her sincerely. "I understand what a tragic loss this—"

She made no move to wipe away her tears. "No, Mr. Jones, you *don't* understand," she said quietly. "He was my last son. My last son! How could anybody ever understand what it's like to lose him?"

It was like a dam had burst. Her body was wracked with sobs, and she stuffed the knuckles of one hand against her mouth to stifle them.

"Mrs. Jacklin." John started toward her, wanting to comfort her, not knowing what to say.

She thrust him away with a violent gesture. "Leave me alone. Please. Just leave me alone . . . !" Her voice tailed away pitifully as she was seized by a fresh round of sobbing.

John left the apartment with lowered head and heavy

heart. It was still raining, thin, mean raindrops that seemed to penetrate inside his very skin. He trudged up the street, not bothering to walk around the puddles. He thought of Mars; more rain had fallen in New York today than the whole Red Planet received in centuries.

Last sons. Yes, he could understand how she felt. He had lived all his adult life as the Last Son of Mars. Is there a difference between grieving for one person and grieving for a whole civilization? If grief is genuine, can it be lesser or greater?

"If we hurt each other," his Martian grandfather used to say, "we hurt the whole Universe."

John came to the end of the street and kept on walking until he was swallowed up by the city.

It would be nice to relate that Lobo and Darlene got officially engaged and that he settled down and gave up all his bad habits, including killing people.

He got a proper job—something in banking—and started saving for the mortgage on a split-level show house in some pleasant suburb. In the fullness of time wedding bells rang. They enjoyed two weeks' vacation on HoneyMoonWorld, memories to treasure for the rest of their lives. Then the patter of tiny feet—or the sound of tiny profanities—brightened up their future.

Dream on, dude.

After the consummation of their deepest carnal desires, Lobo and Darlene retrieved the money from the needleship. Neither Angel Eyes' craft nor the Spazz-Frag was capable of travel, so the young lovers hitched a lift with a miners' shuttle. They checked into a quality space motel, spent several hours "getting ready for dinner," then went out on the town to celebrate both their love and their wealth.

Lobo started with champagne, finished on brandy, and downed several crates of beer in between. Not much of a drinker herself, Darlene was content to just be with him.

They kissed a lot (although his breath was pretty foul), and Darlene didn't complain too much when he started to get fresh. After all, danger had brought them together in a way nothing else ever could. Lobo had realized she was the girl for him; it was time to settle down. She could allow him—and herself—the pleasure of one more night, before celibacy was reimposed until the wedding invitations went out.

Dream on, Darlene.

Eight hours later, she was reporting Lobo missing to the police. They took a special interest in the case, for a couple of reasons. First, a brand-spanking-new Spazz-Frag had disappeared from its owner's parking lot; the cops were hoping for a positive ID on the thief as soon as the owner got out of the hospital. Second, Lobo had the best part of a barrel of alcohol in his belly and eight hundred thousand credits concealed about his person; foul play wasn't suspected, because Lobo took a dim view of anybody playing foul with him and was likely to stiff them, pronto.

Several witnesses claimed to have seen him in the company of a seven-foot brute with fearsome tusks, which was a pretty fair description of Lobo's pal Jonas Glim. A possible lead that had yet to be investigated was the brief stopover by a cargo of pole dancers en route to a Babe World.

Back in her lonely motel room, Darlene found a scrawled note on her pillow. It read: 'Back soon. Wait for me. Bo."

There was a single red rose with it.

She may be waiting there still.

Unaware that Lobo had sent him a postal package containing the money he owed, plus ten thousand creds by way of apology, Al Fretowski changed his name and is working as a plumber on Vega.

On Auriun, unknown to anyone, a host of brainwashed Vrkns continue to dig out biochemical labs and weapons factories. The stone robots are starting to pile up. At current work rates, it will take the Vrkns thirteen thousand years to hollow out the entire planet.

We . . .
  Angry!
  No . . . hope.

The galactic courts struggled to find a jury of its peers, but eventually the Alpha was sentenced to eternal imprisonment in a purpose-built high-security fortress. It was still charged with both Lobo's and the Martian Manhunter's emotional energies, but now lacked the intelligence to understand them. It would spend the rest of its existence trapped in a nightmare of rage and despair.

* * *

And Xemtex?

The remains of Lobo's Spazz-Frag were vacuumed up by an asteroid cleanup crew and eventually dumped on the Trash Moon. There, the bike was stripped by the garbage robots of everything with resale value. The contents of the titanium SSCS tube were emptied into a sludge pail and removed for recycling.

At this very moment, Xemtex is lying in the organics bin of a Gallioz slop shop, awaiting collection for delivery to a factory that specializes in turning offal into shrump.

Lobo may well eat him one day.

This just in: Konik, the hairless M'ryngian barman back at Quarantino's, decided to get out while the getting was good. He'd saved almost eleven thousand credits selling information on bounty hunters' movements to villains; fear of being caught was playing havoc with his health. He fled to the backward planet Earth, where he lives quietly on the beachfront in Haiti with a cat and a dog.

Proving that, sometimes at least, crime does pay.

AUTHOR BIO

Alan Grant was born in Bristol, UK in 1949. Jobs as accounts trainee, bank clerk, student clergyman and door-to-door salesman were aberrations on my path to comics writing. Since 1980 I've written *Judge Dredd, Strontium Dog, Batman, The Incredible Hulk, Superman, RoboCop, Terminator, Lobo, The Demon,* and dozens of others. I've also written around 10 children's books, two Smallville novels and a JLA novel, *The Stone King.* I'm currently writing scripts for the hit kids' CGI TV show "Ace Lightning" and "Dominator: Cradle of Death," the sequel to my independently-produced UK animated hit.

INHERITANCE

ISBN: 0-446-61657-5

By Devin Grayson

BATMAN. AQUAMAN. GREEN ARROW. NIGHTWING. ARSENAL. TEMPEST.

A gunshot shatters the Gotham night as Slade Wilson, the superhuman killer-for-hire Deathstroke, fails to assassinate the young son of a visitng Quarac dignitary. Now three legendary crime fighters, Batman, Green Arrow, and Aquaman—and the three conflicted heroes who had once been their loyal sidekicks—join forces to stop Slade and those who hired him. But as the hunt stretches across continents, opening lost memories and old wounds, it turns into a desperate race against time: for Deathstroke is but one player in a plot to destroy all of Gotham . . .

Available June 2006.